TIDEWA

SHARE YOUR THOUGHTS

Want to help make *Tidewater Tempest* a bestselling novel? Consider leaving an honest review of this book on Goodreads, on your personal author website or blog, and anywhere else readers go for recommendations. It's our priority at Hearthstone Press to publish books for readers to enjoy, and our authors appreciate and value your feedback.

OUR SOUTHERN FRIED GUARANTEE

If you wouldn't enthusiastically recommend one of our books with a 4- or 5-star rating to a friend, then the next story is on us. We believe that much in the stories we're telling. Simply email us at pr@sfkmultimedia.com.

TIDEWATER TEMPEST

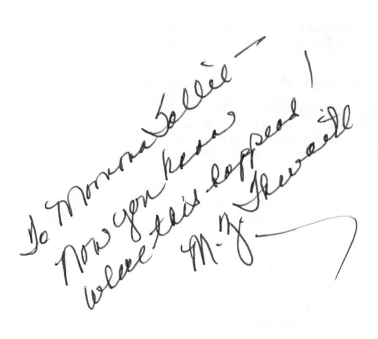

To Morria Sallie —
Now you know
where this happened!
M. Z. Thwaite

M. Z. THWAITE

ISBN: 978-1-970137-20-0

eISBN: 978-1-970137-21-7

Library of Congress Control Number available upon request

Cover & interior design by Olivia Hammerman.

Printed in the United States of America.

For Baerbel, Betsy, Upshaw, Klickie, and Marie.
You all left much too early.

The notes I handle no better than many pianists. But the pauses between—ah, that is where the art resides.
—Artur Schnabel

CHAPTER 1

1991
Tail End of Summer
Atlanta, Georgia

The bead of sweat that rolled off the tip of Abbey's nose plinked onto the blush-pink envelope. The droplet splattered onto her husband's name, dead center on the line above their address, and bled the blue fountain-pen ink like tie-die on cotton. The envelope was small—note-sized, not letter-sized, like the bills that were addressed to him. Curious, she set the note aside on the kitchen counter, gave it a lingering look, and then thumbed through the rest of the mail she had just brought in. She tossed the junk into the trash can, then dropped the Georgia Power bill into a basket labeled "BILLS" under the wall phone. She went back to the letter, ran her fingers across the envelope. It was good stock: Crane & Co. There was no return address, but the ruined fluid script that said "Thomas Clark" followed by Abbey and Tom's address looked to be written by a woman. Abbey sniffed the paper. There was a light floral scent. Rose? She dropped the letter onto the counter where Tom liked for his mail to be left. He couldn't miss it. *I wonder what that letter is about.* She swallowed momentary queasiness.

Sunlight reminiscent of an Arizona sunset played across the Mexican-tile floor. Abbey dropped her shoulder bag onto the sofa, then toed off black flats as soft as kid-skin gloves. The floor felt warm underfoot, the air thick and stale—late-summer air. She hated rooms artificially cooled well below the outside air. The thermostat was set at eighty-two degrees. Outside, it was ninety-five; felt like one hundred and ten. She flipped a wall switch. A ceiling fan moved, began a slow spin, and stirred the air. Abbey removed wrapped items from a paper grocery bag and stuck them in the fridge.

The wall phone rang. When she answered, the caller breathed into the receiver, then hung up. Abbey glanced at the pink note on the counter, then returned the phone to its base. A yellow sticky note beside the phone fluttered to the floor. She picked it up and read: "I'm out of box-ers—again!" It was signed "Tom." *Like I wouldn't know.* She crushed the note into a ball and tossed it in the trash on her way to the laundry room. The plastic basket on top of the washer spewed boxer shorts and white T-shirts. She tossed a load into the washer and closed the laundry-room door on her way out. Heaven forbid the poor guy would have to go commando. Boxers had been an issue as long as she could remember. When she'd suggested that he might learn to operate the washer and dryer if he wasn't satisfied with the current laundry turnover, he had gone out and bought a dozen more pairs.

On her way to the stairs, Abbey thought about the letter. *Who's writing Tom scented notes?* She untied the sash to her wrap-around dress, which she had dubbed a closing dress, like others she had designated for funerals and cocktail parties. The phone rang again when she got upstairs. She picked it up by the bed. Prepared for another breathy hang-up, she all but barked "Hello" into the receiver.

"Well, hello. Bad day?" It was Blix, born Elizabeth Alexander Stouver and dubbed "Blix" by Abbey when they had been in high school.

"Sorry, Blix. I had a hang-up right before you called, so I was ready to give it to somebody. What's going on?" Abbey pulled on shorts and grabbed a sleeveless denim shirt from a doorknob.

"Not much," Blix said. "I went to the dentist this morning, so I feel like Joe E. Brown." Abbey chuckled at the image of Brown, a thick-lipped, elastic-mouthed comedian from fifty or sixty years earlier.

Blix was known for her quick wit. Since they had grown up together, Abbey knew she often used humor to deflect bad news. "Six-month cleaning?"

Blix made no response other than a strong exhale into the receiver.

"Do you still go to your uncle?" Abbey flopped into an upholstered chair, then watched a dust bunny drift across the wood floor.

"My uncle referred me to someone."

"A specialist of some sort?" Abbey waited, and when Blix only offered a soft grunt, she let it go, but it hung in her brain like a to-do memo. "So, any plans for the weekend?"

"Nope. I've had shifts at the hospital all week, so I'll catch up on laundry."

"Whoop-de-do. Now that sounds like fun." Abbey thought about Tom's rather pointed boxer note. "When you're finished there, you can come over here. I'm always behind. Tom's in a boxer deficit."

"Doesn't he know how to run the washing machine?"

"Fat chance."

"All you can do is try. I suppose your gang is going to Kings Bluff for the long weekend."

"Every Labor Day for as long as I can remember and before," Abbey said. "Momma's parents were both big fishermen, so that's how they spent the last weekend before school started, and it stuck."

"How about the boys?"

"I dropped them at Momma's this morning. Tom will bring Momma and the boys on Friday. I'm going tomorrow to get the cottage ready."

"It will be nice for the four of you to get away."

This time, Abbey paused. "You're right. Tom and I need a break. We can use a little together-time without work hanging over our heads."

"Have you thought about putting real estate on hold while your boys are small?"

Abbey's cheeks puffed as she blew air. "Have you been talking to Tom?"

"No. Has it come up?"

"On more than one occasion. I know I don't need to work anymore. That's not the point." Abbey stood and walked over to a window. A yellow car drove slowly past the house. She moved around and watched it drive away. "Do you ever think about when you were little? I mean, in the fifties?"

Blix said, "Sometimes. It was a different world back then."

Abbey said, "I think about it a lot. Daddy worked, Momma took care of us, everybody was happy. Then, one day, Daddy died. Boom. My whole world changed when I was thirteen years old."

Blix exhaled into the phone. "One day, life is one way—the next day, it's another."

Abbey closed her eyes and remembered the jolt she had felt her junior year in high school, when she'd learned that Blix and three other close friends had been involved in a horrible car accident. "Of course, you know. My life-changer was my father's early death. Life as you and I knew it turned upside down, and we had to hit the reset button."

"Damn. Don't I know it." They paused. "But children are only small once. One day, my boys were in diapers, and the next, they were snitching my razors."

"Ugg. Good grief. You are so far ahead of me. Yours shave and mine giggle while they have pissing contests in the toilet bowl." Abbey glanced at the photograph of her two boys on the dresser. "You don't need to remind me these years are precious. Tom does it all the time."

"Maybe you should listen to him. You can always go back to real estate after your two are in school."

"Let's not go there, Blix, okay? Trust me. I think about it. I also think about my mother suddenly becoming a single parent." Abbey went to another window. The grass was neatly mown and edged and a healthy green, except for the spot where the neighbor's dog peed every morning. "And you know what? Momma made sure our lives didn't change so much after Daddy died. We finished high school and college, and she carried the load. It wasn't until I was on my own that I appreciated the sacrifices she made for us. I had always taken my privileged, cushy little life for granted."

"Newsflash, pal. We all rode that magic carpet on our parents' tickets. But now that you're old and responsible and feel remorse for being young and oblivious, you want to make up for it."

"When did you get so smart?" Abbey asked. "I want that good life for my family, like you and I had in the fifties. It was so uncomplicated."

"Hey, life is all about falling down. It's the getting up and giving it another go that's the hard part. All I'm saying is that with your boys, it's your choice. You like your independence. I get that. I just don't want you to kick yourself the day Jimmy heads to college and Walter isn't far behind and you realize you missed how they got there. Think about it."

"Yes, ma'am." Abbey took a deep breath. She had thought about it a lot, and she knew her dogged determination stemmed from having watched her mother meet every obstacle life threw her way. "I got my buttheadedness from my sweet mother, you know."

Blix laughed. "I think you got more than that from her."

"Don't I wish. If I could be half the woman she is, I'd be happy."

"Are you taking Watch Dog with you?"

"No. Rattlesnakes are awful this time of year." Abbey pulled a dead leaf off an orchid plant on her dresser and dropped it into the trash can. "I checked him in at a doggie camp."

"Will you adopt me?" Blix asked, her tone pleading.

Abbey laughed. "Oh, poor thing. Why do you want me to adopt you?"

"Because your dog goes to camp and your children get to go to Kings Bluff, which is better than any camp."

"Why don't you come? There's plenty of room."

"I didn't mean to invite myself on your holiday."

"You didn't. We would love to have you."

"Bunns, you know never to invite me anywhere unless you mean it."

"I mean it. Come on. It'll be fun. Bring that camera of yours. You'll get some great shots."

When they hung up, Abbey grabbed a large L.L.Bean bag from the closet, then collected shorts and T-shirts and all the toiletries and bug sprays necessary for several days at the hunting and fishing club where she was headed. She grabbed a slinky black bathing suit from a shopping bag, then stood in front of the full-length mirror on the back of a door and pressed the suit against her body. Stretched to her full five-foot-eight-inch height, she drew her shoulder blades back and poked her derriere out. *No butt at all.* Nothing, save surgery, would add a nice, tight little round rump. She'd bought the suit when the salesgirl had told her it was a real man magnet. *I need all the help I can get.* She snipped the dangling tags with nail clippers and tossed the suit onto the bed with her other clothes.

On a top shelf in her closet, far from curious little hands, was a blue zippered carryall. She looked inside the bag, inspected the safety glasses and padded ear protection, and grabbed two boxes of Winchester .38-caliber shells from a lidded plastic box and dropped them into the bag. Running numbers on the lock of the compact wooden gun cabinet, she took out a small revolver in a tan cowhide holster and another pistol wrapped loosely in a faded dish towel. She finished packing and put the bags in a corner of the bedroom.

AN OVERLY MADE-UP weather babe on the television looked like freeze-dried kielbasa in her form-fitting paprika-red knit dress. Teetering on four-inch heels, she smiled, and with the sweep of her hand, she indicated swirls and arrows over the Caribbean islands. "This wet weather pattern to the south of us could continue our way and put a bit of a damper on your holiday weekend plans. Though this doesn't look like anything we need to worry about, we are in hurricane season until November, so keep that in mind."

Great. Abbey punched the "Off" button and silenced the babe mid-sentence. *Bit of a damper. Come on. Let's use some*

of that fancy jargon they taught you in meteorology school.
She pulled rain jackets out of the hall closet—two small, one
medium, one extra-large—and dropped them onto the butt-
sprung, faded green corduroy loveseat in the nook off the
kitchen. *A little rain won't ruin our weekend.*

Tom liked to listen to baseball games while he did things
around the house and yard. Abbey found his transistor radio
in a basket by the phone and turned it to Jim Axel on WAGA.
She took a juicy salmon filet and salad greens from the refrigerator. Axel reminded her of a Cub Scout leader as he told his
listeners to be prepared for wet weather. *Great. A weekend on
the coast, and we might be stuck inside.* While Abbey rinsed
lettuce, she glanced at the *Atlanta Journal-Constitution* on
the counter. "HEAT WAVE CONTINUES" was above the fold
in bold black letters. The Gulf of Mexico was reported to be
as warm as bath water. *Not very inviting.*

When the phone rang this time, she said, "Abbey Taylor
Bunn," as though answering at her desk at work. On the other
end was a potential client to whom she had spoken numerous
times. Each time, the woman presented a new argument to
justify the price at which she wanted Abbey to list her home,
a price Abbey insisted was well above market value. Abbey
listened patiently for several minutes, then said, "You keep
mentioning this other agent. If she is willing to list at your
price, then I suggest you talk to her."

"Well," the woman said, "maybe I will."

"Good. I wish you luck. Have a nice weekend and call me
in a couple of months if things don't go the way you plan."
She hung up and stared at the phone, then raked her fingers
through her hair. She had a history of working every prospect, which often meant wasted time and effort. Tom told her
to be more selective, to get tougher. This was her first time

turning down business she thought was a waste of time. *Good riddance. That actually felt pretty good.*

She collected a handful of books for the boys, a well-worn copy of *To Kill a Mockingbird* for her, and a Baldacci novel for Tom, then grabbed two decks of cards and several boxes of puzzles and put them on the sofa with the rain jackets. Tom was not wild about her going ahead without him, but he knew better than to try to talk her out of something once she had made up her mind. The brushed peck on the cheek as he'd hustled out the door that morning had told her Daddy wasn't happy, but she didn't think his mood had anything to do with her going ahead. There was more to it than that. He had been distant lately. She had that creepy feeling you get when you know someone isn't being honest with you but you can't put your finger on the problem.

The yellow car poking by the front of the house popped into her head. She picked up a framed photograph of her and Tom on their wedding day and brushed dust off the glass. Both wore amazing smiles; his arm was draped protectively across her shoulders. She knew they needed time alone, away from home and jobs and distractions, time to talk and hash things out. Something was going on with him, and she intended to find out what it was.

She stuck beers and ice in the cooler on the patio and fired up the charcoal grill. Back inside, she flipped through a stack of CDs and took out Cat Stevens. "Hard Headed Woman" met her in stereo from the patio speakers when she went back outside. A breeze ruffled tree branches and offered relief from the hot, muggy air so typical of the end of the summer in the South. Given the choice, even when it was hot, Abbey preferred to be outside in wide-open air. Distant lightning flickered over the treetops. She settled onto soft chair cushions, propped her feet on a low rattan footstool, and put her head back and closed her eyes. It had been a long day. She nodded off.

Soon, the garage door rumbled. Abbey jerked awake, yawned, and wiped a trickle of saliva from her chin. When Tom appeared, his wrinkled brow and downcast eyes told her something was on his mind. He flung his suit coat over the first chair in his path and looked up. Abbey hoped for the familiar smile she loved so much. One came, but it was different somehow—tentative, maybe, or forced.

"Hi," Tom said, not the *There's my girl* that had been his greeting until the past month or two. She couldn't remember the last time he'd said it.

She smiled, knowing her eyes told a different story. They kissed, sweet, nothing more asked, nothing more offered. Perfunctory. Tom headed to the cooler by the grill and looked inside. He grabbed two Heinekens and motioned toward the chairs. "Shall I use my teeth?"

Abbey fished an opener from the pocket of her shorts.

"It's awfully quiet around here. Where is everybody?"

"I took Watch Dog to camp and the boys to Momma's before my closing."

Tom took a long pull on his beer. "Oh man. That hits the spot." He sipped again. "How'd the closing go?"

"Fine. No surprises." And that ended the discussion. Tom had used to ask for all the details, delighted to hear about real-estate closings, like the time a nursing mother had whipped out a boob at the closing table and fed her baby. Tom said nothing this time—just sipped his beer.

They dined on the patio, then went in to catch the news. The pink letter on the counter could not have been more obvious had it been a long-stemmed pink rose. Tom snatched it up like the last cookie on the plate and stuffed it into his back pocket. *And that's it? You get this note from another woman and don't bother to explain?* He cleared his throat like he always did before he said something that was exactly what Abbey was thinking. They did it all the time, had that kind of connection. He coughed and went to the sofa. She grabbed a glass of water and curled up in a club chair. He clicked on the television.

She stared at him for a moment, fighting to temper what she felt inside. "Who's the letter from?"

His head swiveled toward her. "An old college friend... looking for a job."

Abbey chewed on that one. Did he recognize the handwriting? Or the stationery? Or the rose scent? He obviously knew who the note was from and didn't want to talk about it. She had received letters from old male friends, and it was no big deal, so why should this be any different? But it was. He was defensive. Did he not want her to know? Was he hiding something? She refused to believe that he might be capable of jeopardizing their marriage. *Am I being stupid?*

The news was mostly stories about local murders and a bank robbery. Tom stared at the screen with his lawyer face on. Abbey knew he was collecting details. Like shooting hoops from the foul line over and over again, nightly news was where his trial brain exercised the what-ifs. Tonight, she wondered if his interest was in the news or what was in his back pocket.

When it was clear neither felt like talking, Abbey said, "It's been a long day. I'm going up to shower," a comment that usually had Tom asking if she wanted company.

"I'll be up in a minute," he said as she left the room.

Thirty minutes later, Abbey toweled off and readied for bed. She heard a voice downstairs and went to the bedroom door and listened. It was not the television. She glanced at the clock. Eleven. Tom was on the phone, his tone hushed. She crept to the banister, careful to avoid the spot in the wooden floor that squeaked. His voice droned on but was unintelligible.

CHAPTER 2

A nightmare awakened Abbey at four a.m. No matter how hard she jammed her foot on the brake, the car continued to slide on loose gravel down the one-hundred-foot-high embankment. Her heart pounded. She slipped out of bed and tiptoed to the bathroom and grabbed her robe. A deep yawn interrupted Tom's open-mouthed, back-of-the-palate breaths. He was good for at least another hour, when one big snore would awaken him instantly.

Abbey's bare feet were soundless on the hardwood floor. She grabbed her two packed bags and took them downstairs. If she left early, she might beat the bottleneck that choked downtown Atlanta several times a day. She put water on to boil, then punched the code into the keypad beside the back door and grabbed her bags. Tiptoeing across the dew-damp brick walkway to the garage, she put her bags in the rear of her Jeep. Odors of cedar, sulfur, and salt air escaped her L.L.Bean bag, smells trapped in shorts and T-shirts worn to within a thread of their existence at Kings Bluff and mostly worn only there. She savored the familiar fragrances for a moment, then closed them in and went back inside.

She made her tea with milk and a spoonful of honey, then sat on the sofa that faced the backyard and propped her feet on a wooden chest she had trash-picked and refinished. Lost in a mental checklist to be sure she had done everything she needed to do, she cupped the warm mug in both hands and inhaled the fragrances of black tea and citrus.

A chair scraped the tile behind her. She turned her head and watched Tom bumble past the kitchen island. His hair stuck up Alfalfa-style, and his eyes were puffy. His gym bag snagged on the back of a barstool. He said, "Damn."

"You're up early," Abbey said.

Tom grunted. "I'm working out with a trainer this morning. I must have been tight when I set this one up."

"It's good to get it over with. Sorry I didn't wait up for you last night. I had a long day and was beat." She hoped he'd offer who he'd been on the phone with the previous night.

"No problem. I had a brief I needed to go over, so I was late coming up."

Abbey watched his face to see if there was a tell. He had been talking with someone—at eleven o'clock at night. She had a whole weekend to get it out of him, so she sucked it up for the time being. She didn't want to start anything she couldn't finish. "Here," she said, offering her mug of tea. "This will get your engine running until you can get coffee."

"Thanks." He looked at the steaming mug then at his full hands.

"Come on," she said as she stood. "I'll walk you out." She pushed the garage-door opener, took his suit bag, and walked him out. She hung the bag in the back of his Jeep Wagoneer and handed him her mug of tea.

"I'm leaving as soon as I get dressed, so I'll give you a shout at the office this afternoon after I get settled at the cottage," she said.

"Sounds good." He hesitated. "Are you sure you want to leave today? You could wait and go with us on Friday."

She closed her eyes for a split second and thought about waiting. If she stayed, she'd work. What she wanted was time alone to sort out what was going on with her life; maybe he needed time to himself, too. She opened her eyes and shook her head. "No. I'm sure."

He nodded. Steam from the tea fogged the windshield in front of him. He put the Jeep in reverse and said, "Be careful. Stop if you get sleepy."

She pushed down his door lock. "I'll see you Friday." She mouthed "Love you" as he backed out.

Weather Babe had mentioned rain, so, back inside, Abbey rummaged through a drawer in a chest in the living room and pulled out the brass barometer her mother had given her the previous Christmas, the same one she had given to Abbey's father the Christmas before he'd died. What better place to have a barometer than a cottage on the coast? Better than sitting in a drawer. She gave the heavy brass a quick polish, then wrote Tom a note that said: "Boxers and T-shirts in dryer—in laundry room—still." She stuck it on the refrigerator at Tom's eye level.

FIVE-AND-A-HALF HOURS LATER, she pulled into City Market in Brunswick. The entire drive down, Abbey's thoughts had bounced back and forth between Tom and Blix. She couldn't shake the feeling that something was going on with Tom, and she had a sneaky suspicion that Blix was holding something back. She knew she should let Blix ask for what she needed and wanted. On the other hand, Tom, as she had learned, needed to be pushed about personal things. Being a trial law-yer, he was accustomed to litigation and thought he could work out or around any issues. But what worked in the court-room didn't play out so well at home. Communicating with his wife about the day-to-day was not his strong suit. While Abbey had driven, she had mentally rehearsed different things to say to Tom so that when the time came, one of her lines would roll off her tongue, she hoped.

She recalled the dream that had awakened her that morning. It was one of those "life out of control" dreams where no matter how hard she pumped those brakes, she couldn't stop the car's slide down the crumbly drop-off. *Damn, I hate scary dreams.*

By the time she stepped out of the car in Brunswick, her head felt like a pressure cooker, but she needed dinner tonight and liked to support the local fishermen. Fish-smell plumed through the door when Abbey entered City Market on Gloucester Street. Behind the counter on a high wooden stool sat a white-haired fellow who had worked there for as long as Abbey could remember. He closed a Louis L'Amour paperback when she walked in. Redfish, black drum, whiting, shrimp, and an assortment of other local catch lay on a mound of chipped ice in rows behind a glass partition.

"Well, look here. I haven't seen you in a while, Miss Abbey. Are you down for a break from the big city?"

"Yes, Mr. Ben." She loved the southern properness of the greeting they always exchanged. "You have a good memory."

He smiled.

"I'm headed to Kings Bluff for Labor Day. I'll have a full house by the weekend, but it's just me until then. I hope it doesn't rain the whole time."

"Naw, not the *whole* time. Maybe a little, though. We've been so dry down here all summer, it would be a welcome relief." Ben picked up a white bar towel and wiped down the counter. "It's a good idea to take some time for yourself now and then."

Abbey nodded. Ben studied her while she perused the display of fresh seafood.

"Something bothering you, little lady? I'm not seeing that smile today."

She shrugged. "You're right. I need time to myself." Blix popped into her head. "Have you ever known anyone who seemed to have a black cloud over his head?"

"Sure. Some folks are just that way."

"I have a friend who is the most positive person I've ever known, but bad things happen to her."

"Well, think positive thoughts and send her some prayers. I've had pretty good luck with that, so I'll do a little praying myself, if you tell me your friend's name."

"Blix."

Ben's pale blue eyes searched hers.

"Blix Stouver, or Betsy, if you prefer."

"You got it. Now don't you worry." He grabbed a heavy-duty plastic bag and scooped ice into it. "Tell you what. I know you like to cook your shrimp with the heads on. You by yourself, you said?"

"Yes, so far."

"How about you get started with these tonight. On the house." He dropped a generous scoop of shrimp into a bag, nestled that bag on top of some ice in another bag, and secured them with a twist-tie.

"No, I can't let you do that, Ben. I'd rather pay."

"I insist. You look like you've been thinking about your friend and whatnot the whole way from Atlanta. You go get yourself a nice bottle of wine and cook up these jumbos, then you call your friend and have a talk. This isn't in your hands or hers. Know what I mean?" Ben's bristly white eyebrows raised in a question.

"Yes. I know what you mean. Thank you. You're very kind, Ben."

"No, I ain't. This is my market, and they're my shrimp because I caught them, so I guess I can give some away now and then when I feel like it."

Their eyes met. "Thank you, Ben. You have a great weekend and don't work too hard. Or don't labor too hard, I should say. Be good to yourself." She held up the bag of shrimp. "And thanks for these."

"You enjoy them, little lady. I hope things work out for your friend."

As Abbey walked toward the door, a black teenage boy in an extra-large pink T-shirt walked in. Ben addressed him as Otis and asked if he was shopping for his granny. The boy made eye contact with Abbey, then looked away quickly as she walked past.

CHAPTER 3

In the parking lot behind Atlanta's Piedmont Hospital, Blix hurried to her car and hoped she wouldn't run into anyone she knew. Her appointment had been scheduled early, so she had gotten a good space near the exit. She swiped under her nose with the back of her hand to catch a drip while she jabbed a key into the door lock. She tossed her purse into the passenger seat and slid in. *Lord, why me—again?* Both palms slapped the steering wheel.

From the glovebox, she removed a small pad of tissues, extracted one, and blew her nose hard. She looked in the rear-view mirror. Mascara was smudged below her bottom lashes. One black pupil had contracted to a pinpoint in the diffused light of the garage; the other remained the same, always the same, day or night, stuck in time. She licked her finger and ran it under both eyes, then swiped at kohl-colored smears with the tissue. Her eyes told her past. Details haunted her at times such as this, and today's doctor visit at a hospital she knew all too well had stirred the memory of blaring horns and screeching tires and being tossed around like a small plastic ball in a bingo cage. *Screams. Oh God, the screams.* She replayed her own. A jolt of pain; the stuff of nightmares. Her eyes squeezed shut for a moment. Then, she turned on the ignition and backed out of the space.

Peachtree Street was calm for mid-morning, but the Peachtree Battle Shopping Center's parking lot was active and crowded. Blix drove around until she found a spot. Walking shoes lay on the floor of the backseat of her Monte Carlo. She slipped them on, got out, and headed up the hill to the light and the crosswalk. After her divorce, she and her two sons had moved in with her parents, into the house where she'd grown up. This was her neighborhood. She knew who owned the lovely homes along the street, or who had owned them when she'd been in high school. This was friendly, familiar turf that reminded her of the conversation she had had with Abbey about childhood and the carefree times before life had heaped on its challenges. Blix's tall, thin frame, usually erect, slumped today; her legs moved in halting steps. In front of E. Rivers Elementary, she picked up a long, straight stick and dragged it behind her on the sidewalk. She remembered doing the same thing as a child... and didn't feel like a child now. Adulthood had brought grown-up problems that required life-changing decisions. As she walked, she broke off little nubs that stuck out from the stick until she was left with a nice, straight walking stick. When she crossed Habersham Road, she broke off the stick's skinny tip. At Woodward Way at the top of the hill, she broke off the next section and continued until there was nothing left but a two-inch thumb of wood. She tossed it into the gutter, then jammed her hands into her pants pockets and gazed at the canopy of white-oak limbs overhead. She had only gone two blocks, but that was enough. She knew what she wanted to do. It had shocked her that morning when she'd heard the same words she had heard in movies and had read in books, but her doctor had said those words to her. *You have cancer. Make every minute of every day count. Starting now.* Indecision and time-wasters were no longer options. *To heck with laundry and closets.*

She crossed the park-like median and headed back toward Peachtree Street with a quickened pace. Up ahead, E. Rivers Elementary was in full swing. Children's shrill voices, laughter, and the sound of squeaking swing chains rose from the playground in the back of the school. A bat cracked a ball. Delicious sounds.

Blix went to her car, grabbed her purse from the floor where it had ended up, and went into King's Drug Store. Sunscreen products were picked over this late in the summer, but she found one she liked and took it to the checkout counter. The clerk made small talk as she placed the bottle in a small brown paper bag. Blix spotted shelves of camera film behind the woman. "Do you have Kodak Gold Plus back there?"

"Goodness. Let me see." The woman ran her fingernail across box after box until she stopped and said, "How many do you need, sweetie?"

Blix counted in her head. "I'll take four, if you have them. I'm going to the coast for the weekend, and I want lots of memories."

The clerk rang up the charges. "Are you leaving today?"

"No, Friday. Right now, I'm going to have a milkshake."

"Good for you! Aren't you lucky to be so thin that you can have a milkshake and not worry about calories? You keep up that good attitude."

"I always try," Blix said.

CHAPTER 4

When she left City Market, Abbey proceeded cautiously on U.S. 17. Police lurked behind lush oleander bushes and nabbed unsuspecting tourists more focused on their resort destinations on Georgia's sea islands than on the speed limit. She knew from experience. As she approached the Brunswick River, she automatically looked up and down the waterway to see if an automobile-laden freighter might hold her up on the Sidney Lanier Bridge. The concrete-and-steel vertical lift structure, named for a famous Georgia poet, had been hit twice by freighters and was scheduled to be rebuilt. Today, the coast was clear. As she crossed the bridge, she looked down on white, frothy wakes trailing behind motorboats and gulls that glided and swooped and snatched discarded morsels from shrimp boats headed back to the dock. She imagined living on the coast. Though she didn't put much stock in astrology, she was an Aquarian, a water-bearer, and she loved to be near water. Maybe one day.

Thirty minutes later, lost in thought, she saw her exit at the last minute. The big yellow Stuckey's sign all but shouted for her to turn. Once off the highway, she noticed the change in the way the air smelled. She remembered her father saying her mother's ears would perk up once she turned onto Kings Bluff Road. Abbey felt her whole body perk up. This was her place, where massive live oaks crowded sweet bay trees and hip-high cabbage palms and gray veils of Spanish moss clung to tree limbs and waved in the breeze.

Abbey lowered her window to breathe in the unmistakable odor of good old marsh mud. Farther on, the asphalt cut between sandy flats populated with sawgrass and skittering fiddler crabs whose hidey-holes pockmarked the flats like bullet-riddled cans. A "For Sale by Owner" sign on a side road where an old friend of Abbey's lived caught her attention. Ever the curious real-estate agent, she turned onto the dirt road that was flanked by tall, skinny pines and sword-like palmettos, where turkeys, armadillos, deer, and more snakes than anyone cared to imagine had the run of the land.

Abbey drove up to a tiny makeshift cottage nestled among hardwoods; a fenced garden thrived alongside it. Relieved there was no "For Sale" sign in this yard, she parked and walked to the edge of a garden with row after row of plants. Some were done for the year while others still produced. Smoke curled from the corncob pipe that lay on a stump just inside a crooked, wood-framed gate that was attached by barbed wire to a rickety hog-wire fence. Abbey had known several of the Geechee locals since she'd been a child, and, like her mother and grandmother, she liked to check in on them and oftentimes paid them to do odd jobs for her around the family property.

"Hongry? Are you out there?"

"Here," a small voice called from the other side of a row of plants, from which hung ping-pong-ball-sized green tomatoes. Old ripe-red fruit rotted on the ground. "Who's there?" A sweat-stained brown hat appeared through a break in the aged plants.

"It's Abbey Bunn, Hongry. I just drove down from Atlanta."

A small man appeared at the end of the tomato rows. He smiled and waved and looked all around the ground at her feet. He asked about her dog, which sounded like "dawg," and then he waved her in with his free hand; the other held a long-handled limb lopper.

"I left him home," Abbey said. "Too many ticks and snakes here this time of year."

Hongry looked at her for a minute, and then he smiled and came toward her. "Want some collards?" His voice was as high and squeaky as a juvenile hawk. "I promised some to Roosevelt. I'll cut you a mess, too." Roosevelt was another local who lived down the road.

Abbey laughed. "I didn't come to beg. I saw that 'For Sale' sign and came to make sure you weren't going anywhere."

Hongry shook his head. "No. I ain't leaving. That sign belongs to a neighbor."

"That's good. It wouldn't be the same without you here. Tom and the boys are coming Friday, and I know they want to see you. I imagine Tom will want you to give him a refresher course on picking out crabs." Hongry, with his small hands, was the best crab-picker around.

"He do okay. But I don't mind helping him out none."

"Do you think it'll rain this weekend?"

Hongry nodded. "We're about due. Ain't had none all summer. Watch the birds. They know. Sea birds been moving around, roosting in treetops."

Abbey looked up. Sure enough, white wood storks, their black-ink-dipped wings tucked in to their sides, stood tall and still in the treetops. Hongry lived off to himself, so it was always quiet there, but it seemed unusually so that day. Abbey looked back at the small man, whose attire rarely changed: faded red-plaid shirt, worn green work pants, and briar-scratched brown leather boots. His feet were his only transportation. "I'll take those collards down to Roosevelt for you."

Hongry smiled and pulled a switchblade knife from his pocket. "That'll save me a walk. Let's fetch him some of them greens. You got pepper sauce over to your house?"

"Yes, thank you, I have pepper sauce." *No self-respecting southerner would ever be without a bottle of pepper sauce.* The cottage always had a shaker bottle stuffed with small, red, hot Tabasco peppers and filled to the top with white vinegar. Abbey thought for a minute. "Does your house leak, Hongry?"

"Not too bad."

"Maybe we can get Tom to help you patch it. He likes to do jobs like that." She followed Hongry to a row of substantial-looking foot-tall dark leafy greens. He bent down, whacked a large bunch, and handed it to Abbey, then moved to the next clump and cut again. He walked her to her Jeep. "You say Mr. Tom's coming later?"

"Yes. He's bringing Momma and the boys on Friday. He doesn't want me to have all the fun."

Hongry looked at her kind of funny, then smiled when she grinned. "He likes collards. I know he do. You got to have enough to feed that man, keep him strong."

"He'll be very happy you thought of him. I'll cook them for supper when he gets here."

On their way to the gate, Hongry pinched off several red, green, and orange peppers. Abbey opened the rear of the Jeep and laid the greens on the floor beside her clothes bag. Hongry handed her the peppers. "Case your pepper sauce ain't hot enough."

"Thank you, Hongry. I can't wait." The back of Abbey's jaw tingled at the thought of collards drizzled with hot pepper sauce. "I'll take this bunch to Roosevelt now, so they stay fresh."

Hongry didn't budge from his spot until she was well down the road. In her rearview mirror, she watched him head back to his garden.

The paved road ended under a green-stained wooden sign etched with "Kings Bluff Hunting and Fishing Club, Members Only." Abbey's cottage was just off to her right, but she continued on the road's hard-packed, loamy black sand. Light filtered through thick, opaque green air beneath a dense canopy of trees. She rolled down both front windows and inhaled long and deep. Nowhere else smelled this way. Nowhere.

At the end of the road, she drove up to a freshly painted wood-frame house and parked. Grass protruded from the thick lips of Black Angus cows who studied Abbey with curious eyes as they chewed. A strongly built, white-haired, dark-skinned man walked across the pasture and met her at the fence.

"Good afternoon, Roosevelt."

"I figured you'd be here before long, Miss Abbey."

"My crowd's coming Friday."

"Your momma coming?"

"You think I could keep her away, Roosevelt?"

He smiled. "I'll stop by if I see her having that morning coffee on the porch."

"She'd like that. Before I forget, I have something for you. I stopped at Hongry's." She explained that she'd stopped to make sure Hongry wasn't moving, then collected the collards from her Jeep and handed them to Roosevelt. "He cut these for you about ten minutes ago."

Roosevelt said, "Thank you. Kind of you to save him having to walk. He grows some mighty good greens."

"I can't wait to try them." A cow mooed, then another. "Your cows look healthy, Roosevelt."

"They do, all right. They've got plenty of pasture to graze, and they can get up in the woods for a while to get out of the sun. They're a bit restless right now. Weather's changing."

Abbey thought about the forecast and the patches of rust she'd just seen in Hongry's roof. "I don't want to step on any toes, but I told Hongry that Tom would help him mend his roof if it leaks badly."

"Aww, it ain't bad, though it might not look like much."

"Okay. You ought to know. Enjoy those greens. And do stop by to say hello to Momma."

Roosevelt nodded. "Thank you, Miss Abbey. And thank you for stopping. It's always good to see you."

She drove away slowly to avoid stirring up dust. Her eyes scanned the dense maritime forest for the white-flag tail of a deer leaping over fallen trees or an armadillo scrabbling for cover in the low brush. If you really looked deep into these woods, high and low, there was no telling what wildlife you might see. When she drove up behind the cottage, the river ahead glistened. The cottage's forest-green siding and stark white trim promised calm and quiet. *This is just what I need.*

WHEN SHE RETURNED from her walk, she poured a glass of wine and settled into a rocker on the screened porch. There was a slight breeze. Her shoulders relaxed. She closed her eyes and pulled a mental shade down on real estate, which was easier to do when she was away from home. No shade in the world could block the nausea in her gut when she thought about Tom. Again, she ran over the lines she had rehearsed on the drive down. Surely the appropriate one would come to her when she needed it. After a while, Ben's advice popped into her head. She sipped her wine then went inside. Blix picked up on the second ring.

"Hi, girlfriend. It's me, here all alone in God's country. I hope you know I meant it when I invited you down here."

There was a pause. "I have thought about it. A lot."

"You don't sound so hot. What's up?"

"My appointment wasn't with just a dentist. He's an oral-cancer specialist."

"Damn." Abbey took a breath. "Damn it all. Want to talk about it?"

"Not over the phone. I'm sick of the phone. Word travels fast, you know. Relatives—and friends I didn't know I had—have opinions. And advice. They all know someone who knew someone. I know they're only trying to be nice, but after a while, I run out of things to say. One lady even told me she cures her mouth sores with a dab of Campho-Phenique. I mean, really, folks. We're talking cancer, not fever blisters."

Damn, damn, damn. "That settles it, then. You're coming. It's beautiful here and you can walk without traffic stinking up the air. And you won't have to worry about the phone or the cold-sore lady showing up at your house with a cheesy casserole. You can do your own thing for a whole weekend."

They had a long talk. Blix never cried, at least not in front of friends—who knew what she did in private—but she took her knocks and lived life on her own terms. They reminisced about their trip to Europe at the end of college.

"I should have married that Aussie we met at Oktoberfest in Munich," Blix said.

"He was a hunk. And he was crazy about you. You could have been a butcher's wife and cheered at his rugby matches." There was silence on the phone. *Sadness, regret, confusion?*

Abbey had no answers. "What can I do for you, Blix?" She walked around the kitchen and stretched the curly phone cord to its limit.

Blix finally said, "Just don't coddle me. You know I hate to be fussed over. I want to come down there, but only if you let me help you do everything: cook, take care of the cottage, play with the boys." She paused. "And if anyone steps on a fishhook or gets sunburned, I'll be the on-call nurse. That's something I'm actually qualified to do."

Abbey stopped moving around and pumped her fist. "You're on."

"Good. I'm ready to be there."

Abbey chewed her upper lip and flipped the phone cord around like a jump rope. "You've already talked to Tom, haven't you?"

"Yep. He called this afternoon and told me y'all had talked about it over dinner. He's picking me up sometime Friday before traffic starts."

"Great. We'll have a good time. See you soon." Abbey took a deep breath as she hung up the phone. *Treat her like there is nothing wrong with her.* She left a message for Tom that she'd arrived safely and would try him again later.

After an hour of sweeping up dead roaches and making her bed, she went for a swim. Around eight o'clock that evening, she rang Tom again.

"Hi," he said. "I just walked in the door."

She glanced at her watch. "Did you work late?"

"No, Boonks had me over for supper with her and the boys. What a threesome. I asked those little rascals if they wanted to come home with me tonight, but they said Grandma had to finish a story she was reading to them, so I didn't argue."

Boonks was the nickname Abbey's maternal grandfather had given to his only daughter—Abbey's mother—and the name she'd insisted Tom use.

Abbey knew she'd explode if she passed over another opportunity to confront him. "Tom, are we all right? Is there something I need to be worried about?"

Of course, she was already worried. She wanted him to say something to reassure her. They had both been in marriages before where their trust had been violated. They had worked hard to repair those old wounds, and she'd thought they had, but now she wasn't so sure. When he said nothing, she forced herself to ignore the urge to play peacemaker like she always did.

He took his time. Through the phone, she heard the sofa squeak like it did when he sat in his spot. "What do you mean, Abbey?"

"I... I don't know. We have drifted apart." All she could think about was the letter he had received from an old friend. Just a friend? "We used to talk and laugh all the time, Tom, and lately, everything is so serious and difficult, and we bicker about petty bullshit all the time. Like your boxers, for crying out loud."

This time, he didn't hesitate. "Well, you asked. I work all day so I can support our family, and you work twenty-four seven trying to prove you can have a career and make money and be a mother and a wife and run a house." He huffed into the phone. "It's too much, Abbey. You can't be everything to everybody, or we all suffer. Something's got to give."

She was so blown away that she didn't utter a word about what concerned her.

"You know what Jimmy said at your mom's tonight? He told her you were never home because you had to drive people around and show them houses all the time."

This time, she exhaled into the receiver, then said, "So, you think what's going on with us is all my fault because I'm spread kind of thin."

"No, not at all, but the work thing is your decision. I have told you I don't mind if you work, I just don't want it to interfere with our lives and affect the boys, or me, for that matter."

"So, what else? I know I'm not the only one at fault here. Why don't you tell me about your new pen pal?" When he didn't object, she knew she was on the right track, but she also knew better than to further this conversation on the phone. This one had to be face-to-face.

CHAPTER 5

Early Thursday morning, Abbey went out behind the cottage to the boathouse, a slightly leaning corrugated-metal affair that had been there for years. She dragged open the heavy, rust-hinged door and propped it open with a broken cinder block. Her rowing shell hung from a sling attached to the rafters, a Tom construction that involved ropes, pulleys, and slip knots. The design kept her shell clear of the power boat that her two older brothers, Charlie and Zach, shared with Tom. The dock was empty when she carried down her boat and oars.

As she shoved off, the sky in the east glowed a faint gold over the treetops. By the next day, if not by that afternoon, members of the Kings Bluff Club would dribble in for the long Labor Day weekend and would not waste a minute before putting their boats in. Fishermen were like that. They took every opportunity to be on the water. For now, the river was hers. Her pencil-thin shell glided across the water like a wing through air. Fifty strokes later, perspiration slicked her forehead.

The thermometer in the kitchen window had registered eighty-five degrees when she'd looked at it well before sunrise. The heat would build throughout the day, but the afternoon might bring a thunderstorm to cool things off, if only temporarily. Clapper rails, known locally as marsh hens, moved undetected in the tall spartina grass along each bank and gave away their positions with sharp, screeching cackles—nature's alarm clock.

Seated with her back toward the bow, Abbey glanced over her right shoulder and made a slight course correction to avoid the next dock. Two fishermen loaded their boat with rods, tackle boxes, and coolers. They looked up as she slipped past and stopped what they were doing. Both waved and watched open-mouthed. She nodded. Her hands on the oar handles maintained the set or balance of her shell, a boat that was a curiosity in this prop-driven, gas-fueled fishing world.

The men's voices carried across the water. One of them said if his wife took up the sport, maybe she'd get rid of those flappy things that dangled beneath her upper arms. Abbey chuckled to herself. Everyone thought rowing was about arms. Without any change that an observer would notice, she pushed down harder with her legs, the rower's main power source, and scooted by the men like a blade on ice. This was her realm, her zone.

MID-MORNING, SHE CARRIED a metal-handled plastic bucket to the dock and pulled up the crab trap she'd baited the afternoon before. The small square baskets of her childhood had been fun for a day of attentive crabbing, but the commercial trap did the job efficiently while she went on with her day. "Excellent." She pulled up a load of blue crabs and set the trap on the dock. *There's dinner for tonight and tomorrow.*

Strands of hair tickled her face as she dumped twenty-four snapping, spitting, claw-grabbing male crabs into her bucket. She reminded herself to grab a hat next time. There was still plenty of bait in the trap, so she tossed it back into the river and glanced to the south to see what weather was headed up from Florida. *So far, sunshine and blue sky. Keep it coming.*

***

BACK IN THE cottage, she filled a large pot with water and added a healthy shake of salt, black pepper, Old Bay Seasoning, and a splash of white vinegar and turned on the gas burner. The phone stopped her on her way to the shower. It was Blix.

"Hi, Bunns. I had to call you."

Abbey said, "Are you ready to talk? I know you have had a lot on your mind without me rattling your cage."

"Rattle all you want. It helps to talk, and I know you won't try to tell me what to do."

Abbey sank into a ladderback chair near the phone. "Well, I'm here. So, shoot." The pot of water began to sputter on the stove.

"It's not like I haven't been through tough before, Bunns."

Right. You nearly died the other time. Abbey held back her thought. Blix never talked about herself or the wreck, and Abbey respected her choice.

"After you and I talked, I called my doctor—told him I wanted to know best- and worst-case scenarios."

"And...?"

"It depends how you look at it. Without the surgery, the cancer will spread fast. It's very aggressive. With the surgery, I'll lose part of my jaw. They won't know how much until they get in there. Chances are, I won't be able to chew—for a while at least." She paused. "But what if I can never..." She sighed, then sniffed. "I'll have to do the dining-by-syringe thing again. Hopefully not for that long. Sounds appetizing, doesn't it? I'll have you over for dinner one night. Don't bother to bring anything. I'll provide the syringe and your choice of God-awful, flavor-enhanced goop."

Abbey thought about the corn she'd gnashed into the week before. Blix wouldn't even be able to eat an apple unless it was pureed to a slippery sludge. "Yummy. Sounds great. Are the flavors at least realistic?"

"Doesn't really matter. I don't taste much anyway."

Facial damage from the wreck. "At least they wouldn't have to waste a nurse to teach you how to use the damned syringe."

Blix chuckled. "That's looking on the bright side. 'Patient already syringe-feeding trained.' The thought of having to do that again—well... I thought I was through with all of that years ago."

Abbey rocked back in her chair until it tapped the wall. "How long did you do it after the wreck?" She'd watched Blix fill syringes with her liquid lunches back then with never a complaint.

"As long as my jaws were wired together. Felt like years but was probably several months."

"I remember you carried wire cutters with you."

"I was quite the thing. The only girl who carried wire cutters around in her purse in case she choked."

Abbey shook her head. "You're amazing, dear one. Always have been. Did you ever have to use those things?"

"You mean, did I ever barf on a date?"

Abbey laughed. "Well, did you?"

"No, but guys were fascinated. They all wanted to know how and where to start snipping if I started to choke." She was silent for a beat. "I think I was so afraid that I barely squirted anything in. No wonder I got so skinny." She paused again. "I was afraid of a lot of stuff back then."

There was an eye patch until she got a prosthesis and then rounds of reconstructive facial surgery. "You're the bravest person I have ever known."

"Please don't go all Hallmark on me, or we'll blubber like a couple of idjits."

"Okay, you're right. How thoughtless of me to say something nice to you. So, what's next?"

"Is it raining down there yet? It's supposed to."

"No, blue sky so far. Is it still hot in Atlanta?"

"Steaming. I don't go out unless I have to. If I'm not at the hospital, where they keep the thermostat at seventy, I'm at home in front of the AC."

"We'll be fine here either way. It's great to be away from the city."

"Power goes out here all the time during thunderstorms. What happens down in the boonies when that happens?"

"Candles. I have plenty."

"You're impossible."

Abbey snickered. "Love you too." She sat up, and the chair thumped to the floor. "Oh, and don't forget your rain jacket."

"Already got that, plus my mother insists on filling a cooler for me. Don't worry, I will be prepared. You'd think I was going off for a month. Mother will probably come home this afternoon and sew nametags into my shirts and shorts. She already bought me a stack of Jockey underwear. I swear."

"She's just being a mom. I think it's sweet."

"Real sweet. She bought cotton waist-highs, no less. I'll leave them wrapped and donate them to the Salvation Army."

"Good idea." Abbey went to the shallow drawer near the base of the phone and grabbed an index card and pen. "I'll ask Tom to pick up a generator."

"Don't bother. I'll bring mine."

"You sure?" Abbey hesitated. "You have a generator?"

"Absolutely. I got it in the divorce. That and all of my photo albums."

"All the important stuff." Abbey thought for several seconds. "Why did you ask for the generator?"

"One of life's necessities is a hair dryer. Have you ever known me not to dry my hair?"

"Got it. See you tomorrow afternoon. Keep Tom awake at the wheel. Momma will want to stop at a roadside stand if you pass one."

ABBEY ONLY INVITED those to Kings Bluff who appreciated its rustic, far-from-civilization aspects. She had learned long before that friends who required shops, restaurants, or beaches simply didn't make the cut. Blix had been there before and loved it for what it was, sand gnats, horseflies, and all. Abbey thought Blix would like the small bedroom that adjoined a bathroom complete with sink, toilet, and clawfoot tub. She stripped off the chenille bedspread, grabbed the two lumpy pillows, and went outside and smacked the living daylights out of them. Dust flew. She gave the bedspread a good shake, then draped the lot on the clothesline and left them to air.

At six o'clock that evening, she called Tom. He was on his way out the door to meet someone for dinner and was in a hurry. She got the hint but asked who he was meeting anyway. "It's just Benjamin," Tom said. "I'm running late."

Benjamin was a close friend of Tom's from the law firm. Tom spent a lot of time with Benjamin these days, and Abbey wondered why. "Tell him hello for me."

CHAPTER 6

B runswick, Georgia, the dot at the apex of the bight of the Georgia coast, was the westernmost land on the Atlantic seaboard. It was sheltered from the Atlantic Ocean by two of Georgia's barrier islands, Sea Island and St. Simons Island. Bordered on the east by the Intracoastal Waterway, the city was probably most remembered for the nose-curling, rotten-egg-smelling clouds that belched from its paper mill on the Brunswick River.

From the oven of a compact kitchen in a small wood-frame house near Brunswick's downtown business area, a home-made chicken pot pie exuded the heavenly smells of pastry and baked hen. Nineteen-year-old Otis Simmons twisted the top of a trash bag, then doubled it over and looped it into a knot. He hefted the bag from an oversized plastic bin and carried it out back. His granny, gray-haired and plump, bent over the kitchen sink, her apron dusted with white flour. She didn't so much as look up when the screen door *thwack*ed shut against its frame.

Near a dripping spigot at the rear of the house, Otis lifted the dented lid from a large metal trash can and added to yesterday's deposit, which was on top of several others. He held his breath and clamped down the lid on week-old dinner bones and rotten tomatoes that had baked to a high stink beneath the unrelenting heat.

Brunswick was the only town the teen had ever known. Irene, "Granny" to him, provided the only home he and his three half-siblings, all of whom had different last names, had ever lived in. He had never known his father directly; he only knew about him. Brunswick wasn't that big, and people talked. One of the older fellows in Otis's crowd had spent time in jail with Otis's father. Through the jail grapevine, this man had heard that Otis's father had been knifed "crotch to gullet" in Georgia's Reidsville State Pen. Word had it, the knifing had had something to do with drugs, but it could have just as easily been about a woman, or an old score, or all those things.

Otis was tall for his age. He and most of his friends had bought six-packs and rot-gut wine at a corner store run by an old black uncle who only carded you if you were little and looked like a kid. Otis had studied some of the older under-age boys, how they nonchalantly walked by shelves of chilled cans and bottles as though they had a special kind in mind and then picked up a twelve-pack of Budweiser or Pabst like they did it every day. He'd practiced the way they walked and talked and tried to develop the self-assured air they had about them, as though they could get anything they wanted. From what he saw, they did, especially in the good-looking-lady category. They always scored. And sharp dressers? They wore gold chains on their necks and wrists that must have cost small fortunes. But the best things were their rides, slick and souped-up with shiny hubcaps that sparkled like diamonds when the tires rolled on down the street.

It took a lot of dough to live like those brothers did, but theirs was the lifestyle he wanted and wanted now. He was sick of depending on his granny. He wanted to be on his own. Screw school and all of that shit. He had paid attention, and what he had gathered was that the fastest way to get what he wanted was to sell reefer. Drugs were everywhere, so it couldn't be all that hard to sell them. The real problem was seed money. That was what the brothers called it. He understood it to mean starting-out money, cash he'd need to buy his first batch. He would start with marijuana, none of the hard stuff, and after a sale or two of weed, he'd be able to grow his own. Some of the fellows grew theirs in pots under lamps in their garages. He had a plot of good, fertile land that would outgrow the rest of them put together.

He glanced at neighbors' houses on either side of his grandmother's, then cut through a gap in the greenery no wider than a six-inch board. Granny had a patch back there where she had grown enough vegetables to keep her grandchildren well-fed. The old chicken coop still stood, though it hadn't seen a Rhode Island Red in many years.

Otis came back here often and reminisced about the days when his momma and granny had worked this ground. That was before his momma had begun to act on what she called "the itch." That was what she'd told him when he'd asked where she went all the time. "I just gets the itch." That was all she said. He took her at her word. He'd had a bad case of poison ivy once. He knew you had to scratch a bad itch. It was only when one, then another, then another sibling arrived that he put all that itch business together.

The soil was beautiful. Granny fertilized with what she called Black Gold, which was nothing but seasoned chicken poop from her Rhode Island Reds. That dirt would grow anything. Otis would clean up the weeds and grow primo weed. That was the plan. Then he'd get a fancy car and have his pick of the hot babes he'd fantasized about.

He needed a good think about how to get started. He squeezed back through the hedge and exited the yard where he knew his grandmother couldn't see him from the kitchen window. He plotted scenarios as he walked. Newcastle Street was the heart of downtown. Old buildings still bore the look of the 1940s, some with the establishments' names hand-painted on exterior brick sidewalls, some with the original wood signage still attached. Otis watched dust poof up when a scanty-haired fellow dumped an armload of books onto an outdoor display table. Otis shook his head. Granny didn't tolerate dust.

He glanced in the window at Kresge's Five-and-Dime but kept on walking. Nothing of value there. It was where his mother bought underwear for her brood in plastic packages of five for a couple of dollars. Boys got plain old white. Otis's sister got little ballerinas and kittens and ponies and stuff. His little brothers always begged for one of the store's little painted turtles or bug-eyed goldfish that swam around in a tank decorated on the bottom with fake frogmen and starfish, but his mother said she had enough mouths to feed. *That's a laugh. She don't feed nobody.*

A man behind a sparkling-clean window threw a sheet or something over a counter, but not before Otis caught sight of glittering diamond rings and bracelets. When their eyes met, the man's narrowed. Otis nodded, a tight grin on his full lips. He walked on. Diamonds glittered in his mind.

Down and across the street, a blue neon sign in a window said "Pharmacy." He mouthed the word then looked at the faded hand-painted sign on the brick. "Smith's Drugstore" in tall black letters ran the length of the building. Otis crossed the street and peered through the window. In the way back were rows of brown pill bottles on shelves. *There's got to be some good stuff in there I can sell.*

A cherry-red Impala convertible rumbled down the street. Otis watched the driver, his friend Deke, whose dirty-blond hair swished back and forth as he looked from the storefronts to where he was going. Deke was obviously more interested in the storefronts than in his driving. Otis stepped out and slapped the hood of the car. Deke jammed on the brakes and yelled, "Shit." He grinned when he saw Otis.

"Oh-oh-oh," Otis whined. He folded forward at the waist. "You done injured me, White Boy."

"Damn you, Oh-Shit. Get in here, boy." Deke patted the passenger seat. "Let's ride. We need to talk."

Otis hopped in. Deke, whom Otis called "White Boy" in exchange for Deke's use of "Oh-Shit," was in Otis's class, though he was a good deal older. Deke had had what he considered the misfortune of a teacher who'd refused to pass him from the sixth grade until he'd mastered basic reading and math skills.

"You look all serious today. What's up, big man?" Deke pushed in the car lighter and took the nub of a joint from the ashtray.

"I been thinking."

"Uh oh. Now that's trouble, boy." Deke lit the joint then passed it to Otis. "Thinking about what?"

"This." Otis took a hit, then tapped Deke's right hand with the knuckle of the hand that cupped the joint. "I want to sell some of that so I can afford a cool car like this." He rubbed his hand over the cracked leather seat. "I mean, I'm talking making it big."

"And how do you plan to do that? You know, my old man was a used-car salesman before he dove into the bottle. This car is all that's left of his sorry broke ass." Deke took the last hit, then crushed the final bit in the ashtray.

"I know. But I ain't gonna' end up like him, or mine, either. I'll do it right. I'll grow my own weed and sell it myself. No middleman."

"Well, hell. I can help you get started, man. Let's talk on the way to the beach. You ever been surfing?"

"Surfing? You shitting me? Where you think I'm going to get a surfboard? White Boy, you're crazy in the head."

"Body surf, man. I heard waves is bitchin'. That's surfer talk. Means 'good.' We never get good waves here. Let's go have some fun, and you can tell me about your big plans."

"Where'd you hear about the waves?"

"TV. Atlantic's all churned up. Tropical storm or something is coming. Probably a lot of wind that'll give us some wave action."

Otis was unconvinced. It was a near-perfect day. Why screw it up?

Deke asked, "You swim, right?"

"You kidding me? Sure, I swim." As they crossed the Frederica River, Otis said, "Man, that river looks rough, don't it, with them whitecaps and all?"

"Yeah. That means huge waves." Deke drove to the village of St. Simons and circled until he found an available parking space. When both doors opened, feral cats hiding in the shadows nearby spooked and fled.

"Not many people crabbing on the pier," Otis said.

"Too windy," Deke said as they stepped from the car. "Come on. Let's go see about them waves."

Otis followed about six steps back as they scrambled down to the beach. Sand whipped their legs; salt water sprayed their faces.

"All or nothing." Clad in cut-off jeans, White Boy tossed his shirt to Otis, then high-stepped into crashing waves and dove into the brownish-green water.

Otis watched, open-mouthed, as his friend disappeared. Froth splashed his thighs. Undertow pulled at his ankles and sucked sand from beneath his feet. His eyes darted back and forth, searching. He drew shallow breaths. At last, he saw movement some distance down the beach at the water's edge. Deke's dark form crawled up several feet, then collapsed.

Otis took off, sprinting like he had done on the last leg of the four-forty relay at school, but today on the sand, his feet felt encased in concrete. Deke lay on his back. Gasping for breath, Otis said, "Are you okay?"

Deke's chest heaved; he coughed out water. After several seconds, he said, "Thought I was a goner there for a minute."

Otis dropped to his knees. "Damn, man, why'd you do that?"

"What? I told you we were going body surfing."

"You could have drowned, man. People die every year out here because of that undertow."

Deke grinned. "Aww, did I scare you?"

Otis squeezed a fistful of sand. "I couldn't see you is all. I thought the current done took you away." He tossed his wad of sand. "Damn, man. I don't know about you."

Deke laughed and put out his hand for an assist. Otis stared at the hand. He finally extended his.

CHAPTER 7

E arly Friday morning, Abbey was awakened by the harsh *ke-ke-ke-ke* of marsh hens in their cover of tall spartina grass in front of the cottage. She listened to the clattering of the chicken-sized birds for several minutes and pictured them scurrying around in the river mud, a reminder to get up and moving. Company was coming.

When she and Tom had talked the night before, his brush-off to go meet Benjamin had bothered her. It wasn't like him not to take time for her. Something was obviously going on with him, but she wasn't the type to sit around and stew. She pulled on form-fitting rowing gear and went to the screened porch to look at the water, hoping it was calm. Dawn held a gray tint just past total darkness. A breeze played with loose strands of her hair. She inhaled the complex earthy green scent of decomposition that blossomed in the heavy, damp air, a smell specific to the expansive marshes and caused by the bacterial breakdown of plant debris.

After tea and toast, she wiped down counters in the kitchen until she could see all the way to the other side of the river. She went out and carried her oars and rowing shell to the dock, got in, and shoved off with the outgoing tide. Dead low was in about an hour. Every ten strokes or so, she glanced over a shoulder to check for obstacles. In the early light, the river was a pewter sliver set between slick black mudbanks, where tall marsh grass gave cover to everything from a wide assortment of birds to raccoons and the occasional alligator who had come to the estuary for a saltwater bath. As children, Abbey and her brothers had cut wide loops on water skis at either end of the river, but human alterations to the river's natural flow had changed all that, and mud seemed to be winning.

A *ptuuhh* sound ahead alerted her that she wasn't the only one out that morning. She didn't need to look. In two strokes, she watched telltale rings expand in the water; two more strokes, and a large female dolphin's sleek gray back broke the surface in an arcing roll. Close by, her calf mimicked her and added a flip of its tail. All of nature was out feeding in the early-morning hours. Abbey was accustomed to the three-to-four-foot sharks. Her boat was a lot bigger than they were, so she paid them no attention.

Elegant white egrets on toothpick legs unfurled long, slender necks and darted their beaks into the shallows to capture minnows. A shrimp-pink roseate spoonbill wagged its distinctive bill back and forth, eating as it strolled along the water's edge. Abbey never tired of her close-up views of nature.

Several bends later, a crab man pulled his trap and dumped its contents into his boat, the blue crab one of many sea creatures that flourished in the nutrient-rich estuary. The man looked like Ben from the fish market, so she stopped and waved. He looked at her for several seconds, then waved before he moved on to his next trap. At the docks at Taylor's Point on the north side of the club's property, she stopped for a drink of water. She always carried a bottle in the boat. In the absence of exertion, she felt the river's movement. Low swells rocked her twenty-seven-pound boat in a long, slow, rolling rhythm. Ben's boat had disappeared around the bend, probably headed back to Brunswick, and there hadn't been any other boats to have caused a wake. *That's odd.*

Using one oar to turn her shell one hundred eighty degrees, she could see in the direction in which she had been headed. Still, she saw no other boats, yet the gentle swells continued. Vertigo on tidal waters was something she had experienced before but attributed to competing movements, the tide going one way and her shell the other. But this sensation was different, like when you sat on a waterbed and it took several minutes for the water inside the plastic bladder to calm. But this didn't settle. It continued to roll.

Determined to figure out what caused the continuous waves, she let the spoon-shaped blades of her oars lie feathered on the water's surface and waited for the rolls to flatten. She wondered what kinds of things the shore birds mined from the pluff mud. A sole pelican tucked and dove into the water, then retreated with a fish captured in his distensible pouch. She wondered if Tom felt captured like that fish. Did he have reservations about joining her after their talk? Surely not. Close to five minutes passed, and the roll still hadn't played out. There was too much to do to waste any more time. The tide had turned and would assist her return.

WHEN SHE GOT back, a stocky young man stood in a boat tied to the community dock in front of her cottage while an older version of the same body type passed rods, cooler, and a bait well to him from the dock. "Hi, Mr. Jones," Abbey said to the older man as she drifted past. "Beautiful day to be out on the water."

"Yes, it is, Abbey," he replied. "We're getting out while we can. Rain's headed our way."

She drifted toward the end of the floating dock where Tom had attached a low-profile platform to accommodate her low-riding riggers. Getting in and out in the current was difficult, but she had a system that worked, most of the time. She hopped out, removed her oars, and lifted the shell to the top of her head. She walked up beside the men. "I've been out since sunrise, so I haven't heard the latest forecast."

"Weather folks are still tiptoeing around, like they do when they don't want to make a call," Jones Junior said. "Especially since it's a big holiday weekend and all. They won't say anything for sure because they don't want to call it wrong, but it acts like a slow-moving front."

Mr. Jones said, "Local feller I listen to over in Brunswick agrees with my son. He says these slow-movers are the worst because all the rain they bring in makes for floods, and floods cause more deaths than wind damage. Now, that's not what I would have thought."

Abbey adjusted the boat on top of her head. "And if we get much wind, we might lose power because of all the old trees here."

"That's right," Mr. Jones said.

"Rain won't change things for the weekend, will it?"

"Not really," Mr. Jones said. "Course, everything's weather-dependent. We're going ahead with the kids' fishing tournament because it's all done off this dock, so that's good."

"Thank goodness. I have two little boys coming down here from Atlanta, and they'll be disappointed if they don't get to be in the fishing tournament and the raft race."

Jones Junior cleared his throat. "Um, they did call off the raft race for tomorrow morning."

"Oh." The stern of Abbey's boat swung when she turned to face Jones Junior, and it almost hit Jones Senior in the head. "Oops. Sorry. I forgot about my hat."

Jones Senior chuckled.

"It's too bad about the raft race," Abbey said. "Why cancel unless it's pouring and there's lightning?"

"Guess you didn't see them," Mr. Jones said.

"See what?"

"Portuguese men-o'-war. Lots of them. We've been standing here watching them sail by for thirty minutes or so. About the time the tide turned, those fellows started blowing in here like little ships. I haven't seen them in here in years, but once they're here, they're here for a while."

"All I noticed were the unusual swells. What do you suppose they're about?"

"Yep. We were just talking about that, too," the younger man said. "That's really what we're keeping an eye on. Those swells are probably caused by weather out in the ocean way out yonder."

"Thanks for the update. I need to go break the news to my husband before he leaves town with the boys. Good luck fishing." *Wouldn't you know it? I hope I can catch Tom.*

CHAPTER 8

It was close to 8:30 in the morning by the time Abbey got back to the house, and it was already hot and sticky. Every stitch of clothing she had on was wet—a salty white strip encircled the crown of her baseball cap—but a swim had to wait. Tom had said he'd hoped to pick everyone up and be on the road by eleven o'clock at the earliest. His secretary put Abbey right through when she called him.

"Hi," Tom said when he picked up. "Uh, what's up?"

"I had a good row this morning and it's beautiful here, but I just talked to two fellows on the dock who seemed a little apprehensive about the weather." She half-expected him to say he'd rather be at home if it was going to rain.

"Have you looked at the forecast?" Tom asked.

"Not yet. I just put my boat away."

"What did the men on the dock say?"

"As far as they know, the fishing tournament is on, but the raft race was called off because of a Portuguese man-o'-war invasion. They're everywhere out there, Tom."

"I've never seen one. What's the problem?"

"They look like a flotilla of little purple balloons, and each one has long, thin filaments that trail along behind and stick to your skin. They burn the dickens out of you. I got into them in the ocean once and I panicked for a minute. We can't put the boys in that water."

Tom sighed. "Where'd they come from?"

"The ocean, most likely."

"So, waterskiing's out, too, I suppose," Tom said. "Maybe we should cancel the whole deal, Abbey. Our guys won't be happy if they can't ski or do the raft race, and they'll drive us crazy if they're stuck inside."

"I know. That's all they've talked about." She thought for a minute. "But I almost hate to disappoint Blix more than the boys."

"I forgot about her. Listen, I've got to go. Call me back and let me know what you decide. I'm good either way."

She called her mother and told her about the jellyfish. Boonks held the receiver away from her mouth while she explained the cancellations to the boys. Squeals of protest were loud and negative.

Abbey listened to her mother calm the boys with a distraction. "Okay, boys, why don't you two put out some lettuce for the turtle while I finish talking to your mother. Lettuce is in the fridge." There was conversation that Abbey couldn't make out, and then Boonks came back onto the line. "Sorry. I'm here."

"You have a pet reptile?"

"Well, no, I don't *have* him. When he shows up, I put out lettuce and water in an aluminum pie pan."

"And you used to scold me when I left milk out for a stray cat, Momma."

"I know. We're both softies." There was little-boy laughter in the background. "'Turtle' sounds much nicer than 'reptile,' sweetie."

"I beg your pardon, Momma." Abbey chuckled. "A visiting turtle."

Boonks asked, "So, what do you think?"

"That's what I wanted to talk to you about. I need to let Tom know if you and I come up with another plan. Blix needs to get out of town to do some thinking, so I'd hate to disappoint her."

"And it wouldn't hurt you and Tom to do the same," Boonks said.

Abbey hesitated before she responded. She respected her mother's opinions about most things. "What do you mean, Momma?"

"I try to stay out of my children's business, but it won't hurt for you to have some alone time."

"It's that obvious?"

"Let's just say you and Tom seem a little prickly around each other."

"Okay. Thanks."

"But about this weekend, sweetie. I just happen to have another option that might make the boys happy."

"I'm all ears."

"You remember my dear friend Lila, who has a cabin on a blueberry farm in the mountains?" What ensued was a detailed description of Lila's invitation to Boonks and her family to spend the weekend at Lila's farm in Highlands, North Carolina.

"She has two black labs and two miniature *burros* that James and Walt will have so much fun with," Boonks said.

While Boonks talked, Abbey began to feel relieved. Without the boys, she and Tom might be able to focus on what was going on with them, and Blix could use the time to figure out what she wanted to do. "Momma, I'll call Tom, but I'm sure he won't mind. Tell Lila we'd like to come get some of that mountain air sometime, too."

CHAPTER 9

Boonks's comment about Abbey's marriage was a wakeup call. Abbey leaned against the doorframe between her bedroom and the screened porch and stared at the futons she had made ready for the boys. The whole weekend had changed. Tom or Blix might want to take a nap or lie down and read on the porch, so she left the futons made. She turned on the big box fan she'd brought from home and plopped into a rocker. She closed her eyes and remembered the noisy rotating pedestal fans she and her brothers had carefully arranged here to blow across the Army cots where they'd slept at night and played spades and gin rummy during the heat of the day. Buck, their Grandmother Taylor's yardman, had shown them how to make smudge pots by stuffing Spanish moss into a coffee can, impaling the can on a big stick, and jamming the stick in the ground on the windward side of the porch. When the moss was lit with a kitchen match, it smoldered and deterred most of the biting sand gnats. Of course, the three of them had smelled like smoke a good bit of the time, but a dip in the pool had cured that.

Abbey allowed herself a short mope because Boonks and the boys weren't coming and got over it when she pictured them in Lila's kitchen in the mountains. They would insist on showing Lila how to make pully candy, a specialty Boonks had learned from her mother-in-law. Abbey's mouth watered, the smells of melted sugar, butter, and vinegar fresh in her memory.

Okay, time to shop. Years of selling real estate had taught her that when one deal died, you moved on to the next. Blix and Tom would arrive in the late afternoon. There was already a mess of cooked crabs in the fridge, and there would be more. The kitchen smelled of Old Bay and vinegar. To her working grocery list, Abbey added both vinegar and Old Bay, chicken backs for crab bait, Hershey's powdered chocolate, and ice. Tom loved Boonks's chocolate sheet cake, and the recipe was on the fridge. Abbey's mouth watered just thinking about the moist, gooey chocolate cake.

She went to the boathouse on the back of the property and slapped the rough board walls to scatter any snakes that might be coiled up inside. Tugging open the structure's sagging metal door, she located an extension ladder and climbed to the cobwebby rafters, where she grabbed two large coolers and lowered them to the dirt. She picked up a red gas can from a back corner, thinking that if Tom got bored, he could mow the grass. She hosed off everything and loaded it into her Jeep.

On her way out of the driveway, Snag Privit, the fishing club's president, intercepted her.

"You leaving already?"

"No. Tom's coming this afternoon with a friend of mine from home, so I'm making a food run. Because of the jellyfish, Momma is taking the boys to a friend's cabin in the mountains."

"That's a shame, but they'll have fun up there." Snag tapped the side of his door with an open palm. "Now don't you go buying no bait. I'm going to the dock right now to clean fish, so I'll put all the heads and backbones in your crab basket."

"That'd be great. Chicken backs were on my shopping list."

"All right then. Scat."

Traffic on I-95 North was moderate. The southbound flow was heavier—people headed to Florida beaches for the last couple of days before school started. The drive from Atlanta had almost emptied the gas tank, so Abbey stopped at the first station on U.S. 17 and filled up. Winn-Dixie's lot was packed. No one wanted to get caught flat-footed on a holiday weekend.

While Abbey shopped, she thought about stopping in at the local Board of Realtors to introduce herself. How many times had her broker in Atlanta stressed the importance of networking, anywhere, anytime? *Why not? It might pay off someday.*

The board office was nearby. She went in and was met by business as usual. Voices talked over ringing phones and grinding office machines. Abbey approached the woman at the reception desk and handed her a business card with her local number handwritten on back. They introduced themselves.

"Pleased to meet you, Sally. I'm an agent in Atlanta, but I have a cottage at Kings Bluff just south of here."

"The hunting club," Sally said.

Abbey wasn't surprised she knew about the club. Most folks around here were familiar with the names of the hunting and fishing clubs in the area. "That's right. I'm down for the Labor Day weekend, and the jellyfish sort of put a damper on some of the activities."

"I heard they're all over the beaches," Sally said. "Just blew in this morning. Nasty little things, but kind of pretty."

"I guess they are. But listen, I don't want to take up your time. I stopped in to introduce myself. You never know when you might need a name and a phone number in our business."

Sally flicked the corner of Abbey's card with her fingernail. "Your name is very familiar." She thought for a minute. Abbey knew where this was headed. She'd made the local papers several times in the past couple of years.

"I know," Sally said. "You were instrumental in the arrest of that scoundrel developer and his wife down in St. Mary's several years ago, weren't you?"

Abbey nodded. "Lucky me."

Sally smiled. "You're sort of a celebrity around here, you know. I'll hold onto your card. You got another one I can add to the office rolodex?"

Abbey took another card from her wallet, wrote her local number on the back, and handed it over. "I'd love to hear from you."

"Thanks, Abbey. Nice talking to you." Sally's vowels were soft, broad, and soothingly southern. "If we need help, or come up with a good referral, we'll give you a call. Thanks for stopping in."

"Thank you, Sally. It was a pleasure to speak with you."

Back in her Jeep, Abbey sat there for a moment, pleased she'd taken the time to stop. In real estate, contacts were important. Then she thought again about what Boonks had said. *Tom and I are prickly around each other? She would have only brought it up if it were obvious. I need to slow down and take a good look at my life.*

She glanced at her watch. It was still early. She didn't want to get away from civilization only to remember something she'd forgotten when she was halfway back to the cottage. *If it rains hard, the cottage might lose power. We'll need flashlights... already have Momma's nubs of candles.* She popped into a pharmacy and got what she needed.

Toward six o'clock that evening, she set the table, then filled her new flashlights with batteries and stuck them in a drawer in the kitchen. She heard the hum of rubber on asphalt. A horn tapped three times. *They're here.*

CHAPTER 10

Several hours later, while dishes air-dried on threadbare tea towels, Abbey shooed Tom and Blix out of the kitchen. As she closed the lid on a container of what was left of Hongry's collard greens, she imagined herself in Blix's shoes. What would be going on in her head, had she just been told she had an aggressive cancer but could prolong her life with surgery? Blix was like Abbey in many respects. Neither wanted to be fussed over. Blix's diagnosis hadn't come up over dinner, but Abbey was eager to talk to her about what she imagined could be terribly disfiguring surgery.

With a final look around the kitchen, Abbey headed out the door. In the still, sultry evening air, the tap of her Topsiders on the dock's wooden walkway was barely audible over nature's sounds. Insects hummed, frogs peeped and croaked, and a chuck-will's-widow beckoned his mate. Lights flickered in the cottages along the bluff. Cars and trucks pulling boats on trailers continued to trickle into the club. Most of the members were hunters and fishermen who lived within an hour or two of the club and drove down on weekends and holidays after they got off work.

Though the sun had been down for a while, sweat trickled down the middle of Abbey's back. She wiped her forehead with the back of her free hand; the other grasped a bowl of dinner's discarded shells that were destined to go back into the river. Scavengers would nibble on the bowl's contents, a practice that kept stinky crab and shrimp shells out of the garbage can in the kitchen.

Blix and Tom's low voices carried over the water. "Any cooler out here?" Abbey asked when she joined them. Tom and Blix sat on a wooden bench that bore years' worth of the carved initials of teenage sweethearts.

Tom eyed the bowl in Abbey's hand. "I'm sorry you had to bring that down. I said I'd toss them."

"No problem."

"Tomorrow, I'll do all KP duty," Blix said.

"No way," Abbey said. "You're company."

"Since when? I'll go home if you treat me like a guest." Blix and Abbey exchanged a look.

Abbey gave back a single nod. She would be the same way, were the situations reversed. She dumped the bowl's colorful, aromatic contents into the river. "It's still hotter than the hinges of Hell in the house. At least the air moves a little out here."

"A little is right," Tom said. He and Blix joined Abbey at the rail. "Blix and I noticed how high the tide is tonight."

Moonlight made it possible to see across the river. "It is a pretty high tide," Abbey said, "and the moon isn't even full until Sunday night, when it'll be even higher."

Blix said, "I listened to the news last night while I packed, and the weatherman said to expect higher tides than normal—moon tides, or something like that."

"It's a gravity thing," Abbey said. "Full moons mean higher tides and lousy fishing. If you have high winds, tides will be even higher than our normal seven-to-eight-foot swings."

"Just ask nature woman," Blix said, tipping her head toward Abbey.

"Give me a break. You learn that stuff when you grow up with a bunch of fishermen." The breeze tapped a loose piece of tin roofing. Abbey glanced at it. "Somebody ought to tack that thing down."

She headed down a ramp to the long floating dock. Blix followed. Abbey asked, "Are you feeling okay?"

"Honestly, I don't feel any different physically, but if I slow down and have too much time to think, I imagine things." Blix picked up a dried-up barnacle from the dock and tossed it.

"There's usually marsh grass sticking up all along the other side of the river there." Abbey pointed. "Tonight, it's covered. It's that moon thing." She bumped Blix's shoulder with hers.

"Moon tide," Blix said. "I like that. Water wouldn't come up to the house, would it?"

Abbey felt the wonderful warmth of her friend and smelled the shampoo Blix had used that morning. Herbal Essences, if she remembered correctly. "It all depends. I suppose it could, though I've never seen it get that high."

Blix glanced up to the main dock, where Tom lay stretched out on the bench. She took a deep breath, then gave Abbey details about the procedure her doctor had suggested. They talked quietly for several minutes.

"My sister-in-law had a friend who went through something similar, Blix. She was a heavy smoker, and I only know about the results secondhand. I'll be honest with you: it sounded pretty grim."

"That's what I gather." Blix said. They walked back to the main dock and stood at the railing. Blix fiddled with a broken length of rope left by some crabber. "Thing is, it's all or nothing. I have the surgery, and I live for who-knows-how-long. Anybody's guess. I don't have the surgery, and I'm out of here. Adios. Pretty quickly."

Abbey hesitated, then looked at her friend and said, "I know this is all you have thought about, but are you really ready for this?"

"For what?"

"Death," Abbey said.

Blix hesitated for only a moment, then said, "Death. Yes." She bumped Abbey with her hip. "Thanks. That's the first time I have said it. It's so damned final."

They talked about death as though it were just another road trip, an adventure, destination only imagined but guaranteed. Abbey stared at headlights miles and miles away, as the crow flies—vehicles trusting I-95 to lead them across Georgia's irregular, water-riddled, marsh-covered edge—and she thought about how life was so much like that road. Roads required that you make decisions. She thought about the choice Blix had to make, to have surgery or not to, and the consequences of each decision. She wondered what she would do. She wondered if the surgery was worth it.

Finally, Blix said, "Abbey, can I take a walk by myself? I mean, is it safe?"

"Sure. Nothing will eat you. Just follow the white shell road, Dorothy. Look out for roots and pointy shells, though. I trip on them all the time when I jog. And don't venture off the road. I'd hate to have to pull you out of the marsh. That mud would suck you right up, and the fiddler crabs would nibble your ears and toes all night."

"Gross. Don't worry. I won't go off the road."

When Blix left, Tom joined Abbey. "What's going on?" he asked.

"She told me about the surgery. It sounds gruesome, but she doesn't have much of a choice. She's a goner if she doesn't do it."

"Huh," Tom grunted.

"I came right out and asked her if she was prepared to die."

"Damn." Tom crammed his fists into the pockets of his jeans. "What did she say?"

"She said yes."

"Well, hell, you're going to tell her not to give up, aren't you?"

"I won't give her false hope, Tom. She has seen a specialist."

"Well, shit, you have to tell her to have the surgery. They're doing tons of research, and they're curing a lot of diseases these days. She needs to buy time. Tell her to go for it. What's she got to lose?"

"Spoken like a true lawyer," Abbey said. "I won't tell her to do anything. It's not my decision, it's hers. What she needs now is a friend to talk to, not someone telling her what to do. She has to make up her own mind."

A pelican the size of a small child hit the water then skimmed away with his catch. Hearing the edge in her voice and remembering that Tom hadn't known Blix for as long as she had, Abbey said, "She will have to take food through a large syringe. Everything will be liquified into a nondescript milkshake."

"Oh, come on, I'm sure they flavor that stuff." Tom crossed his arms. "And it's temporary. She'll be able to eat again after she heals."

Abbey turned to him. "How the hell do you think she's going to chew? I don't know about your teeth, but mine are attached to jawbone. She'd lose a good chunk of hers."

Tom's hand went to his cheek. He and Abbey made their way back to the cottage in silence.

Thirty or so minutes later, the screen door on the porch squeaked open and then *whack*ed shut. Blix walked into the living room, where Abbey and Tom sat in front of the TV, Tom in a chair, Abbey on the sofa. "What's going on?" Blix asked.

"Just catching the news out of Jacksonville," Tom said.

Abbey patted the cushion next to her. "Have a seat."

Blix nodded toward the front of the cottage. Abbey followed her to the screened porch, where they both dropped into rocking chairs.

"You okay?" Abbey asked.

"I'm not ready to decide about this surgery yet, Bunns."

Abbey let the thought settle, then said, "Take your time. You'll know when you know."

"I think so," Blix said. "Right now, I just want to enjoy every second of every day."

Abbey said, "As you should."

Blix grabbed her hand.

"You'll know, Blix. You're one brave woman. You'll know."

They sat in silence. Abbey tried to imagine what might be in store for Blix but realized she couldn't. All she could do was be a friend. "If there is ever anything you need or want, all you have to do is ask."

Blix nodded.

"As long as it's legal," Abbey said. Both of her eyebrows went up and down to accentuate her teasing tone. Their eyes met. They laughed. Then they cried.

Blix said, "Thank you. I needed that."

By the time they went back into the living room, Tom was watching an old John Wayne movie.

"If it rains, we might be watching a lot of The Duke, ladies. They're running a special on him this weekend."

"That might be sort of fun," Abbey said. Then she got the barometer and motioned for Blix to join her at the dining-room table. "Let's figure out how to read this thing."

CHAPTER 11

The next morning, Abbey and Blix were walking back from the dock with their coffee as Snag drove up in his truck and rolled down his window. "Heard the latest news?" he asked.

"Doubt it," Abbey said. "Snag, this is my friend Blix. Blix, Snag. He's the president of Kings Bluff."

They said hello.

Abbey asked, "What did we miss?"

"Fellows in Brunswick are in a radio club." Snag threw the truck into park. "They've been listening to broadcasts from the Caribbean, and it sounds like a tropical storm just nicked them down there, and it's headed our way. Might be building as it goes."

"Did it do much damage?" Abbey asked. "I saw a little film footage on the news, but it was just palm trees blowing around and rain."

"All I know is it's that time of the year," Snag said. "I suggest you keep a radio on. Things can change minute to minute."

"Thanks for the heads-up," Abbey said. Snag waved and went on.

Tom was watching the news when they walked in. "Weather folks have changed their tune," he said. "They say be prepared for high winds and rain with flooding in some areas. People in Florida are already bailing out."

"Has the governor called for an evacuation?" Abbey asked.

"No, but people they interviewed said they didn't want to chance it, so they're leaving."

"Good grief," Abbey said. "Maybe we ought to go see what they think in Brunswick." She had no interest in going to Brunswick, but she was fishing for a response out of Tom, any response. She didn't like the vibes she was picking up from him.

"You two go on," Tom said. "I need to check in at the office."

Abbey studied her husband's face. That was a response, all right. Was he eager to get her and Blix out of the house so he could talk in private? "Is anyone even in your office today? I mean, it's a holiday weekend."

He looked at her. "I just need to make some calls, Abbey, okay?"

Tom's expression was blank and gave Abbey no hint of what he was thinking, save annoyance. Even more concerning was the fact that his hands hadn't so much as grazed her body since he had arrived at Kings Bluff, and now that she thought about it, it had been quite a long time since he had shown any interest in intimacy, and that was odd for him. Puzzled, she nodded. "Sure. Blix and I will see what's going on in Brunswick."

As opposed to the last several days, when everyone on the interstate had been headed south, traffic today was a steady northbound stream. "I can't believe everybody's leaving," Abbey said. "But if you stay and it floods, you'd better have a boat in your backyard so you can escape, because there won't be anybody left to rescue you." She glanced at Blix. "You know, if things start to get dicey, all we have to do is head home. Right?"

"Sure, but I have been thinking. Suppose things turn bad. I'd like to see if they could use some help at the hospital."

"That's a great idea," Abbey said, "and if they don't, maybe they know someone who does, like some emergency-preparedness group."

They drove to the hospital. Inside, rubber-soled shoes squeaked on polished floors. A volunteer at the information desk made a call, then directed Blix down the hall to an office. Abbey found a vacant seat in the reception area, which was almost as crowded as the highway had been. Children bounced on hard-cushioned chairs, babies cried, and elders folded their arms across their bodies and cat-napped, unbothered by all the activity around them.

"If the mayor says I'm supposed to go somewhere, where does he suggest I go?" asked the ebony-skinned man seated across from Abbey to the fellow next to him, whose skin tone reminded her of walnuts. "I ain't got no place else to go, Sam. How about you?"

"Naw. I ain't got no place to go, neither. And my meds is about to run out." The fellow named Sam turned both his palms up, then clasped them in his lap. His shoulders rose and fell with an audible sigh. Abbey imagined what would happen to the two old men if a disaster hit. Surely there was someone who could take them in.

Twenty minutes later, Blix appeared. Straight-line lips replaced the smile she had worn in. She looked around until she found Abbey, shook her head, and walked over. "Too much red tape." Blix looked around the packed room. "I bet these folks have been here for hours. You can't tell me they don't need help here. Maybe I ought to set up a little MASH triage unit out in the parking lot."

"Don't go getting any ideas," Abbey said. However, once outside, she stopped.

Blix asked, "What are you thinking, Bunns? I know that look."

"I just had an idea, or rather, you said something that gave me an idea. There were two older gentlemen sitting near me in there. They were talking about not having anywhere to go if an evacuation is called. You can't tell me there aren't a lot more people in the same situation."

"So… what do you have in mind?"

"They probably belong to a church. Why don't we go back inside and talk to them and see if we can't come up with some way to help them?"

Blix smiled. "Great minds."

They went back inside and approached the two men. "Excuse me, gentlemen. My name is Abbey, and this is my friend Blix." Two pairs of yellow-stained eyes looked up. "I couldn't help but overhear you several minutes ago about not having anywhere to go if things get bad. Do either of you attend a church in town?"

The men looked at each other and nodded. "Yessum. We attend Good Shepherd AME. We both sing regular in the choir."

Abbey and Blix exchanged looks. "About how many are in the congregation at Good Shepherd?" Abbey asked.

The men mumbled between themselves, and then the one named Franklin said, "Somewhere in the neighborhood of twenty-to-thirty—on a good Sunday."

Abbey asked Blix, "Could we figure out a way to help twenty people, plus-or-minus, for several days?"

"I don't know why not," Blix said. "You and I both have more than that when our families get together for holidays."

"All right, then," Abbey said. "I'm thinking out loud here, so this might sound kind of crazy, but if something happens and a group of you needs a place to go, would your pastor open up his church to those who can't get out of town? Maybe let folks bring bedrolls, sleeping bags, what-have-you, and stay there? In the church? It would help if there was a kitchen."

The two men mumbled to each other again, and then Sam said, "I'll talk to our preacher myself. We did this once before when a storm came through and we was out of power for five, six days. Everybody brought stuff from home because it'd spoil anyway, so we just cooked it all up and kept everything on ice. We had a fine time. I know he'll do it."

Blix asked, "If we can make this happen, can y'all get the word out?"

"No problem there. We have one of them phone trees. Need be, we can get the word out fast."

"Shouldn't you ask the preacher first?" Abbey asked.

Franklin nodded. Sam stood, looked across the room, and asked in a loud voice, "Brother Isaiah, you opening up the church if the storm hits? Some of us ain't got nowhere to go if we supposed to leave town."

Abbey looked across the room. A large black man in a dark pinstripe suit looked up from a row of young women who sat against the wall. Each either had a baby in her lap or one in the oven. Brother Isaiah held a gray felt hat to his belly. All eyes turned to Sam and the two white women standing by his side. The women with the babies nodded and began to chatter among themselves. Brother Isaiah said something, and there was a great deal of head-nodding and talking among the women. He strode across the room with purpose, his hat now clasped in both hands behind his back.

"What do you have in mind, Brother Sam?" the pastor asked.

"I don't know. I was talking to these ladies here, and they suggested we hold the church open for those can't get out of town if the storm comes in here."

"I see." Brother Isaiah seemed to give their idea some thought. "And who are these two Florence Nightingales?" Even, stark-white teeth showed between his full lips.

Abbey extended her right hand. "Reverend Isaiah, I'm Abbey Taylor Bunn." His large hand swallowed hers in a firm but gentle grip. "My mother has a place at Kings Bluff just down the road. My husband and my friend Blix here and I came from Atlanta for Labor Day weekend."

The preacher nodded.

"Blix is an emergency-room nurse at Piedmont Hospital in Atlanta." The preacher listened patiently; his eyes never left Abbey's. She glanced at Blix. "We thought we might be able to help somehow if this storm hits. I, uh, I overheard Franklin and Sam talking, and I figured maybe I—" She looked at Blix. "—we might be able to help them out. It was just a thought."

Reverend Isaiah held up his hand. "Okay. Relax." He looked directly at Abbey. "You said Abbey Taylor. I assume that's a family name."

"My mother's maiden name is Taylor," Abbey said. "Bunn is her married name."

"Your people from Wayside?"

"Yessir. Momma's from there." That seemed to satisfy him. Abbey wondered why but didn't ask. Her mother's family had lived in this corner of Georgia for centuries, and her grandfather had been heavily involved in land preservation and tree-farming. She hoped the preacher saw those as good things.

"I see," he finally said. He hesitated for several seconds. "What would you need? At my church, I mean."

Abbey faced Blix. "Why don't you tell Reverend Isaiah what you think you need, Blix."

Blix snatched a quick breath. "Well, let's see." She stared at the floor for several seconds. "Your congregation will need to bring some things from home, whatever they can't do without for several days. Also, creature-comfort items like pillows, blankets, toiletries. They'll need their meds in prescription bottles with their names on them. Clearly printed. And their dentures, glasses, things like that. They can put them in individual bags or sacks, whatever they have. No need to buy anything. The bags should be clearly marked with their names and contact information." Blix thought for several seconds. "Prosthetics, inhalers, anything they use daily that would make an extended stay difficult if they had to do without. Diabetics, anyone who injects or needs to refrigerate meds—tell them to bring a little cooler. We'll need to pick up enough ice to last several days." She paused again. "And copies of any paperwork related to their medical histories, if they have it." Blix looked at Abbey.

"Driver's licenses, homeowner's insurance papers, that sort of thing," Abbey said. "If they don't have or can't make copies, maybe I can do that for them at the Board of Realtors."

Reverend Isaiah did a slow head-turn toward Franklin and Sam. "Y'all just met these two nice ladies?"

Franklin and Sam nodded.

"Huh. The Lord works in mysterious ways. I'll show you the church, if you'd like to see it."

ABBEY FOLLOWED THE white Eldorado's back bumper as closely as she dared. She'd been to Brunswick many times, mainly to the seafood market or the downtown area, but she didn't know her way around that well. Reverend Isaiah drove slowly and nodded or waved to folks walking down the sidewalks or in passing cars. Blix was quiet. Abbey looked over. Her friend's lovely, gentle hands were clasped in her lap, her fingers long and slender, her nails neatly polished in a taupe shade that blended with her smooth, even tan. Familiar tunes played one after the other on an oldies station. The lot was full at the Piggly Wiggly grocery store they passed.

Several minutes later, the reverend's right-turn signal blinked. The small wooden church wore a fresh coat of white paint. Its shutters were a deep Charleston green, almost black. Azaleas in the yard had been trimmed and banked underneath with long-leaf pine straw. The reverend unlocked the front doors of the church and showed the women in. Wooden pews gleamed a rich, lustrous brown, and the air smelled of lemon oil. They walked through the sanctuary then down a short hallway to a spacious room where tables and chairs were neatly stacked against one wall. A kitchen was visible through a door at the back of the room. "This is the church hall, where we have our weekly suppers. I imagine between the sanctuary and this, we have enough room to make folks comfortable."

Abbey thought of her mother, who pronounced supper as "*suppah*" like Reverend Isaiah. Her eyes traveled from wall to wall. "What's the size of this room, about thirty-by-thirty?"

He gave her a slow nod. "Precisely." He studied her as though trying to figure her out.

"I sell real estate. I measure a lot of rooms."

He smiled, said, "I see," and steered them to the kitchen and showed them the stove, refrigerator, pantry, and storage room.

Blix had been quiet for the entire time. She pointed a finger at a back corner in the kitchen and went there, then explained where everything should be arranged along the wall. She opened the refrigerator door. "We can store milk, yogurt, meds if necessary, that kind of thing here. If we lose electricity, which we probably will, we will need coolers and loads of ice. We can go to several grocery stores to see if they will donate what we need." Blix finally stopped and looked at her companions, who both grinned as they watched her. "What?"

"Nothing. It's fun to see you in action," Abbey said. "But I was thinking, what if there's no evacuation?"

The pastor, with his hands clasped behind his back and his head bowed and eyes closed, took several seconds and then asked, "But what if there is?"

"Right," Blix said. "Nothing will go to waste."

"Okay. Let's go start asking," Abbey said. "But we might need a truck."

Reverend Isaiah said, "Most of the congregation shops at the Piggly Wiggly we passed on the way here. They're good folks. Always willing to help. And I have a truck."

Abbey had seen a late-model truck parked behind the church that looked like it hadn't moved in years. "The one parked out back?"

He chuckled. "No, no, no. That's my project. I have one at home that actually runs. I'll call my wife and get her to bring it over."

BY THAT AFTERNOON, the church's kitchen was filled with enough supplies to last thirty-or-so people several days. Sam and Franklin split the phone-tree list and gave out specific instructions. So far, about twenty adults and several mommas with infants had said they would be interested, should an evacuation be called, and they knew more mommas and older folks would show up once word got out. Abbey and Blix left with a key to the church and Reverend Isaiah Johnson's home phone number.

It had been a long day. Blix's head dropped to her headrest before they hit the Sidney Lanier Bridge. Abbey took a deep breath. Though she exercised almost every day and often experienced long and physically wearing days showing houses, she was exhausted. Blix had been going at it all day and had not stopped for a minute. *Impressive.* Blix's diagnosis hadn't slowed her down at all. Again, Abbey wondered what she'd do if the choice were hers. She imagined the actual surgery. Blix would go into it looking one way, but no one knew what she'd look like when she came out. And then what? More surgeries? Chemo? In the background, the radio droned on about the deteriorating weather conditions. Abbey tapped a pre-programmed button on the radio: an oldies station. It never took her long to recognize a song. This one was by Maurice Williams & The Zodiacs. She sang softly. "Stay, just a little bit longer..."

With her eyes still closed, Blix joined in. "Please, please, please, please, please..."

CHAPTER 12

The Brunswick River separated the city's downtown area from a broad expanse of wetland marsh. Though it was unsuitable for development due to its quicksand-like mud base, people enjoyed watching the birds and raccoons who thrived in the grassy tidal environment. Saturday morning, shrimpers, fishermen, and sailors steered their vessels slowly down the river to comply with the no-wake zone in the vicinity of the downtown marina.

Headed downtown from his home, Otis Simmons sauntered down the cracked sidewalk on L Street and eyed each house, curious how his granny's little wood-frame home compared to the neighbors'. He took care of basic maintenance at the house, like touch-up paint jobs and keeping the gutters clear and tending the yard, and he had enough pride to want to see how his work stacked up. He also knew his granny trusted him, and she'd made no bones about who her will directed to be in charge once she was gone, which, according to her, was no time soon. Otis suspected that being in charge meant more than taking over upkeep of the house. He'd need to provide care and a home for his siblings, just like Granny had done for all of them.

Granny had been up early, fussing around room to room. She had sent the younger children to play in the yard, where she could keep an eye on them, and shooed Otis out after them. She'd told him it was too pretty outside for him to hang around the house when rain was on the way and he'd be stuck inside. He knew why she'd been touchy that morning and had wanted to be left alone. He wasn't all that happy himself. His momma hadn't come home the previous night.

At least her absences were predictable. They coincided with paydays at the paper-and saw-mills. That was how he'd figured out what his momma was up to a while ago; the previous night, the red, pointy-toed shoes with the skinny heels had been a dead giveaway. He'd seen a shiny red toe sticking out of the large handbag she had carried with her. She'd looked him straight in the eyes and told him she'd be working late and not to wait up. She hadn't fooled him for a minute. Not anymore. Nobody could work in shoes like that unless... He didn't even want to think about that option, but he couldn't help it, couldn't stop his imagination from working around the idea of his momma being with some man. She was always after him to get a damn job, so what was so different from what she was doing and what he wanted to do? Not much. Both illegal. *Shit*. He wiped sweat from his face with the bottom of his T-shirt.

He kicked a rock and sent it scuttling down the sidewalk. Up ahead, pavement and buildings gave way to the sparkling river. Seagulls glided overhead, on the lookout for lunch. Otis walked to the edge of the bank and inhaled the salty air, and then he grabbed the front of his oversized T-shirt and pulled it away from his damp body. It caught the wind through the armholes and luffed like a sail. He repeated the motion several times, then glanced at an old, white-haired black man sitting nearby in a collapsible chair under a live oak tree.

The man held a cane pole and watched the boy cool his body; his white-toothed smile said he knew how good that air felt. Attached to his line was an orange-and-white float the length of a man's shoe that bobbed in the water. A glass juice bottle filled with ice and a caramel-colored liquid sat on the ground within easy reach of his chair.

"Feels good, don't it," the man said. "I recollect doing the same thing when I was your age and didn't mind a bit showing off my middle. No sir. Sure do feel good."

"Unh-hunh," Otis said. "I ain't never been so hot."

"I was once. Long time ago. I was little, but I remember. Sure do. This heat we been having reminds me. You don't forget something like that."

Otis's shirt luffed again. "Like what, old man?"

"Like the storm that formed up behind all that heat." The man lifted the tip of his cane pole. The hook was bare. "Doggone yellowtail—maybe a crab—done stole my bait. You mind fetching me another shrimp out of that little cooler over yonder?"

"What's your name, old man?"

"That'll do. I'm a man... and I'm old. I reckon I earned that nickname."

Otis spotted the small Igloo cooler nestled in the roots of the oak tree. Inside the cooler was a handful of dead shrimp bait and a can of Coca-Cola. He grabbed a shrimp and threaded it onto Old Man's hook.

"When was this storm you been talking about?"

Old Man muttered "Thank you" and lowered the hook into the water. "A good while ago—1898. Like I said, I was just a little feller, but it like to scared the living daylights out of me. I was lucky, though. My daddy hitched up his mules, and we skedaddled out of town before the water come in here too bad. Got to sixteen feet, they said afterwards. We was lucky. It killed a lot of folks."

"Killed them how?"

"Some got hit by stuff flying all around. They was signs and roof shingles and limbs and stuff like that blowing around like it was dust." He paused. "Goodness, the limbs. It sounded like a war, the way they was cracking and breaking. Trees was picked up clear out of the ground and tossed around like they was nothing to them. But most of 'em drowned when they couldn't get to higher ground." Old Man shook his head. "Awful thing, that was, people stranded on those islands and all."

Otis stared at Old Man. "When did you say this was?"

"Eighteen ninety-eight. That's right." Old Man nodded. "That was a bad storm year."

Otis made some calculations. "That's a long time ago, Old Man. That makes you about..."

"Ninety-seven." Old Man looked directly at Otis. "For another week or so, anyway. I be ninety-eight, end of September. That's how I remember that storm. It was near my birthday." He raised the tip of his pole. The shrimp was still there. "What's your name, son?"

"Otis Simmons."

"Otis. I always liked that name."

"My momma says she likes some singer got that name."

"Yes sir. Otis Redding. One of the best. 'Sittin' on the Dock of the Bay,' just like we're doing right now. That's a fine name, son. Suits you."

Voices drifted up from the marina, but the breeze made it difficult to hear what they were saying, so Otis just watched. "What're they doing?"

"That's what they call a day dock. Those are transient boats."

Otis looked at Old Man. "What's that mean, 'transent'?"

"Transient. It means just passing through on the way up and down the Intracoastal Waterway. Your eyes are better than mine. Look at where some a' them boats is from. It's written on the stern. That'd be the back end."

Otis cut Old Man a look, said, "I know where the stern is," and then walked back and forth on the bank. "Some of them are from Georgia, and those are from Maine, New York, New Jersey, Delaware. What're they all doing here?"

"A lot of folks live up North, but it gets too cold up yonder in winter, so they brings their boats to Florida over the winter, and in springtime, they takes them back up to Maine or some such place as that. I reckon those boats out yonder are getting a head start going south for the winter. That dock will be like that all fall—people stopping in to pick up water and groceries or go to a restaurant in town. They might hold up here a day or two, enjoying the company of other folks. They'll start to party after a while. Just you watch."

"Hunh. Like they're all in some big floating hotel or something."

"That's what I reckon. Those are mighty expensive boats out there; cost more than your house and mine put together—and that's before you put in gas."

Otis looked on, open-mouthed, as men steered stream-lined boats into position and bumped up alongside the day dock. Another boat lifted from the water, strapped beneath a mechanical hoist. Sure enough, Otis saw a man with beer in-hand hop aboard the sailboat tied up behind the one he'd just secured. "Party time," Otis said below his breath. Then he said, "I don't know much about sailing. I was at the beach the other day with a friend, and the waves were huge. I can't imagine being out in the ocean with all of them waves and no land in sight."

"You got that right. You best watch yourself near that ocean, boy."

"How come, Old Man? I can swim."

"Because you'll be one more damn dumb drowned fool, that's how come."

Otis thought for several seconds. "I was with this white feller. He dove in. Looked to me like he got churned up pretty good."

"Nobody with any sense ought to be in that ocean. You hear me?"

"Naw. I knows how to swim."

"In a pool, maybe. Not in that ocean. It's tricky."

"Water's water. It don't make no difference."

"Do too. That undertow gets ahold of you, it'll carry you away. I'm telling you. Don't do it." Old Man raised his pole to check his bait. Still there. "You see them men tying up them boats? Ain't no use if we get some weather in here. Water will gobble them up sure as I'm sitting here and you're standing there."

Otis stared at the old man. "Ninety-eight, huh? Same as that storm you told me about."

"That's right, but I ain't there yet, so don't rush me. But I'll tell you, I learned a thing or two in all those years."

"I reckon you ought to."

Old Man raised his pole and swung the baited hook toward Otis. "I got to get on home. Been sitting here long enough for my legs to stove up on me."

"I'd better get on home, too," Otis said.

"All right, then. Take care of yourself, Mr. Otis Simmons, and you stay away from that ocean, you hear? There are some places you ain't got no business being."

Otis nodded, grabbed the line that dangled several feet in front of him, and flipped the mangled shrimp into the river. "Looks like Mr. Crab been playing with your bait."

"I felt him. I was hoping he'd steal it and save me the trouble of taking it off my hook."

Otis wrapped the line around the pole and secured the hook. He picked up the cooler and chair, looked around, and asked, "How'd you get here?"

"My wheels." Old Man tottered toward the live oak. A beat-up old black bicycle with a wire basket lashed to a rack over the back wheel leaned against the tree's trunk.

Otis helped him attach his gear to the basket with the length of dirt-blackened cotton cord that was loosely knotted there. "Nice talking to you, Old Man." Otis turned to leave.

"You live with your momma and daddy?" Old Man asked.

Otis hesitated, then said over his shoulder, "My granny. She looks after me and my brothers and sister."

Old Man asked, "She a good woman, your granny?"

"Yessuh. She's a good woman," Otis said. "A real good woman."

"You ain't going swimming in that ocean and make trouble for your granny, is you, boy?" Otis felt Old Man's stare on his back. "You take care you don't disappoint Granny. You hear me, Otis Simmons?"

Otis turned and looked at the old man. "Naw," he said as he walked away. "I won't."

"Where you going now, son? I imagine your granny could use some help around the house, being it's Saturday and she probably cleaning and all."

"I got to go work on my garden."

"Garden. You a gardener?" Old Man called, but Otis paid him no attention.

Ever since he'd ridden around with White Boy and told him how he wanted to make it big, he had thought about that garden, and now he'd met Old Man. *"Take care you don't disappoint Granny." Shit bucket, Old Man. Why'd you have to go say that?*

Several streets later, downtown all but hummed. Everyone was busy moving things from here to there and engaging in hand-waving conversation. Having nowhere to go and nothing to do, Otis felt conspicuous among those who did. Although it was still hotter than blue blazes, he decided to get to work on his plot of ground. White Boy had promised to donate a dozen marijuana plants to their new partnership, and Otis wanted the ground to be perfect.

Two blocks from his granny's and deep in thought, he saw a red car pull away from the church and thought it was White Boy until he realized it was a Jeep. There were two white women inside, talking to beat the band. *What they doing at that church?*

Then he noticed who was coming toward him on his side of the street: his pretty neighbor, Latisha, and her little boy. Otis hadn't known the baby's father, but he had heard he'd been a cop and had been shot and killed during a drug bust.

"Hey," Otis said with a wave as Latisha turned toward the church. "What's going on?"

"I'm just helping out at the church."

"Huh. What's going on, bake sale or something?"

"No, silly. Lots of folks are planning to stay in the church if the weather turns. Your granny probably got a call from Sam and Franklin."

"Because of a little rain?"

"Where you been, Otis? Everybody who can git done already gone. Ain't you listened to the news at all? We're preparing for a lot more than just rain. Reverend Isaiah's gonna open the church to his congregation if need be, so we're getting the church ready just in case. We gots food, water, a roof over our heads if a bad storm develops, and we'll at least all be together."

"I know what's going on, Latisha. I ain't deaf or blind neither." He crossed his arms and balled his fists. Latisha glanced at his biceps. "Granny might be interested, but I ain't spending the night in no church."

"Okay, then," Latisha said, and she kept walking. "Suit yourself."

Otis relaxed his fists and stared at the floral pattern on Latisha's short skirt. *Granny grows those.* He watched roses and hydrangeas sway back and forth on Latisha's slim hips as she and her little boy walked up the steps of the church. Her firm, round calf muscles brought coffee ice cream to mind. He turned to go, lest he be caught staring. "Umm, umm, umm," he mumbled. "That's one fine woman."

CHAPTER 13

As Abbey drove up behind the cottage, she watched Tom's Jeep Wagoneer come down the dirt road in front of the row of cottages and stop at the mailbox. She had never seen him look in the mailbox here before. Several minutes later, he pulled in beside her Jeep and parked. The sound of power saws and pounding hammers all along the bluff drowned out the usual bird calls and insect buzzes that were part of life on the estuary.

Abbey said to Blix, "I have no idea how or if Grandmother ever did anything to prepare for high winds. We were in Atlanta, so I'm certain Momma never came down here to help." Abbey's grandmother had given the cottage and the club membership to her only daughter, a godsend to Boonks and her three children after her husband had died.

"It looks like they're boarding up windows," Blix said.

When Tom joined them, he held a batch of slick advertisements from a local Dodge truck dealer. Abbey asked, "Are you expecting mail—down here?"

Tom squinted and his lips parted, but he didn't take the bait. "No." He handed her the trash. A truck pulling a trailer crept toward them.

Blix said, "He's got a heavy load. Looks like wood. Who is that?"

"You met him. It's Snag," Abbey said. The truck drove onto the property and pulled up beside them.

"Hey," Abbey said. "Looks like you've gone into the lumber business."

"Something like that. I picked up more talk on my radio last night after I heard the governor's warning. This feller was talking about what he thought might be moving on up into Florida and heading our way, so I went into town first thing this morning and bought up everything I could carry in one load. If we don't use it all, we can store it. There'll be a time for it."

"Want to sell any of it?" Abbey asked.

"Nope, but I'll give it to you. I bought out every piece of quarter-inch I could get my hands on. How much you need? I've got plenty."

Abbey asked, "How much do you want per sheet?"

"It's on the house for members."

"Momma's the member, and she's not here."

"And for children of members. Club has a reserve fund for things like this, and the board approved it. They hope afterwards, members will come help clean up."

Abbey noticed Blix walking around the side of the house as she and Snag continued to talk. Moments later, Blix reappeared and said, "There are twenty-two windows, including the one from the front bedroom to the screened porch."

Abbey grinned. "My handywoman. Thanks, Blix."

"All right then," Snag said. "Let's pull off what you need so I can get on with my delivery. I'll be back around with my saw. While I'm gone, y'all get a rough idea how big those windows are so we can cut the boards. I suggest you just put up enough to block anything flying but leave space to see out of and get some light through; otherwise, it'll get claustrophobic inside the house."

Tom had been quiet, but he pulled off half a dozen plywood sheets and stacked them.

"I'll get pencil and paper from the house," Blix said.

"I have a tape measure in my car," Abbey said. Tom followed her.

"What the hell was that about?" he asked.

"What?"

"Don't play games, Abbey. You know good and well what I meant. Your comment about the mail."

Abbey slung open the door to her Jeep. "You're telling me not to play games? That's choice. I get hang-ups on the phone at home and you're getting perfumed mail, and you have the nerve to tell me not to play games?" She grabbed a tape measure out of the glovebox and slammed the door.

Tom looked gut-punched. "You didn't mention a hang-up. When?"

"Make that plural. The last one was when I got home from work Wednesday evening, same day as the letter. The caller even breathed into the receiver before she hung up. She wanted to make sure I knew she was there." She stomped off.

"Abbey, wait. When was the other time? Please stop. This is important."

"You're damn straight it's important. And I think someone's casing our house. The same day, Wednesday, I was on the phone with Blix, and a yellow car went poking by our house like it was checking it out."

Tom's mouth dropped open. His eyebrows creased.

"I don't know what, but something's going on, Tom."

His face looked pained. "Please, Abbey. When was the other hang-up? It's important."

"Beginning of the week. Monday, I think. She seems to know when I get home."

Tom ran a hand over the top of his head then chewed his lip. Abbey left.

"I need to make a call," Tom said to her back.

Abbey struggled with whether to shout after him or cry. Instead, she pulled the tape out and let it snap back several times, then found Blix in the front yard, staring at the screened porch.

"What do we do about the porch?" Blix asked. "These screens have seen better days."

"Forget about them. With any blow at all, they'll be ripped to smithereens. They need to be replaced anyway."

Tom reappeared with his hands dug deep into his pockets and a frown on his lips. "If you two measure windows, I'll look for nails."

"There are jars of them in one of the corner cupboards in the dining room."

Tom's forehead creased. "What's a corner cupboard?"

Abbey glanced at Blix, eyebrows raised. Her brain said *Einstein,* but she held her tongue. "There are cabinets in two of the four corners in the dining room. They have doors, and the last time I looked, they had old kerosene lanterns on top of them."

Tom cleared his throat like he knew exactly what she was thinking, and he probably did.

By the time Snag returned with sawhorses and a circular saw, they were ready to cut. The cottage's near-hundred-year-old windows had thick wood mullions that held rippled glass panes, two-over-two, in double-hung sashes. Layers of white paint helped hold the windows together. "One thing's obvious," Abbey said to Blix. "Windows aren't made to last like this anymore. Obsolescence is now a built-in feature, so things have to be replaced regularly. Makes no sense."

***

LATER THAT AFTERNOON, Snag dropped by. "I think we're in pretty good shape here," Tom said. "Can I help somebody else?"

"Matter of fact, if you can drive a boat or pull a trailer, we can use you. We're moving boats behind the caretaker's house, and we're short of drivers."

"I'm happy to help," Tom said.

As they drove away Blix said, "Boys always get to do the fun stuff."

Abbey looked at her for a minute. "Not always. We've been working all day, and there's not a whole lot more we can do. There are a lot of fun things we haven't done, so I have an idea."

"When do you not have an idea?"

"Have you ever fired a gun?"

Blix thought about the suggestion for several seconds, then swaggered off, turned, and struck a bow-legged stance with her thumbs hooked in her belt loops, comical with her skinny chicken legs. "You can call me Dale. Evans, that is."

"Hold that pose, girlfriend," Abbey said as she swiped the small, ever-present camera from Blix's back pocket. *This is the Blix I want her boys to remember.* "Smile for the birdie."

Click, click.

CHAPTER 14

Abbey and Blix went back inside and loaded up with sunscreen and bug spray. "Are you ready to become a sharp-shooter?"

Blix screwed up her lip and looked at her hostess as though she'd been sitting around waiting all day. "Well, heck yeah. Let's go."

"I'll be right back." Abbey went to the open-fronted bureau in her bedroom and took the Derringer wrapped in the tea towel from the bottom of a stack of her shorts, and then she rejoined Blix.

"Are we doing dishes before we go?" Blix said.

Abbey unwrapped the dish towel.

"Oh." Blix stared at the small pistol. "Do you always keep your gun wrapped in a dish towel?"

"Tradition." They got into the Jeep, and Abbey placed the gun on the backseat. "That's how Grandmother Taylor kept it in the drawer of her bedside table."

Blix chuckled. "That fits. You had a pistol-totin' grandmother."

"Sure did. She was all alone in that big old house of hers, and she didn't want any surprises."

"I remember her house. Your mom had dances up in the attic, didn't she?"

"Yep."

"Did your grandmother give you her gun?"

"She did. I haven't fired it in a while, and a gun is like anything else with moving parts. It needs to be used. If I'm working, I carry one of mine with me."

"You have another gun?"

Abbey nodded.

"Where do you keep that one, in your makeup kit?"

Abbey pointed under her seat.

Blix looked down. "I don't see it."

"Don't worry. It's there."

"So, you always carry one of those around."

"Most of the time. Think about it. I don't know my clients half the time, and when I hold an open house, I'm a sitting duck. There was an agent in Atlanta a while back who showed a prospect a vacant townhome, and it wasn't until she didn't show up to cook dinner that her husband called her office to see where she was. They found her in the basement of the property she'd shown. She'd been raped and strangled to death." After a pause, Abbey said, "I had a close call several years ago."

"The developer. That was near here, wasn't it?"

"Yes. My gun evens the playing field." They turned off the meandering tree-shaded road behind the cottages and onto another dirt road that ran arrow-straight between rows of planted pines with charred bases. "That char on the bottom is from a controlled burn. The club does them to get rid of grasses, limbs, and anything else that could fuel a fire after a lightning strike."

"Has one of those burns ever gotten away from them?"

"Oh, sure, and that costs us. Harvesting those trees is how the club supports itself. California wildfires burn out of control all the time because tree-huggers out there don't believe in controlled burns."

"What about the animals? What happens to them?"

"Most run, but others go underground. There's a whole ecosystem that depends on the habitat created by the deep

taproot system of those longleaf pines. Gopher tortoises bur-
row way down below the trees, and snakes and bugs crawl
down into those tunnels and live there."

Blix rubbed her skinny thighs like she was the next up
to bat. "What an adventure this is. I love it down here." She
looked at Abbey. "You don't, by chance, have a holster, do
you?"

I love showing her my other world. "I do. It's little and
sticks in your waistband. Want to try it?"

Blix smiled. "Sure."

Abbey reached under her seat and pulled out a small, tan
suede holster with a wood-handled pistol inside. They were
only going twenty miles-per-hour, so she extracted the pistol
and handed the holster to Blix. "See the clip on the back? Hook
the clip on your shorts, in front of your right front pocket."

Blix fussed with the holster, then pulled down the visor
and aimed its mirror at her hips. "That is so cool."

Out of the corner of her eye, Abbey watched Blix reach
toward her hip, point her finger-pistol, and make appropriate
sound effects. She did this several times. Abbey imagined
enemy cancer cells lurking among the pines and being blown
to bits. "Did you get them?"

Blix looked at her. "Every last one of them."

"Good girl. That holster makes you look like the real deal."

The road forked and appeared to eventually disappear
into a dense maritime forest. Blix turned in her seat. "Where
does that road go? I don't know how in the world you know
where you're going back here with all these little side roads
and the trees. It all looks the same to me. I'd be lost in two
seconds flat."

"Remember when we went fishing the last time you were
here, and we saw Cumberland Island?" asked Abbey.

"Yes. I remember it looked like a big long hump, like a whale. Can we go back there when we get through with my shooting lesson?"

"Sure." They pulled up to a raised wooden platform that looked out over a mown open area edged on either side by thick palmettos and brush. Soil had been pushed to the back to form a berm that stopped fired ammunition. "Come on. Let's load up."

Abbey placed the pistols on a raised counter on the platform, then retrieved a rusted real-estate sign from the rear of the Jeep. She walked off four paces from the platform into the range, pushed the metal legs of the sign into the ground, and went back. "Come on up here out of the grass, knucklehead. Stand out there much longer and you'll need to de-tick tonight."

Blix's face scrunched up as she did a little two-footed hip-hop in the tall grass and scooted up the platform's warped steps. She ran her hands briskly up and down her bare legs.

"Don't worry. They'll let you know they're there."

Blix looked at Abbey like she'd lost her mind. "Are you serious?"

"If you have any, they'll sort of tickle when they start to crawl around, or you'll just start to itch somewhere. They love to get under elastic bands in bras and underwear."

Blix frowned and scratched the middle of her sternum.

"Take a bath in a quarter-cup of Pine-Sol tonight, and that'll take care of them."

"Seriously? It'll take care of my skin, too. Doesn't it burn?"

"No. But it sure kills the ticks." With a glance at Blix, Abbey put on protective plastic glasses then pulled on padded, sound-absorbent headgear. All went quiet. Her ears felt like they were encased in foam-rubber pillows. "When you fire a gun, you need ear and eye protection." She dug in her gun bag and took out a white tube, from which she extracted a pair of orange foam earplugs. She handed them to Blix. "These guns are loud. Roll the tapered end around in your fingers to make a point and stick that pointy end in your ears. Keep your sunglasses on. The gun ejects a spent cartridge, and you don't want to catch one in the eye." *Shit.* "In your face."

Blix moved her sunglasses from the top of her head to her nose.

"Now, watch what I do. I'm aiming for the capital letter 'E' on the bottom line where it says, 'Real Estate.'" Abbey slowly got into position and fired one round. The bullet hit approximately two inches high and right of the E. She heard soft clicks behind her. *Camera queen.* She waited for the clicks to stop, then fired four more rounds in quick succession. She lowered the pistol. The E on the sign was no more. "Looks like I hit the bad guy."

"You killed the sucker. Now you have a 'Real state' sign."

Abbey grinned and shook her head. *Blix humor.* "The objective is to kill the sucker, as you say. Cops shoot to kill, but I can't say I wouldn't just unload to try to wound an intruder. Then I'd pray like hell I had scared the bejesus out of him, and he'd run like hell out of my house."

"But you got it right there in the middle." Blix pointed, then took a picture of the shredded target. "It sure is loud."

"Hence the ear protection. Now watch again." Abbey reloaded, then spread her feet shoulder-width apart and extended her arms comfortably in front of her. Blix stood behind her. *Click, click.* Abbey glanced around, made eye contact, and shook her head.

"Sorry."

Abbey fired five more times and then loaded one bullet into the chamber and explained all the safety precautions used when you handle a weapon. Blix repeated what she had heard.

Abbey said, "And never put your finger on the trigger until you are ready to fire." Blix repeated. Abbey put the pistol into Blix's hand, showed her the grip, and then posed Blix in the proper stance. She steadied Blix's arms and hands toward the target and said, "Now, take a deep breath. Remember, this is not a jerk. It's a slow and steady squeeze with that index finger." Abbey stared at the target and counted in her head. *One, two...* On *three*, the pistol jumped, and there was a loud, muffled explosion. Dirt kicked up six feet behind and to the right of the sign.

"Whoa!" Blix said. She placed the pistol on the counter in front of her, then massaged the web between her right thumb and index finger. "I did it. That was fun. Boy, it's loud. Did I hit it?"

"You were a little high and to the right, but you did great. All you need is a little practice." Abbey worked with Blix one shell at a time until most of her shots hit the sign and rewarded her with a satisfactory *ping*.

A box of shells later, Blix placed her spent cartridges in the empty ammunition box and tossed it into the plastic trash can at the base of the stand like she'd done it all her life. Abbey collected the battered sign and tossed it into the back of the Jeep.

"So, what'd you think?"

Blix loved it and wanted to go again in Atlanta. She said, "This has always been on my bucket list."

"No kidding," Abbey said. "Check it off, then."

"I never had anyone invite me to go shoot guns before. This was fun. Thanks."

"You're welcome. You never know when knowing how to handle a gun might come in handy." Inside the Jeep, Abbey patted Blix on the thigh and drove off. She turned onto a narrow road that was hugged on either side by the dense forest where massive, curving limbs dripped with Spanish moss and thick, ropelike vines.

"The beauty of renting a gun, Blix, is that you can try different calibers and different kinds of guns, revolvers and automatics."

"Uh-huh."

Abbey looked over and stopped talking. She recognized the numbed response, had seen it before. Blix was in another time, another life, maybe a "*What if?*" trance. These old woods had a way of working their way into one's psyche. At a small aquifer-fed pond, Abbey turned onto another road and hit the brakes. "Turkeys!"

Blix startled. "What?"

"There." Abbey pointed. "Coming in from the edge of the woods." Four tall brown fowl trotted across the road and into the woods on the opposite side.

"Are you sure they aren't buzzards?" Blix asked. "They don't look like any turkeys I've ever seen."

"That's because they're wild, not the big old fat farm-raised domestic birds we eat for Thanksgiving. Those are the real deal. That's what people hunt."

"Oh." Blix thought for several seconds. "Do those taste as good as the domestic ones?"

"Can't say. I've never eaten a wild one."

"You're a different breed, Bunns."

Moments later, the road ended at a narrow river with a broad expanse of marsh on the far side. A phalanx of pelicans, their profiles like paper cutouts against the blue-gray sky, careened toward the north. Blix was quiet for a moment, and then she said, "Thank you for inviting me down here. I don't like Atlanta right now; too many people, too much traffic, everybody in a hurry to get somewhere. This place is so real." She flicked a finger under her eye. "It's all about life, here. Good, healthy life. I could get used to this."

"I've thought the same thing many times. You can chill and let everything else go." Abbey looked south, where a black bank of clouds inched toward them from Florida. "Of course, soon, that weather system we've been promised might be all we're thinking about."

WHEN THEY GOT back to the cottage, they emptied the crab trap and put it away.

By the time Tom walked in, there was a platter of crab bodies and claws in the middle of the dining-room table and Blix was putting the finishing touches on a bowl of coleslaw. She chattered away over dinner about how much fun she'd had at the firing range. Abbey made an occasional comment to Blix; she and Tom avoided looking at each other.

After dinner, they turned on the news and watched days-old footage of whipping palm trees and heavy rains in Cuba and the same as the weather pattern crawled up the coastline of Florida that afternoon. As of yet, there was no threat to Georgia, though the weatherman mentioned several times that these were the conditions that had preceded hurricanes in the past.

"Wonderful. So, what's that supposed to mean?" asked Blix.

"That means they don't have crystal balls, but they don't want to catch the blame if this thing gets big," Tom said.

"I need to call Momma," Abbey said.

"Tell the boys I love them."

"They should have been in bed hours ago," Abbey said.

"Maybe. Thank Boonks and tell her to have fun." Tom changed the channel. "Do those kerosene lanterns you were talking about work?"

He listened to me. "Of course they work." Abbey thought about the times her parents had fired up the lanterns when she'd been a child. She remembered the smell of the black smoke that had risen when her father had lit the wick. *That was a long time ago.* Not wanting to give Tom any reason to get peeved with her, she decided to play it safe. "I should say, they did work."

"When, Bunns?" Blix asked from the living room. "First World War?"

"Very funny. No, Daddy used them one time when our power went out."

"And he's been gone since when?" Tom asked, inches behind Abbey.

She startled. She hadn't heard him come into the room. "Nineteen sixty-four."

Tom chuckled. "Okay, so it has been a while."

Abbey watched Tom carefully lift the old lanterns. She couldn't read his face, but she found it hard to believe he was cheating on her, after all the talks they'd had about his first wife and her dalliances. Part of Abbey believed there was an explanation and wanted to give him the benefit of the doubt. *You wouldn't do that to me, would you?*

CHAPTER 15

A bbey and Blix walked to the pool under the light of the near-perfect moon. It was ten o'clock, and the thermometer in the kitchen window still read ninety degrees. The cottage had never been air-conditioned, so it was customary to go for a swim before bed to cool off. Abbey dove in and swam to the deep end underwater, easy in the backyard-sized pool. When she surfaced, Blix said, "This feels like a mountain stream after a snow melt. How do you jump in like that?"

"It's the best way," Abbey said. "All or nothing."

She treaded water and watched Blix lower herself in an inch at a time until she was fully submerged. "It's freezing," Blix said.

"Swim down here and you'll warm up," Abbey said.

Blix had just made it to the other end of the pool when Tom ran up, yelled, "Geronimo," and cannon-balled eight feet from them. Waves splashed over the low, rough sides of the pool, whose tabby construction replicated that of a popular oyster-shell-and-sand concrete used in the coastal southeast in the fifteen-hundreds. Abbey turned her head but still got a face full of water.

"There's one in every crowd," she said.

"It has to do with gender," Blix said. "My sons would be right there with him to see who made the bigger splash. Annoying is in their DNA."

Tom swam over. "How high did it go?"

Abbey and Blix exchanged a look. *Now he wants to play chummy.* "Gosh. I forgot to look. Did you see his splash, Blix?" Abbey open-palmed a blistering sheet of water into her husband's face.

"Spoilsport." Tom swam to the shallow end and stepped out. "I'm going in."

"We're right behind you," Abbey said.

"Now that I'm in, I hate to get out," Blix said.

"We don't have to. There's no clock on us."

Blix talked about her doctor, how he looked like a teenager playing a role but had graduated at the top of his class at Emory. They spoke in depth about the procedure, and Blix allowed that her reservations were because of the unknown extent of the disfiguration the operation would cause.

Thirty minutes later, inside and in dry clothes, they joined Tom in the living room.

"Y'all won't believe these crazy fools," Tom said. "They went surfing in those damned giant waves."

"Where is this?" Blix asked.

"Jacksonville, this afternoon."

"Those waves were caused by the big black clouds we saw when we went for a ride, Blix," Abbey said.

"Oh, by the way, Boonks returned your call," Tom said.

"Is everything okay?"

"She was just checking in. Wanted to know if we plan to go home."

TEN MINUTES LATER, Abbey returned, smiling. "The boys rode the *burros* today, and now they want a pair. They think we should fence this yard and build a barn, and they'll do yard work at home to pay for grain and hay. They've got it all figured out."

"Fat chance," Tom said. "But I like the yard-work idea. What else?"

"They chilled a watermelon in the creek while they rode the *burros*, then they cut the melon and ate it sitting on rocks in the creek and had a seed-spitting contest."

Tom smiled. His eyes met Abbey's, and his brow furrowed. The look confused her. She forced her lips to relax, an almost smile. She hoped he would open up and tell her what was going on without her having to push.

The mayor came onto the screen and did the requisite introductions for the chief of police, the head of the Georgia DNR, and the head of GEMA. Network cameras flashed. The mayor spoke about the deteriorating weather conditions in Florida that showed all the signs of developing into a hurricane, and then he issued a mandatory evacuation of the entire Georgia coast by noon Sunday. He warned that those who chose to ride the storm out did so at their own risk. There would be no emergency staff to come to anyone's rescue.

"There you go," Abbey said. "We have about twelve hours to pack up and get out of here, if that's what we decide to do. Regardless, we need a game plan."

Tom glanced at Abbey. "Hell, it would be crazy to stay. We need to pack up in the morning and get on the road. Traffic will be bad, but easier to deal with in daylight."

The two women looked at one another the whole time Tom talked—silent communication. "Call me crazy, but I had hoped we'd stay," Blix said. "I feel like I'm supposed to help the folks at that little church."

Abbey nodded. "That's good enough for me. I vote we stay. We have food, ice, candles. And who knows, we might really be of help to someone."

Tom stared at the floor. "You two are crazy. Sleep on it and see if you feel the same way in the morning."

Abbey disappeared and returned with three plates, forks, and the remainder of the chocolate sheet cake. "We need to keep our strength up."

When the last crumb was gone, Tom headed for bed. Abbey turned out the lights, and she and Blix settled in with John Wayne.

CHAPTER 16

Late that night, Otis peered through a dense privet hedge and watched a small white circle of light jiggle down the exterior of his granny's house. Metal scraped across concrete and was accompanied by a male voice's curse. Otis pictured the trash can at the back door.

"Back here," Otis said.

"Where the hell is here?" asked the voice.

"Look for my light." Otis zigzagged his white beam in the sky.

"Light? Hell, I don't see nothing," the voice said. "You got a lightning bug in a jar or something? Damn, man."

"Look here," Otis said. "There's a cut in the hedge right where I'm standing. I'm fixin' to shine my light through it." He shone his light through the break in the hedge and moved it up and down.

"Okay. I see it now." Deke pushed through the tight opening. "I like to broke my neck trying to find your damn path, as you call it." Deke moved his light around the garden plot. "Hey, man. I smell smokes. Gimme one."

Otis flipped a Marlboro from a pack. His friend snatched it, waited for Otis to fish a Bic from his pocket, and leaned in for a light. The flame lit Deke's fish-belly-white face.

"Did you get them all planted, like I told you to?" asked Deke.

"Over yonder." Otis motioned with the ember end of his cigarette.

"Well, show me, bro. I got to make sure you done it right."

The light from Otis's flashlight swept across Deke's eyes.

"What the hell, man. You trying to blind me? Damn."

"Sorry." Otis lowered his light to the ground. "This way." He led them to a cleared patch of dirt. Two straight six-foot rows of precisely mounded dirt held healthy young cannabis plants; yellow marigolds occupied the four ends.

"What the hell?" Deke asked. "Are you growing flowers or weed, man?"

"Both. Flowers is just my cover-up. Granny will want to know why, all of a sudden, I'm into gardening, so I figure after I'm through tending my livelihood out here, I can cut some flowers to give her. That way, I'll keep her from being too curious."

"If you say so." Deke walked up and down the rows, then came back to Otis and dropped his cigarette butt on the ground.

"Hey. Don't be littering my garden." Otis picked up the butt and dropped it into a coffee can half-full of butts at the end of the row.

"You ready to ride?" Deke twirled a keyring on his index finger.

"I reckon. Where we going?"

"Town, bro."

Otis led the way through the gap in the hedge. Both boys wore black head to toe, per Deke's instructions earlier that day. Single-bulb porch lights were still on in several of the small wood-frame houses along the street, most of which were dark inside, save for the occasional fluorescent flicker of a television screen. Across from Granny's, a candle flickered on a front porch where a swing's chain creaked back and forth in a slow summertime rhythm.

"Who's over there swinging?" Deke whispered.

"My neighbor."

"No shit, dumbass. I mean who is it?"

"Just a girl."

"Your honey, big man?"

"Naw. Just a nice girl. Real nice girl. She's got a baby."

"Well, well, well. Baby got a daddy, bro?" Deke socked Otis's arm.

"What do you think, White Boy? I reckon it has to, don't it?"

"Ooo, touchy touchy. Never mind, big fella. Sounds like you sweet on that bitch."

"Naw, I ain't, and don't be talking about her like that. Her husband got killed, that's all."

"I'm just fooling with you, Otis. Come on. Car's around the corner."

"Why you park so far away?"

"I don't want your granny looking out the window and seeing my ride. Last thing we need is her or your girlfriend noticing it."

"Oh. Okay." Otis got into the passenger seat. The engine roared. As they rumbled down the street, Otis shook his head. "If you don't want to be noticed, why the hell don't you replace that busted muffler? You'll get a ticket for that one of these days."

"I like the way it sounds."

"You're going to pay for that sound one of these days is all I'm saying."

Downtown Brunswick was empty and locked up tight; most of the windows had been boarded up or taped. "What the hell good is that tape supposed to do?" Otis asked. When they were a bit farther, he said, "Only lights on are ones directing traffic."

"Yeah." Deke lowered his window all the way down. "And ain't nobody around, neither. My old lady had the TV on. The mayor told everybody to evacuate. Looks like most everybody did, don't it?" Otis nodded. "Damnation, it's hot."

"I reckon Granny would have taken all of us somewhere if we'd had someplace to go." Otis lit two cigarettes and handed one to his friend. "But we ain't got no place to go." *That ain't right. I guess we can go to that church. Granny'll like that.*

"Me neither, man, but here we are with all of downtown to ourselves." Deke drove slowly. Businesses and shops had been closed for hours. "No place to go and nobody cares. Shit. Everybody will probably drown if we have one of those tsunami things anyway. You know about them?"

"Naw. What's a soomamee?"

"A damn wall of water a hundred feet high, or something like that. They had one in Japan a while back, tore up buildings and streets and drowned thousands of people. Hell, the pictures on TV 'bout scared me to death just watching." The car slowed. Deke turned at the next corner. Halfway down the street, he pulled into a driveway and parked behind a boarded-up house. "Come on."

"What are we doing here?"

Deke reached into the back seat. "Take this." He handed Otis a large wood-handled hammer and a short crowbar and reached back again. "And this." He dropped a scratchy white pillowcase that reeked of mildew onto Otis's lap. Granny's pillowcases were soft as silk and smelled like fresh air.

A prickle irritated Otis's nose. He sneezed. "Excuse me. I'm allergic to mold."

"Bless you." Deke dropped a pair of latex gloves onto Otis's lap. "Put these on." Otis pulled on the thin, transparent gloves. "Now, move it."

Otis stumbled out of the car, eyes squinted and mouth half-open as though asking a question that wouldn't come out. His heart pounded. Old Man's words popped into his head like the occasional Bible verse did when he was about to do something that he knew in his heart he shouldn't do. *"Don't disappoint Granny." Dang. This don't look too good. That's just what I'm fixing to do.*

They walked through the backyard of the vacant house, then emerged into a worn graveled alley. "Left here," Deke whispered. Though there was no one around, it became clear to Otis that what they were doing required quiet concentration.

It was so dark that Otis had to follow White Boy's light and his chalky face, which flipped around now and then and asked, "You still back there?"

"Yeah, I'm here. Where are we going, man?"

The alley ended behind a group of low, attached brick buildings. Otis glanced back toward the street where they'd left the car and saw nothing unusual. Ahead of him, there was one quick pop; glass tinkled onto concrete. His head whipped back around. *Holy shit.*

Deke whispered, "Dammit."

Otis caught up. Deke had one finger in his mouth; his other hand reached through a broken window beside a door. "Door's chained," Deke said. He wiped the bloody finger on his pants several times, then inserted his crowbar between the door and its frame and pried until the chain gave and the ruined door creaked open.

"Where are we?" Otis asked.

"Jewelry store. Come on. We got three minutes inside."

Otis stopped dead. "You kidding me? Alarms'll go off any minute now. Cops'll be here before we even get back to the car."

"Naw, they won't." The other boy moved through the darkness like a creeping rat. "Keep moving. What in hell do you think I been doing all night, smoking in my garden like some folks I know? Electricity's off, alarm's disabled. I been busy."

Mimicking White Boy's bent-over stance, Otis followed.

"You go down the left side of the room along the wall, I'll do the right," Deke said. "Display cases are covered with white sheets or some shit in the front of the store. Toss the cover off, then sweep with one hand and hold the pillowcase open with the other. Don't be picky. Just sweep. This place has good stuff. We'll make a killing. We have exactly two minutes left, so move it."

What the hell am I doing here? Sweat dribbled down Otis's temples, tickling.

A car drove slowly down the street. "Drop down," White Boy said. The only sounds in the room were their elevated breathing and the regular *tick-tock* of a clock.

With a head that throbbed as he fought the urge to pee, Otis swallowed the bitter bile in the back of his throat to staunch his urge to throw up.

"Okay, go," White Boy said as he snatched the white cover off the case on his side. Otis did the same opposite him. He had seen the diamonds in the case when he and the store owner had had a stare-down the other day, so he knew what was there. His eyes moved over bracelets, rings, and necklaces. He took a breath. Sweat streamed down his sides. His hand slowly went toward a row of necklaces. *Bong, bong, bong.* He jumped as though he had been struck.

"Shit. What was that?"

"A clock, dumbass. Now hurry."

He stuck his hand into the case and felt plastic things like the bird perches he'd seen at the pet store. He remembered how the glittering jewelry had been displayed. Metal clinked repeatedly as White Boy dropped jewelry into his pillowcase. Otis's heart raced. He wondered if he was having a heart attack. *I'll die right here in this damned store where I ain't got no business being.*

A flashlight moved down the sidewalk across the street. "Lights off," Deke said. "Across the street." Both boys squatted on their heels. After several seconds, Deke said, "Dog-walker. He's gone. Sixty seconds and we're out of here."

Otis swallowed spit and counted off seconds as he worked his area. He had only gotten to fifteen when White Boy said there were thirty seconds to go.

Hallelujah. Otis had long arms and accurate pitcher's hands. Objects dropped without a sound into his pillowcase as he went through the motions.

"Hey, we'll sort it all out later. Sweep, man! Take it all. Don't be picky. Fifteen seconds and we're outta here."

Sweat washed down Otis's face and neck. He took a deep breath, smelled the stench of his own body, breathed out through his mouth, and mentally ticked off the final seconds.

Deke said, "We're outta here."

Otis dropped the white cover back into place over the case.

"Good idea." Deke did the same. "That'll keep them from knowing anything for a little longer. Give us more time."

Otis's hands quivered as he knotted his pillowcase like he'd done the garbage bags at home. He thought of Granny. He forced his breaths deeper.

They exited the way they'd entered, this time with bulging pillowcases inside their shirts and their shoulders hunched to help conceal their illegitimate babies. Race-walking back to the car, they dropped their loot into the trunk. Deke slipped the car into neutral and told Otis to push. Two blocks later, Deke said, "Jump in."

A police car cruised down the cross street a block ahead. Otis said, "We're dead." He held his breath. The cop drove on.

"How you doing, Oh-Shit?" White Boy grabbed another cigarette from Otis's pack on the dash and turned on the car.

"I ain't never stole before, except a pack a Juicy Fruit gum at the five-and-dime when I was a little kid and didn't know no better." *And a bottle of Granny's wine one time. Damn.*

"Well, hell, boy, that was good practice, I reckon. Stealing's stealing, but you just graduated to the big time."

"What do we do with it now we got it?"

"Well, I've been thinking. You know that church over near where you stay?"

"Uh huh." *Please don't let Latisha or the preacher man see me doing nothing.*

"There's an old truck parked behind it," Deke said. "Preacher of that church used to work on it all the time, kept it running pretty good."

Otis opened his window all the way and rested his arm on the door. "I hear he's fixing it up. He takes all the little children for hayrides on Halloween." He thought about that truck loaded up with little girls dressed like Snow White and little boys like Superman and Spider-Man. "You dress up like that when you was a kid, White Boy?"

"Yeah. My mom was into all that shit. We used to wear costumes to school and all and go around the neighborhood and get tons of candy." Deke drove on. "When I got older, me and my buddies would go out and roll neighborhoods instead—cover them up totally with toilet paper."

"I take my little brothers and sister. Momma likes to go, too, when she's home. She likes to see all the children in their costumes." Thinking of her made him feel sad. And guilty. He sure couldn't point any fingers at her after what he'd just done.

"Aww. How sweet." Deke chuckled.

Sometimes I want to punch you in the mouth.

"Okay now. We'll hide this stuff in the preacher's truck for now and figure out what to do with it all later, after we've had some time to think on it. No one will ever look in that old truck."

Yeah. Truck's parked behind the church where Granny and Latisha go. I ain't a praying man, but please, Lord, don't strike me dead for this. It wasn't my idea.

CHAPTER 17

Early Sunday morning, Abbey and Tom jogged slowly through air thick enough to slice. They had been out for almost thirty minutes, heavy breathing their only communication. Tom had been at Kings Bluff for less than thirty-six hours and wanted to leave. Between them, the energy was taut enough to pop. It was clear his focus was on getting back to Atlanta, not on their marital issues.

Abbey finally asked, "Are you having an affair, Tom?"

He stopped dead. "What the hell? No, dammit."

Panting and dripping sweat, she spun and faced him. "Then what's with that letter you got at home from some woman? And the damn hang-ups?"

He threw back his head and took a deep breath. "It's not what it looks like."

She took a step and began to jog. "Surprise, surprise. That's not very original, Tom. You ought to be able to come up with something a little more convincing."

He caught up. "I know it looks bad, but it's not. I'll be able to explain, just not right now. Please believe me."

"That's a giant ask," she said. Frustrated by his complacency and immersed in thoughts about how she should go forward, Abbey mentally blocked Tom's presence from her mind and picked up her pace. *Believe him? Why can't he just tell me what's going on? And what's with all the damn secret phone calls he's making?* For the remainder of the run, she tossed possible scenarios around in her head and didn't like any of them, but her gut still told her not to say or do anything she'd regret.

By the time they called it quits, their clothes stuck to their skin like cellophane on bacon. Back at the cottage, they were met by the aroma of fresh-brewed coffee. "Yay," Abbey said. "The coffee fairy is up."

"And her twin sister, the breakfast fairy." Blix danced around the kitchen, waving a spatula like a magic wand. "No-calorie cinnamon buns are in the oven."

"You're hired," Tom said, his voice scratchy. He filled a mug. Aromas of cinnamon and sugar in the kitchen had temporarily replaced that of Old Bay.

"Tom, you had a call from a guy named Benjamin at your office."

"Okay, thanks." His eyes darted to Abbey's, and hers asked a silent question. He left. Moments later, the hall shower turned on.

"Bunns, you had a call from the Brunswick Board of Realtors. They want to know if you're available."

Abbey grabbed a coffee, made the call, and identified herself. She was asked if she was available to make some calls. "Sure. I'd be happy to. I just came in from a jog, so I'll shower and head your way. See you soon."

She hung up and said to Blix, "Most of their staff is leaving town, and they need someone to contact local real-estate offices for them, so now we both have jobs to do."

SIXTY MINUTES AND a platter of cinnamon buns later, Abbey and Blix rode in silence, which was unusual for them. Tom had thrown his gear into his Wagoneer, taken cinnamon buns in a sheet of paper towel, and left. Prior to his departure, while he'd packed his suitcase, he and Abbey had argued about her decision to stay. Since Blix had been changing in the bedroom next to theirs, they had gone outside and walked. "I need to do this for Blix," Abbey had said.

Tom had argued that she wasn't thinking clearly by putting herself and Blix in danger. She'd said, "I would never forgive myself if we left and Blix told me later that she regretted not having stayed. Please don't ask me to carry that burden." Tom had gotten in his Wagoneer and left.

Other than a drug-related shooting, the Jacksonville station's main story was the weather pattern that had stalled over the southern tip of Florida but threatened to creep northward like a steel-toed boot cocked back and ready to kick. High winds buffeting the reporter's microphone made it sound like she spoke from inside a wind tunnel. The reporter cautioned about the potential of flooding, severe wind damage, and numerous other hazards that could occur when and where the storm landed, though due to its fickle nature, these hazards had yet to be determined. Depending on numerous weather-related factors, the storm could either swing toward the Gulf of Mexico, spin out into the Atlantic, or barrel straight north and take a swipe at Georgia, South Carolina, or beyond.

The reporter compared current conditions to those of historic hurricanes that had hit both Galveston, Texas, and Brunswick, Georgia. When his report was over, Abbey switched to a music station. "Damn. Surely we're better able to predict the weather now than they were back then."

"Those were awful," Blix said. "And both were preceded by massive heat waves. I don't ever remember it being this hot. Maybe this summer was a setup and we're in for it."

Abbey thought about her two boys and how they had begged her to turn on the sprinkler the previous weekend.

They'd been playing soldier in the boxwood hedge in the front yard and had found her and Tom weeding in the side yard. The little guys had been red-faced and sweaty, and their shorts and T-shirts had been as red as their faces from good old Georgia clay. Abbey had pulled out the hose and the sprinkler and let them play until the mosquitos had chased them all inside at sundown. *I'm glad you two are safe with Momma.*

Overhead, the sky's normal blue tint was a grout gray. Traffic on I-95 limped along, all vehicles headed north. Their sheer numbers meant service stations would have a tough time meeting demands for gas.

"Check out these cars, Blix. They're all packed to the hilt, like they've got almost everything they own."

"I'd leave my clothes," Blix said. "I was never a fashion plate anyway." Several minutes later, she added, "I have plastic bins at home with secure snap-on lids. If a storm like this was headed for Atlanta, I'd dump all the junk stored in those boxes and fill them with my picture albums and take them with me. You can't replace memories."

Abbey glanced at her friend. "Do you remember the time in college when a group of us was at Kings Bluff and we wired up our braided pigtails with coat hangers?"

Blix said, "Yes!" She used her hands as she talked. "We bent the wire over our heads, then worked it through the braids and bent the braids straight up. I have those pictures." She chuckled. "I'd forgotten about that. We had a good time that weekend. I need to show those pictures to my sons when we get home."

They were silent again for several minutes. Abbey swallowed the lump in her throat. She knew by her friend's inflection that she wasn't finished.

"I want them to remember me like I am right now: happy, well, and whole."

Whole. Has she decided not to have the surgery? Abbey reached over and squeezed Blix's arm. "Now, listen: if things start to get scary, we'll head north like everybody else. We might have to crawl our way back to Atlanta, but that's okay. We can always sleep in this Jeep if we get stuck."

They got off the highway and onto U.S. 17. As they crossed the Sidney Lanier Bridge, an indecisive wind toyed with the Jeep; the steel-and-concrete bridge swayed and didn't feel capable of holding them out of the churning waters below. Abbey glanced in her rearview mirror, half-expecting to see Tom following close behind. But no, he was gone. She took a deep breath. Since they'd been married, she had experienced a few anxious moments, and most of those had been real-estate-related. This was much worse.

"Interesting," Abbey said after they crossed the bridge.

"What?"

"There aren't any cars at the parking meters and only a few people on the sidewalks. What would you say is the average age of most of these folks?" Abbey swept her hand toward the sidewalk on Blix's side of the car.

"Well, they're all old."

"They're probably the ones who can't leave. Reverend Isaiah might have a full house."

"Oh boy," Blix murmured.

Abbey drove into the swept-dirt yard in front of the AME church. She rummaged in the glove compartment and took out a clunky sport watch. "This is one of my spares. Why don't you put it on? There's a button that lights it up so you can read it in the dark. It's waterproof, too, and that might come in handy."

"Very encouraging. Thanks."

Inside the church, soft lights glittered. A worn red runner with vacuum tracks ran the center aisle to the front of the church, where a black Jesus, his face contorted, his body bloody and torn, hung high on a rough-hewn wooden cross. Several dark faces turned toward Abbey and Blix as they walked down the aisle. Reverend Isaiah looked up from a young woman seated in a pew with a child in her lap.

"Ah," the preacher said. "Our Florence Nightingales. Welcome. Will y'all be staying with us today for a while?" He handed the Bible he held to the seated woman. "Some of the sisters are preparing a pot of soup, and I saw a skillet of cornbread go in the oven. We'd love to have you join us."

The fat-cheeked toddler in the woman's lap had dark brown eyes that studied Abbey and then Blix. He stopped there, perhaps intrigued by her faded facial scars or curious about her eyes, which reflected so much life—one that was locked in the past, or the future, or nowhere at all, but was somehow different from the other. Two chubby fists grabbed his mother's shirt, and with a grunt, the little boy pulled himself up, slapped his little feet down on the pew, and reached for Blix. "Unh, unh, unh." He bounced up and down between grunts. The mother and Blix exchanged looks.

"Go on, ma'am. He usually don't like nobody except me handling him."

Blix picked him up. "And what's your name, little fellow?"

"Joseph," his mother said. "Like in the Bible."

"Joseph. What a nice name. You have a lot to live up to, with a name like that." Blix swayed slowly back and forth with the boy on her hip. One of his tiny hands wound around in her hair while the fingers of the other went into his mouth.

Blix said, "I'll be here most of the day, Reverend. Abbey's coming back for me around three o'clock." The preacher nodded.

"I'll be at the Board of Realtors, Reverend, in case you need anything," Abbey said.

"Not showing houses, I hope."

"No, just making some calls for them."

"I've been here at the church for a while," the preacher said. "Has anything changed in town?"

Blix said, "Everything looks boarded-up, but people seem to be going about their business."

"Until it hits," Reverend Isaiah said in his deep baritone. "Then things'll change in a hurry."

Abbey said, "Survival mode does that to people." She patted Joseph on the back. "See you this afternoon, Blix. Until then, you and Joseph stay out of trouble and don't do anything I wouldn't do."

Blix grinned. She and Joseph and the preacher walked Abbey to the door, and Blix said, "So, it's okay if I turn into a one-woman rescue-and-recovery team for the next couple of hours."

Abbey shook her head and said, only loud enough for Blix to hear, "Gosh darn, Thelma. Every time we get in trouble, you go blank or plead insanity or some such shit."

Blix laughed out loud. "Gosh darn?"

Abbey shrugged and said, "Well, we're in church."

Several steps behind them, the reverend's eyebrows cocked; he looked confused. "Did I miss something?"

"I just reminded Blix of a line from a movie. Did you see *Thelma and Louise?*"

The preacher shrugged. "No, I don't think I saw that one."

Abbey turned as she walked, and she said to her friend in the church's doorway, "Don't even think about any heroics, Blix. And I mean it." She got a thumbs up in return. To Reverend Isaiah, she said, "It's a great movie."

As she drove away, Abbey noticed a black teenager in baggy shorts, a baseball cap, and an oversized pink T-shirt.

She probably wouldn't have noticed him were it not for his tough-guy glide, where one shoulder rocked back each time the opposite foot stepped forward. Maybe he was a model working on his runway style, but chances were, he was just some dopey kid imitating a tough older man he'd seen around town. When he glanced toward the church, she recognized him. *That's the same fellow who walked into the fish market the other day. Otis, Ben called him. I wonder what he's up to.*

THE BRUNSWICK BOARD OF REALTORS was quieter than the last time she'd been there. A different woman was at the front desk. When Abbey introduced herself, the woman said, "My name is Rebecca. They told me you were coming to help us. It's very generous of you."

On their way to the conference room, Rebecca explained that, to help the community, the board had come up with an idea. Abbey was to call each broker in the county and ask them to contact their agents. The agents were to call their clients with a checklist of items to take with them if they evacuated. In front of one of the leather chairs at a banquet-sized table, there was a neatly printed spreadsheet with information filled in under column headings: "Name, Office, Address, Phone Number." The final larger column with the heading "Comments" was blank.

"This is very well-organized. Thank you," Abbey said.

"It's about all we can do," Rebecca said. "Have at it. You know where I am if you need anything."

After several hours, Rebecca came in with a deli sandwich and a large iced tea.

"I ordered out for everyone, Abbey. I can't thank you enough for helping us. We're a little short-handed because most of the staff have children, and naturally, they headed out of town the minute schools were closed. I can't say I blame them."

"Certainly not. You can't take chances with children." Abbey thought of her boys, safe in the mountains with Boonks. *Thank goodness.* "Will you stay?"

"Yes." Rebecca tapped a pencil in her palm. "My husband and I talked about leaving, but we're in a new house on a high bluff, and we're confident the water will never reach us, or at least he is, but who knows. He wants to see how our supposedly hurricane-proof windows hold up. I hope we're not sorry." She rapped the conference table with her knuckles on her way out.

CHAPTER 18

With Joseph still on her hip, Blix went back to the little boy's mother inside the church and introduced herself. "My friend and I met Reverend Isaiah the other day at the hospital. I told him I'd be happy to be on hand if he needs help."

The young mother looked her up and down but didn't make eye contact. "That ain't what he said." She held out her hands and took Joseph back.

"Oh." Blix folded her arms across her body. "Well, what did he say? I don't want to make him out a storyteller."

The woman looked at Blix and almost smiled, but not quite. "He told me you and your friend—I reckon that's the lady just drove off—that y'all done met at the hospital, and you offered to be here with us case we need any nursing. That's what he told me."

"That's close enough," Blix said. "I know your son's name, but I didn't catch yours."

"I'm Latisha, Latisha Jones."

"Well, Latisha, company's coming. Why don't you and I get things ready."

Though Latisha followed, she shook her head. "What company?"

"Oh, I was just being..." Blix stopped talking when she realized the odd look on Latisha's face was confusion. "I just meant other folks in the congregation. I hope they'll come. It'll be a lot more fun with a full house." Blix realized she needed to curb her wisecracks. *This isn't home,* she reminded herself. *No one here knows me or my sense of humor.*

"Oh, okay." Latisha's full lips eased at the corners.

"He's precious, Latisha." Blix nodded toward Joseph. "I know you're proud of him." Latisha's lips tightened; she nodded. Blix knew better than to ask if the baby's father would join them. Assumptions sometimes proved embarrassing, so she didn't pry. "Let's see what's going on in the kitchen. Something smells awfully good." As they walked, Joseph stared at Blix. She waved to him with her fingertips. He smiled and imitated her with a backward wave to himself.

Several ladies talked and chuckled as they chopped vegetables on sturdy wooden cutting boards atop a long Formica counter. A ham bone bubbled in a large pot of water on the stove. "Latisha, why don't we get out bowls and spoons for lunch? That okay with you?"

Latisha nodded. "I reckon."

At the corner of the kitchen where Abbey and Blix had organized paper goods the day before, Blix stopped. The neatly stacked supplies had been ransacked.

Latisha said, "The reverend found it this way when he opened up this morning, and ain't nobody had time to straighten it up yet." Her eyes flicked toward Blix, then to Joseph's foot that gently tapped against her hip. "I meant to straighten it up, but people kept on coming in, and I got busy with them." Her fingers played with the baby's tiny toes.

"Don't worry about it, Latisha."

"I don't know who came in here and done this. I reckon they must have took some stuff, by the looks of it. It was all straightened up nice when I was in here yesterday afternoon."

Blix did a quick mental calculation of what was missing. "Maybe they need it more than we do."

Latisha mumbled, "Huh. Still ain't right, stealing from a church and all."

They gathered paper bowls, napkins, and spoons and put them on the counter near the stove. Blix opened the refrigerator door. "Latisha, our thief likes milk. At least he left us one gallon."

Latisha looked in. "Our thief is one sorry human being is all I got to say, stealing from a church." Joseph reached toward a block of cheddar cheese inside the refrigerator. "Come on, baby. Help me straighten up this mess, then maybe I'll give you a cracker with some of that cheese on it." Latisha smiled at Blix. "He's a fool for cheese."

Around noon, more people wandered in. They were pretty much what Blix expected: old folks and young mothers. Latisha eagerly pitched in and did whatever Blix asked of her. Joseph speed-crawled behind Blix, as close to her feet as he could get. She turned to him and did a Donald Duck quack. He laughed, then looked at her and waited. She quacked again. He laughed and clapped twice and waited. Blix's boys were almost grown. She hadn't had a baby to fuss over in years. She scooped him up and carried him around on her hip while his mother took charge and helped people roll out their bedrolls, blankets, and sleeping bags.

After lunch, Blix and Joseph made the rounds, and she found out if anyone had special medical needs. The church began to look like a high school sleep-in, with cased pillows and an assortment of bedding materials on every pew and in every corner; one or two pillows had books on them, worn Bibles and paperbacks. "Are you okay here?" Blix asked a diminutive woman on the first pew, who looked up from the open hymnal in her lap. "Do you need anything?"

"No, thank you, I'm fine, but I thought Gracie would be here by now. She told me she would catch a ride into town with her neighbor."

Latisha walked up, shaking her head. "Irene, ain't no neighbor bringing Miss Gracie. She live too far out."

"Where does she live?" Blix asked.

"About ten miles out in the country. You know Darien?"

"I was there once a long time ago, for the blessing of the shrimp fleet. It's just up U.S. 17, right?"

"That's right. And I know they do that blessing of the fleet. Anyhow, she stays up there by herself."

The reverend came up to see what all the talk was about. Blix told him she'd be happy to go for Gracie if she had a car. He offered his and handed her the keys to his Cadillac.

"I need to stop at the store to replace some things anyway. Are you sure you don't mind?"

"Not at all. I filled it with gas yesterday, so enjoy the ride."

BLIX FOLLOWED REVEREND ISAIAH'S directions to Highway 17 and headed out of town for a twenty- to thirty-minute drive. Once out of Brunswick, the marsh-bordered two-lane road shot straight north. She didn't remember the water being so close to the road before, but then, it had been a while since she'd been there. It felt good to be out of the confines of the church and behind the wheel. She settled into the cushy leather seat and felt like she was flying a private jet. After a while, she knew she was close to her destination when she saw the tall shot tower on her left, a leftover landmark from the Revolutionary War, where colonists had fashioned ammunition from lead. Soon, she crossed the bridge into downtown Darien. Shrimp boats were secured stern-to-bow along the length of a dock. *So far, so good.*

Several minutes later, she turned into the dirt driveway at the mailbox with the pot of pink geraniums at its base, as directed by the reverend. The yard was neatly raked, and more pots of pink geraniums occupied the ends of the single step to the front porch. The screen door rattled when she knocked. A large handbag sat in a chair just inside the door. Though Blix's sense of smell wasn't great, she was sure she smelled smoke. She knocked again and pushed on the door. It opened. The kitchen was straight ahead.

"Gracie?" A coffee pot bubbled over on a flaming gas burner. Blix grabbed a hot pad, removed the pot, and turned off the burner. She went through the house, calling Gracie's name, and then went back outside. Set back from the house, an old, rusted tractor sat under a roof that was attached to a neglected barn whose door was partially open. As she approached, she heard a low, rumbling growl, then a hacking sound. She peered around the warped garage door. An elderly woman chopped the ground with a long-handled garden hoe. On the ground was a very large, very dead bloody rat. A hefty striped cat eyed the decimation of the rat; its bushy, tangerine-colored tail whipped back and forth, and its throat rumbled like a Model-T Ford. Blix knocked on the garage door. "Gracie?"

The woman turned, her mouth set. Still gripping the hoe, the woman looked comical dressed up in hose and heels and a blue dress with matching hat. "I was afraid he was too much for Geraldine to handle by herself." Gracie leaned her hoe against the wall, and Geraldine moved in to explore the inert mess.

GRACIE TALKED THE whole way back to Brunswick while Blix listened. She figured Gracie had an adrenaline rush from the rat episode and needed to work it out. The water was higher than it had been earlier; Blix had heard about road washouts caused by abnormally high tides, so she paid attention. Abbey had shown her how to tell if the tide was coming in or going out. A clump of marsh grass moved to the right, which meant the tide was still coming in. Both her hands clutched the steering wheel, white-knuckled. Blix slowed. River water that had breached the ditches and filled a dip in the road drummed the underside of the Cadillac.

"We've gone down in the marsh," Gracie groaned.

"Not quite." Blix maintained steady pressure on the gas pedal. "We're fine, Gracie. It's just a little water over the road. Nothing to worry about. This car's a tank." Gracie looked somewhat relieved.

BLIX STOPPED AT a small grocer she'd noticed on her way to Gracie's and bought items to replace those that had been stolen from the church, as well as provisions for dinner and several items for entertaining the children. When they got back, Gracie looked around the sanctuary and asked, "Is this the hotel you told me about? I believe I've stayed here before with my late husband. It smells so nice and clean. This is lovely."

"This is where your friends are, Gracie, and this will be your home for the next several days."

"Oh yes. There's Irene." Gracie's dainty high-heel-clad feet minced their way to the front of the church. "Here I am, Sistah. A nice cab-driver lady picked me up and brought me here. We even went by the ocean. I haven't been to the ocean in the longest time."

Blix and Irene exchanged a look, and Blix shook her head. Irene said, "Yes, dear. Have a seat right here. Did you bring sleeping things and toiletries?"

Blix nodded and mouthed, "In the car." While Gracie and Irene talked, Blix retrieved Gracie's personal items and gave them to Latisha, who made a place for Gracie near her friend.

After Blix gathered the groceries from the Jeep, she found Reverend Isaiah in the kitchen, putting leftover soup in the fridge. "I picked up extra paper goods and several cut-up chickens, potatoes, and salad things for dinner," she said. "Maybe we should bake the chicken and roast the potatoes, make it easy."

"No, ma'am. Don't you worry about another thing." He rubbed his hands together like he was getting ready to dig in. "You done more than your part. We're on my watch now. I'll take care of the cooking for this evening, sure will. You go rest for a bit." Reverend Isaiah waved her away, then pulled things out of the grocery bags and sorted them on the counter. "This'll do just fine," he said under his breath.

Satisfied that the preacher was bound and determined to do the cooking, Blix picked up the small paper bag and the butcher paper she had brought from the store and went back out to the sanctuary. She rolled out the paper and took a large box of crayons from the bag. Children gathered around her, their eyes wide and staring at the crayon box full of rainbow colors and the expanse of clean, unmarked paper on the floor. Within minutes, Joseph and the other children were on knees and elbows and hard at work. A colorful, uninhibited masterpiece began to take shape.

Sometime later, the reverend found Blix with the children and said, "I know I told you to take it easy, but would you mind going for some vegetable oil? I thought I had plenty, but what's here has gone rancid."

Blix said, "That's no problem at all. This is just another excuse to drive that beautiful car of yours." The reverend handed her his keys.

CHAPTER 19

That afternoon, Abbey heard Tom's voice and put down her pen. *What's he doing here?* She glanced at her watch. It was almost three o'clock. Tom had been gone since about eight o'clock that morning—almost seven hours. She looked up from the paper-strewn table. Tom stood in the conference-room doorway, hands in his pockets, concern on his face.

They looked at each other for a moment. How she longed to see his crooked, smart-aleck grin. "I'm surprised you came back."

He walked in and looked around. "Nice conference room." He nodded toward the piles of papers on the table. "What's all that?"

"It's what I have to show for the day. I called brokers and asked them to get their agents to tell their clients to keep their important house documents safe and dry." She tamped her papers down, then secured them with paperclips. "All I can do is suggest."

Tom leaned against the doorframe. "Traffic crawled on the interstate."

Gave you time to think, didn't it? She collected pens and returned paperclips to their box.

"Abbey, I know I've been an ass lately." They made eye contact. "I thought about what Blix said about helping people, so when I got to the second Brunswick exit, I got off and went back to the downtown marina." He came into the room and picked up the bundle of pens and box of paperclips. "I've been helping them pull boats out. Some folks are staying put, others plan to go north to try to stay ahead of the weather. There's a pretty good wind out there already, and the sky is all weird; looks like a big nasty bruise." Abbey listened patiently, relieved he'd come back. Tom grabbed her purse as though he did it every day and slung it over his shoulder.

"Thanks," she said as she stacked her papers. "Nice look."

Tom glanced at the purse. "Doesn't match my shoes."

Abbey grinned. *There's my Tom.*

As they walked out, Tom said, "The tide is already very high; if just one of those boats pulls away from its mooring, they'll have a mess. If it's okay with you, I'd like to go back to the house and catch the news. All I've had all day is radios."

Abbey said, "Of course it's okay. Blix expects me to pick her up, so in case she wants to stay at the church a little longer, do you mind following me over there? I'll leave her my Jeep, and she can come back to Kings Bluff when she's ready."

She found Rebecca and explained her shorthand and the notations on her lists. "Please call me if you need me again. I'm happy to do whatever I can."

"I can't tell you how much I appreciate your help, Abbey," Rebecca said. "Anything we do at a time like this is great. It helps the community, and it certainly can't hurt our image."

"I hear you. People think all we do is collect commissions. They have no idea what goes on behind the scenes."

ABBEY GLANCED IN her rearview mirror several times. This time, Tom was there. She was relieved he had come back and was hopeful they'd talk on the drive back to Kings Bluff. Since he'd said he could explain, she promised herself she'd remain calm and hear him out. When they got to the church, Tom pulled up beside her and motioned that he'd wait in his Wagoneer. She went inside and found Reverend Isaiah in the kitchen. He told her Blix had gone to get some cooking oil and should be back shortly. Abbey was eager to have Tom to herself for a while.

"Tell you what, Reverend Isaiah. Tom is waiting for me out front, so I'll leave my Jeep here for Blix in case she has any other running around to do, and then she'll have a way to get back to Kings Bluff. I'll jot down directions in case she needs a reminder."

"She told me the way earlier: I-95 south and left on Kings Bluff Road. She'll be fine," he said.

"From the look of things here, it seems word has gotten out that your doors are open," Abbey said.

"Oh, yes. My congregation is special. They're all devoted to one another. They made sure everyone knew they could come here."

Abbey handed him her car keys. "Before I go, is there anything you need?"

"Not that I can think of. We're in good shape." The reverend paused. "Now I don't mean to be nosy, but I believe Miss Blix has had her own trials in life; it means so much to me to have her willing to help us out in our time of need."

"You noticed her scars," Abbey said.

The preacher nodded. A little girl ran into the kitchen and turned around and left when she saw Abbey and the reverend.

"I'll walk you out," Reverend Isaiah said.

Abbey said, "She was in a horrible car accident when we were in high school."

"That poor child."

"I don't think she'd mind if I share something else, Reverend. She has just been diagnosed with some sort of cancer in her mouth. She hasn't shared what kind, and I didn't want to push. It seems her odds of surviving are nil unless she has surgery, but she's undecided whether to have it or not. The facial alterations could be significant."

He closed his eyes. "That explains some things. She's making her peace." Reverend Isaiah walked Abbey to the front door. "I've never seen anyone so sincere and so loving. Thank you for bringing that sweet lamb into this house. Her love and care will not be wasted. We will look after her, so don't you worry about that."

"Thank you, Reverend." At the front of the church, Abbey said, "When she gets back, please shoo her out the door so she can get back to Kings Bluff before dark. These roads are tricky if you aren't familiar with them, and no matter what any of us says, we don't see that well after dark."

Reverend Isaiah nodded. She handed him one of her business cards.

"My local number is on the back. Please call me if you need me."

As THEY DROVE back through Brunswick, Abbey and Tom were both quiet. The pensive look on Tom's face was as good as a "Do Not Disturb" sign, so Abbey let it be. Something was on his mind. When they got on the highway, Tom said, "We're the only ones going south."

"They won't close highways, will they?"

"I don't know, Abbey. I've never been through anything like this, but I imagine they could."

"Surely we'll get some warning." She turned on an AM radio station, listened to a political rant for several seconds, and then turned it off. "I guess we'll play it as it goes. Situations can change in a hurry." She noticed Tom's grimace and wrestled with the feeling that everything that came out of her mouth these days had a double meaning. He reached over and grabbed her hand. *He's thinking the same thing.*

Several minutes later, Tom said, "We need to talk." He glanced at her. "But I could use a beer."

Courage in a can, Abbey thought. *Well, here goes. I'll stay calm.*

When they turned into Kings Bluff, there were cars and trucks parked outside the clubhouse, and the people inside were visible through the windows. "Wonder what's going on," Tom said.

"Let's go find out," Abbey said.

Twenty or so men and women stood inside the clubhouse, talking in small groups. A transformer had been taken out by a tree up the road, so Kings Buff was without power. The group planned to have a potluck with what folks had in their refrigerators that might go bad before the power could be restored.

"What time?" Abbey asked.

Snag said, "Around six. It'll be dark by the time we all head home, so bring flashlights."

WHEN THEY GOT back to the cottage, Tom went to the porch to work on the lanterns while Abbey assembled their contribution for the dinner. When she finished, she found Tom fully engaged in his project. For a moment, she stood in the doorway and watched the back of his head and the movement of his broad shoulders. She remembered the days when she had first met Tom and helped him piece together details of the one-car accident, not far from Kings Bluff, that had killed his wife. Had he accepted her offer because he'd been at loose ends after his wife's death and had been grateful that she'd been willing to help him? Or had he had more in mind, since, all of a sudden, he'd been single?

Abbey tucked her hair behind her ear. *How could he possibly have had any more on his mind? He'd just lost his wife, you idiot. Nope, I was the one with more in mind, fresh out of my damned divorce. But he made the first move.* She felt a trickle of guilt, then came back to the present, to her and Tom. If she had to put a date on when she'd noticed a strain in their relationship, she'd put it around the beginning of July. She remembered because it had been Independence Day, and they had been at Capital City Club in Atlanta for the Fourth of July picnic. She and her boys had sat on the lawn and watched fireworks while Tom had had a head-to-head with his friend Benjamin. She remembered that the fireworks finale had just begun when Tom had sat down beside her. She didn't remember his expression. Why would she?

Totally unaware of her presence, Tom worked on. A sweaty strand of hair flopped down on his forehead and made him look boyish. Abbey remembered the first time he had called her. He'd fumbled around and asked her out to dinner, sounding like a kid asking a girl out for the first time. She cherished the memory. *Okay, he came back today. Ball is in my court.* She moved up behind him, placed her hands on his back, and dug her thumbs between his shoulder blades. It felt like the first real touch in weeks. He responded with an appropriate flex and groan.

"Thanks," he said without looking up. Blackened wicks lay on the chair near his discarded flashlight; new white replacements dangled in glass lantern bases at his feet. They were half-filled with liquid. "I thought you'd gone for a walk or something."

"Nope. I finished what I was doing, so I've just been standing here watching you."

"How come?"

"Just remembering how I got you."

He looked up, a question on his face.

Abbey said, "You showed up here at a meeting at Kings Bluff, remember?"

He nodded. "I was trying to figure out how the hell my wife had died."

"I offered to help you," Abbey said.

"You knew the area, so I took you up on your offer." He picked up a lantern. "I never could have sorted it all out without your help."

Abbey knew that guilt-ridden, how-could-I-have-been-so-stupid tone and didn't want him to get hung up on his past when there was so much to discuss about the present. She sat down across from him and said, "You would have figured it all out eventually, but it would have taken a lot longer. You made me your partner, remember? You told that tow-lot operator you were an attorney and I was your partner. Woo-woo!" She circled her finger in the air. "Shortest leap ever to partner in a law firm."

Tom pulled a pack of matches from his pocket. "Watch this." He struck a match and put it to each wick. "These things are almost foolproof, and they're cool. We should get some for home. Our little guys would love them." The boyish grin was back.

"Tom, I helped you sort all of that out. Don't you think it's time to sort out what's going on with us?"

Tom blew out the lanterns, then looked out at the river. "Not now. I know I have been a jerk, but I can explain it all to you. And I will. Soon."

Exasperated, Abbey raised both palms.

"Look, Benjamin is working on something for me. I called

him today from Brunswick. Please be patient. Soon, I will explain everything. I promise."

Abbey left him sitting there with his lanterns. She walked to the dock and stared out at the marsh. *I will not blow a gasket. It's important that I try to trust him, even though I am beginning to have my doubts.*

CHAPTER 20

Reverend Isaiah poked his head out the kitchen door, holding a large frying fork by his side. He wore a white apron over khaki shorts and a faded blue denim shirt. His grease-smudged apron barely covered his knotty knees and muscular calves. He pointed at each guest in the room as his mouth formed numbers. "Looks like about twenty-five teens and adults, five children, and four babies. That match with what you figure, Miss Blix?"

Blix looked up and did a fast head count. "Sounds about right."

"Dinner tonight is compliments of our helper and art teacher, Miss Blix, from our capital city in Atlanta. And I guess it's no secret I'm frying up a mess of chicken for dinner."

"You been driving us crazy, Rev, making us smell that chicken frying," an adolescent boy said.

"What time are we eating?" asked another.

"When it's ready. Last batch is in the skillet and the taters are cooked, so let's say in about thirty minutes. You boys go wash up, now. We got to feed Miss Blix so she can get on to where she's staying."

Blix and Latisha got to work on a salad. When the phone in the kitchen rang, Blix couldn't help but overhear the reverend's pulpit-practiced keep-them-all-awake voice as he talked. Her interest piqued when he said, "That's okay, Franklin. No, no, I understand. Don't you worry about it. I'll get someone over there directly to pick y'all up." He hung up the receiver and stood there for a minute, shook his head slowly, and then looked around until he made eye contact with Blix.

"Ah, Miss Blix, might I impose on you one more time?"

"Certainly, Reverend. It sounds like someone needs a ride." She reached into her pocket for Abbey's keys.

"You remember Franklin and Sam? You met them at the hospital the other day."

"Yes. I remember."

"They went to their weekly card game, and time got away from them."

Blix grinned. "That happens when you're having fun."

"You're an angel. They thought they could catch a ride here with one of their friends. Neither drives. Nobody showed up to play except the two of them, so they got to playing gin rummy and whatnot, and now they're stuck. I'd go, but I've got to go get my wife clear over on St. Simons. Franklin sounded a little upset, and I don't want him and Sam to fret. You understand. They're old men, Miss Blix. I imagine they're somewhat embarrassed, maybe even a little frightened, what with the evacuation and all."

"No problem, Reverend. I'd be happy to get them if you tell me where to go."

"I know you want to get on home, but it's not far. There's a little clubhouse in their neighborhood where all the fellows congregate. Now you be on the lookout for stuff in the road. That wind's been picking up all afternoon, and after this heat and the dry spell, limbs will come down, so you be careful. I really appreciate all you've done for us." He told her how to get to the men's clubhouse.

***

REVEREND ISAIAH'S DIRECTIONS were precise and included memorable landmarks; left at the pink house, pass the hot-dog stand on your right, turn in at the fish mailbox. It took Blix less than fifteen minutes to find the house—the only one on the block that had a huge green fish with a gaping pink mouth in which to drop letters. Behind a small, red brick house was a turquoise-blue wooden shed with an unpainted metal roof. The two men sat in green metal lawn chairs in front of the shed under a hand-painted sign: "CLUBHOUSE – MEMBERS ONLY. NO TRESPASSING! AND THIS MEANS YOU!!"

Both men looked up when she pulled into the driveway, and they stood when she got out of the Jeep. "Franklin, Sam, remember me?"

"Yes, ma'am," Franklin said.

"Sure do," said Sam.

"Reverend Isaiah sent me for you two. Are you ready?"

They wobbled toward her.

"I bet y'all are hungry." She helped them buckle their seatbelts and get comfortable.

"I hope we can get supper or something to eat tonight," Franklin said from the rear as they drove away. "We plum lost track of time and forgot to eat."

"Don't worry. I happen to know where they're serving fried chicken and potato salad."

The wind had picked up considerably. In the time it had taken Blix to get to the clubhouse, debris had blown across the road and blocked it. From the backseat, Sam directed her another way. No other cars were out, and there were no streetlights or house lights on. Neighborhoods that were usually active were quiet. Brunswick looked like a ghost town. "The power must have gone out while I was coming to get y'all," Blix said.

"Sure has," the men echoed.

"Where'd everybody go?" Sam asked.

"I guess most of them evacuated when the mayor said to go," Blix said.

When she drove up to the church, Reverend Isaiah's car was gone. *He went to get his wife.* She parked behind the church, beside a red pickup truck in whose bed grew tall grasses and a pine sapling.

As she grabbed her purse, she noticed the shattered door at the back of the church. She pictured the storage room on the other side of that door and the kitchen through yet another door. She turned in her seat, placed her finger to her lips, shushed, and pointed.

Her passengers murmured, "Uh-huh."

She felt around under her seat, then retracted her hand and made a handgun with her thumb and index finger and pointed under her seat. Sam whispered, "We're both retired United States Army, Miss."

"Okay." Blix grabbed Abbey's Smith & Wesson and a box of shells from under her seat. They got out and left their doors open.

As they crept to the destroyed door, the holstered pistol dangled by Blix's right thigh. Voices loud enough for them to hear argued inside: a man and a woman. Blix raised the pistol and tried to remove it from the holster. Her hands shook. "It's loaded," she said.

Franklin gently took the gun from her, removed it from the holster, and handed it back. Sam led them through what remained of the exterior door's frame.

They heard a woman's heated plea to leave her alone and a man's gruff response. There was a persistent *thunk... thunk... thunk*, like water dripping into a large metal sink, but louder. The three of them huddled at the interior door, ready to enter, their nervous eyes darting from one to the other.

"No!" the woman shrieked. There was a loud clap—skin on skin. "Don't you touch me again, you damned white devil!"

"You'll pay for that, bitch."

Blix whispered, "That's Latisha."

"I said, don't touch me, you devil. You do that again and I'll cut you bad."

A baby squealed. Blix lurched forward, led with her free arm, and butted the door wide open. A white teenage boy's blond head swung around; his eyes met Blix's.

"No, Miss Blix," Latisha yelled. "He got a gun."

In one motion, the teen whipped around and leveled a pistol at the newcomers. Blix's hands snapped out in front of her. Instructions, *"Cops shoot to kill,"* and Abbey counting all flashed through her head as she squeezed the trigger. *Kerboom!* She flinched. Though her arms shook, she held their extended position. *Did I hit him? Should I shoot again?*

Fine white powder showered down from the ceiling and covered the teen's face and head. His free hand went to his eyes. Sheetrock dust coated his hair and eyelashes. Latisha's hand flew up as she lunged forward and slashed with the butcher knife in her hand. Red seeped through mid-gut on the white boy's T-shirt. He screamed and staggered backward; his pistol clattered to the concrete floor. "You bitch! You goddamned bitch! You knifed me!" Tear tracks made his newly powdered face look morbidly clownish. He fell back against the counter with both hands clutching his stomach. "I'll kill you for this."

Franklin took the pistol from Blix's trembling hands and held it on the teen. Shaken, Blix went to Latisha, took the bloody knife from her, and tossed it onto the counter. She wrapped an arm around Latisha's shoulders and said, "Sam, there's a gun on the floor." Sam retrieved the gun and stuck it in his back pocket.

"You take it easy for a while, Ms. Blix," Sam said. "Keep an eye on him, Franklin. I'll get something to put on that cut."

"Hold a clean cloth firmly on the wound," Blix said. "I'll be there in just a minute."

"Take your time, ma'am," Sam said. "You done enough for one day." Sam grabbed clean dishtowels from a drawer, then pried the boy's hands from his body and pressed the towels to the wound. People from the sanctuary wandered into the kitchen like curious calves.

His voice authoritative, Franklin said, "Ain't nothing you can do here except get in the way. Everything's under control." No one left, but they did at least move to the back wall, where they watched and murmured.

"He'll need stitching up," Sam said.

"I'll do what I can until we get help," Blix said. She gave Latisha a squeeze and said, "Are you sure you're okay?"

Latisha nodded. "He busted in here." She choked back a sob. "That piece of white trash was on me before I knew what was happening. Where's my baby at?"

Blix looked around the kitchen and saw Joseph in the corner, banging a wooden spoon on a large soup pot. She went over and picked him up. He grinned and tapped the top of her head with his spoon.

At that moment, a young black man walked through the storage-room door, followed by an older woman and several young children. "What's going on in here?" he asked. "I thought I heard a gunshot. How come the door is all busted up?" He stopped and met a roomful of alarmed stares.

Latisha said, "Where you been, Otis?"

Happy to no longer be the center of attention and curious about who this new young man might be, Blix stepped away with Joseph and watched.

Otis went to Latisha while the older woman with him herded her wards toward the folks in the back of the room. Latisha grabbed Otis around the waist and buried her face in his chest. His grin said he was pleased by the reception but confused. He patted Latisha's back while he looked around.

Blix squeezed Joseph. *What must this Otis fellow think? I'm holding Joseph, Franklin is pointing a gun toward Sam, and Sam is kneeling on the floor beside a fellow I tried to shoot and Latisha whacked with a butcher knife.*

The white boy cried out between moans and nonstop cuss words. Otis detached himself from Latisha and went to Sam. "Holy shit." Sam continued to swab the wound in the boy's gut, which by now looked like a slice of rare roast beef. "What the hell? What's going on here? White Boy, what did you do, you damned fool?"

"You weren't home, so I came here looking for you. You know why. That bitch there—" He glared at Latisha. "—was out back messing around that old truck."

"Uh-uh," Latisha said. "I was getting a ball one of the children threw in the back of that truck earlier. That's all I was doing, and he come up and grabbed me from behind. Like to scared me to death, his hands all over me like that and me not knowing who it was. I got away, but he followed me back in here."

"Whore cut me." The boy's face contorted in pain and rage. "I'll get her for that, I swear I will."

Latisha stood behind Otis. "He was after me, Otis. I got away from him and locked the door, and he busted it open and come after me, waving that gun around like he's gonna kill me. Miss Blix done come in and fired that shot. I reckon she either saved me from getting raped or that white-trash friend of yours from getting killed. Killed by me. I'd have done it. That's the truth. I'd have done it sure as I'm standing here."

I'd better go patch that fellow up. Blix went up and handed Joseph to Latisha. "I'll take it from here, Sam. You've done a good job staunching the blood." She collected the first-aid kit from the storage room and reentered the kitchen at the same time Reverend Isaiah walked in from the front of the church.

"My wife is getting our things out of the car," Reverend Isaiah said, and then he stopped. "What's going on here? Is everything okay? I smell gunpowder."

Blix said, "We've had a little excitement, but I think everything's under control now."

The congregation still stood speechlessly against the back wall. While Blix and Sam doctored, Franklin filled Reverend Isaiah in on what had happened.

"Well, patch him up good, because the hospital has been evacuated along with everything else," the pastor said. "There's no one in town to do any doctoring, so I'm afraid you're it, Miss Blix."

Blix taped the bandage while the preacher located lengths of rope. Sam bound the boy's wrists and tied him to a stove leg. "He ain't going nowhere soon."

Otis grabbed Joseph and his pot and left the kitchen with Blix and Latisha. In the sanctuary, Reverend Isaiah made the rounds to settle everyone down and make sure they were comfortable. When he got to Irene, she looked around the room, and her expression changed. She shook her head and mumbled loud enough for Blix to hear, "Esther ought to be here by now, Reverend. I know she was coming today."

Blix didn't hesitate. "Reverend Isaiah, if you give me directions, I'll go for Esther, then get on back to Kings Bluff." She glanced at the oversized watch on her thin wrist.

"You've done too much already," the pastor said, "but I don't feel like I should leave, what with this new situation." He glanced toward the closed kitchen door. "I might need to calm some nerves."

THE MINUTE THE kitchen door closed, Deke began to work the ropes that bound his hands and feet, like a snake slithering through a mouse hole. Then he waited.

CHAPTER 21

When the Kings Bluff group reconvened for the potluck, they ate while they listened to a transistor radio one of them had brought. It seemed the storm had finally made up its mind on where to hit. "Listen up," one fellow said loudly. "Mayor's coming on."

Utensils stilled and conversation hushed. The air smelled of grilled pork, fried fish, and grease. Local officials had gathered at the news conference with the mayor. Someone turned up the volume on the radio as the mayor said, "The folks at the weather bureau are cagey. They don't want to get this wrong. Three days ago, they said there was the potential for a tropical storm that could turn into a hurricane. Tonight, they issued a hurricane warning. That means we could have winds of seventy-plus miles-per-hour and anywhere from a Category 1 to a Cat 4 hurricane. Whatever happens, it looks like we're in for a pretty good blow, and flooding to boot. I don't advise you to try to leave town now; it's too late for that. Stay where you are and don't drive unless you have to in order to get to shelter. They predict this thing will come right at Brunswick, though outlying areas will feel some effects."

"Okay, that's it," said Snag. "Let's get this cleaned up. Look around, see who's here, and let's get on back to our houses and get ready. We'll get some of whatever is headed for Brunswick, that's for sure, because it'll get to us first. The eye will either pass over us or skirt by us and keep on going. Either way, we'll get something. Put flashlights where you can get to them easily. That's about it. You all know what to do, I reckon."

"I know you grew up in North Carolina, Snag, but have you ever been through anything like this?" Abbey asked.

"No, but my daddy spent more time down here than me, and he always talked about high-marsh hen or moon tides in the fall, when the river came over the bank and flooded the road out front there. Now I don't want to scare anybody, but if the water does come up like that, it'll come up in every creek around here, and there are lots of creeks. After it blows on through, watch your step."

A woman said, "Okay, Snag. What are you hinting at?" She and the man to her left chuckled as he zigzagged his hand in front of them.

"Anything that lives near or under the ground is going to be looking for someplace to go—as in, higher ground," Snag said.

"He means snakes," Abbey whispered not-so-quietly to Tom.

"I figured," he said.

"We have no idea what time this thing might hit, and there's always the chance it'll stay offshore. Remember, we're here for each other. I'll patrol off and on all night, so don't get spooked if you see my headlights going up and down the road out front. It ain't a haint, so don't shoot!"

Abbey collected her bowl, and she and Tom headed to the cottage. "I kept expecting Blix to walk in while we were eating," she said. "I'll put these things in the kitchen, then let's go sit on the dock and get some fresh air while it's still light."

"Sounds good."

Tom waited for her in the yard while she put her bowl in the kitchen. When she came back out, he followed. Abbey had a feeling he was scanning the ground for that one rattlesnake that had it in for him. Her inclination was to tease him about it, but she didn't want to make him defensive and delay whatever he had decided to tell her.

"The water's already almost up to the bottom of the dock," Abbey called back from the wooden walkway. Tom caught up.

Just below them, waves rocked the marsh grass and crested halfway up the bank. "This is bizarre, Abbey. It feels like we're standing on the ocean."

"I've never seen it like this." A gust tipped her backward into Tom. "Whoa. Sorry. Wind's out of the south right now. It's pretty powerful to knock me off-kilter." Dark, menacing clouds tumbled and rolled overhead; the scents of a recent burn hung in the air.

"We'd better go back in before you get blown away, honey."

"No argument here," Abbey said, pleased to hear "honey." It had been a while. "It is a little frightening, I have to admit."

As they stepped back onto the road, a group of young people approached on a leisurely stroll. Their laughter and conversation stopped when they neared the two adults.

"Y'all be careful out here," Abbey said.

"Yes, ma'am. We're just walking to the other end and back."

"This wind is strong enough to bring down old dead limbs," Abbey said. "Any of you ever heard of a widow-maker?"

Heads shook. There were three "No, ma'am"s.

"If you walk under a tree and a broken limb drops and falls on you, you're a goner. They call those widow-makers because a lot of people have been injured or killed when they were out for a walk in the woods," Abbey said. "See the broken limb in that big tree over there?" She helped them locate a big sweetgum tree in her front yard.

The children nodded. "Yes, ma'am."

"That's a widow-maker. I was going to hire a tree man to cut it down, but I bet it'll be on the ground by tomorrow morning, if this wind keeps up. So y'all be careful on your walk. If you hear any cracks or loud noises, move. Fast." She ran her arm through the crook of Tom's elbow, and then, realizing what she'd done, she started to retract it until he snugged it to his side. "Have a good night," Abbey said to the children as they looked over their shoulders at her and continued on their way down the road.

"You just couldn't resist, could you?" Tom teased.

"No. I couldn't. What if we woke up in the morning and found out one of those children had been killed by a falling limb?"

As they went up the front steps, Tom said, "Well, I think your little warning worked. Look." He turned her. "They're coming back."

"Good. I know it's exciting and all, but it's dangerous. Their parents ought to have their heads examined, letting them out on a night like this."

Inside, Tom went to the kitchen. "Would you like a glass of water? Something I ate over there was really salty."

"The green-bean casserole. I took one bite. I'd love a glass of water." She grabbed their books from inside and settled into a rocker.

Tom reappeared with two glasses and sat beside her. "Do you think folks five miles inland from here are worried about this thing?"

"Probably not. It's just a news item for them."

Draining his glass, Tom said, "I can't believe that's the same river we ski on. It's rougher now than I've ever seen the surf on St. Simons."

"Water's powerful," Abbey said. "That current will take you away before you even know you're in trouble."

Kings Bluff was eerily quiet; the sky had gone positively black. Wind played with the screen door—pushed it partially open then *thwack*ed it shut. "That will drive me crazy." Abbey retrieved a pair of flip-flops from the bedroom and jammed one underneath the door. "Blix should have been back long before now."

"I'm sure she's okay," Tom said.

"I hope. We can sit here and watch the sky change while we wait for her."

Tom's brow furrowed as he looked around the yard beyond the screen. "What's that noise?"

"Sort of a moaning?" Abbey asked.

"Yes, I guess. It's eerie."

"Probably a pine tree being pushed around, or a limb rubbing against another limb. I brought your book out, if you feel like reading."

"Okay. I never got my beer. You want one? I sweated off ten pounds moving boats around today." When he returned, he said, "I bet those kids are glad you sent them home."

"I didn't send anybody home."

"No, but you scared the fool out of them, so you might as well have."

She looked at him. "I didn't try to scare them. I just warned them."

"Uh-huh." He took a sip. "You're right. You saved them from themselves."

"Maybe I did."

"No, you're right. It was a good lesson."

Her head tilted up. "Smell that?"

"Smell what?"

"That unusual combination of sulfur, cedar, and marsh. It's almost thick enough to cut."

CHAPTER 22

B lix glanced at the clock on the dash. It was almost six-thirty. Abbey and Tom were probably already worried about her, but there was nothing she could do about that now. Driving as fast as she dared, she made a plan. She would collect Esther, deliver her to the church, and still get back to Kings Bluff before dark. Reverend Isaiah's voice giving her directions boomed in her head as though given from the passenger seat. Knowing that Blix was nervous, the pastor had given her basic directions, without the shortcuts known by locals. The St. Simons causeway took her from the mainland to the island across the churning, frothy waters of the Frederica River.

Once across the river, she met only one other car. They exchanged blinks, a greeting or warning under normal conditions; today, it could be either or both. She looked through the windshield at tumbling gray clouds and hoped the rain would hold off.

Trees alongside the road thrashed wildly in the willful wind; brittle limbs snapped and littered the ground. Blix white-knuckled the steering wheel as gusts pushed and shoved the Jeep. Pinecones and dense green clumps of pine-bough tips darted like swallows and smacked the windshield, startling her until she figured out what they were. She took a deep breath. *I can do this. Esther's probably scared to death. Shoot. So am I.*

Bennie's Red Barn Restaurant came into view. *"Right on the first dirt road past Bennie's. Go to the creek. Esther's house is on the left."* She tapped the turn signal. A faded white sign with a red arrow pointing down the road advertised "JOE'S FISH CAMP – FRESHWATER POND (No Dogs! No small children!!! Gator in residence.)" Deep ruts defined the way. *What if I get stuck?* Blix's heartbeat quickened; sweat stung her underarms and forehead. Imagining a spinout and the Jeep bubbling out of sight in one of the water-filled ditches on either side of the road, she slowed.

Take your time. She forced a deep breath and thought about the little old lady sitting at home all alone, probably scared to death and not knowing whether anyone even cared. The car shimmied then found its footing. Glancing at the gas meter, Blix turned off the air conditioner and then lowered the two front windows slightly; warm air scented with cedar and pine whistled through the openings.

"Oh damn!"

She slammed her foot onto the brake. A large object lay across the road. When it moved, she yelped. A gigantic alligator raised up on its short legs, lumbered a short distance, and slid into the drainage ditch. Blix remembered the fish camp sign. *Get back to your damned pond.* She took another deep breath and released it slowly.

"Okay."

She drove on. About twenty yards later, an apparent washout had taken away most of the road. A late-model Buick was canted to one side, stuck on a high hump in the middle of what had been a road but was now a pond connected on either side to wetland swamps. Blix got out for a look. The passenger-side door of the stranded vehicle was turned up and totally out of the water. Blix decided not to chance driving farther. She'd feel like an idiot if she got stuck.

She grabbed a flashlight from her purse, just in case, then tossed the purse to the floor. *Oh God. What if she's in the car?* Blix looked at her footwear, happy that she had paid attention to Abbey's suggestion and worn sneakers. She stepped into ankle-deep water, relieved she hadn't tried to drive through. She looked around for more gators, banged on the hood of the Jeep, then waded to the stranded car. The driver's-side door was two-thirds underwater. A quick look told Blix there was no one in the car. The oil slick on the water's surface suggested there was a busted oil pan. She sloshed ahead until she came out on higher ground in the road. Several small wooden houses showed no signs of anybody home—no cars, no dogs, no lights. Farther down, there was an opening. She heard the gentle lap of water and saw a wide area of marsh beyond the opening. Then, to her left, though almost obscured by a gigantic oak tree, there was a small house.

Blix walked around the oak's wandering limbs until she came to a brick walkway that led to a front porch overlooking the creek. Light flickered through a window. Blix knocked on the door. Nothing. She called loudly, "Esther, my name is Blix Stouver. Reverend Isaiah sent me to get you." While she waited for a response, she glanced down. A pair of muddy black patent-leather high heels were beside the door.

A latch threw, and the door squeaked open. A petite gray-haired, dark-skinned woman in her Sunday best looked up. "The reverend sent you? Won't you come in?" The fact that an unfamiliar, disheveled white woman with a flashlight in her hand stood at the front door didn't seem to faze Esther one bit.

Inside, every horizontal surface in the cozy house held lighted candles of all shapes and sizes, the overall effect of their light that of gold fairy-dust. The air smelled of vanilla and ocean with a hint of biscuit. "Would you like a cup of tea?" Esther asked.

Blix was so taken by the atmosphere and Esther's soft voice that she almost said yes. "Another time, maybe, but we should get back to the church, Esther. Reverend Isaiah is worried about you."

"Oh, that's right. There's that storm. I watched it on TV earlier, and when I tried to leave, well, I got my car stuck. You must have seen it on your way in."

"I did." Blix scanned the tidy space and wished they had time for tea and biscuits. "I'm glad you were able to walk home."

Esther turned up her ankles to show Blix the raw red cuts she'd gotten when she'd tried to go barefoot to save her patent-leathers. Blix recognized the orangey antiseptic that Esther had used—Merthiolate—as the one her own mother had used on her when she'd been a child. "I think I busted something underneath my car when I tried to get through that washout in the road. I hope I didn't ruin my shoes. I had to leave them on the front porch to dry out. I'll clean them later if they aren't ruined."

"I think they'll clean up fine. Do you have some boots or rubber-soled shoes you can put on to walk to my car?"

"I got some old boots what my husband used to wear. He wasn't a big man, and I wear them sometimes in the garden."

"Let's try those. And get a pair of socks, so you don't rub blisters."

Thirty minutes later, Blix had snuffed the candles and Esther had changed into her gardening clothes and her husband's boots and fishing hat.

"Now you look like you're ready for a little walk."

The two women set out side by side. They exchanged unfamiliar, space-filler conversation as they made their way over ruts, potholes, and broken limbs. Unpredictable wind pushed them backward, sideways, forward. Esther stumbled. "Oh my." She chuckled. "TV said a hurricane's coming. It's good the reverend is taking folks in at church. He's done this before."

Surprised by Esther's tight grip on her forearm, Blix patted her hand. "Just hang on a little longer, Esther, and don't let go of my arm. You're doing great. We're almost there." Blix adjusted the fabric straps of Esther's small duffel on her shoulder.

"It was nice of you to come after me," Esther said. "But now I have gone and forgotten your name."

"It's Blix, Blix Stouver. I'm a nurse. I offered to help Reverend Isaiah."

"They're good folks at my church." Esther stumbled. "My husband loved these boots I'm wearing."

"They'll do you a lot more good tonight than those pretty black patents I saw at the door."

"Oh Lord. I do hope I haven't ruined them." Esther sighed. "I'm a little clumsy in his boots is all. He wore them all through basic training at Fort Benning, always kept them ready for inspection. I hate to think how many times he had them re-soled. Funny how you gets attached to things. Even boots."

Several minutes later, Blix said, "There's your car, Esther."

Esther looked up and said, "Sure is."

"My Jeep is there on the other side."

"Oh yes. I see it."

"Take my hand now, Esther. I think we stand a better chance walking through this little bit of water than trying to walk around in the swampy area on either side. You just hang on."

"Whatever you say, Miss Blix." Esther chuckled. "I never been to church dressed like this before."

"Well, when there's a hurricane bearing down and the mayor says get out of town, people do all kinds of things they wouldn't ordinarily do. People don't usually sleep in churches, either, unless the preacher is a bore, right?"

"No." Esther laughed. "I suppose not."

Wet drops tapped Blix's forehead. She ignored them. They stepped into the water and walked slowly on the cratered roadbed. Suddenly, Esther gasped and fell sideways, taking Blix with her. Blix splashed to her feet and grabbed Esther by the elbow. "Are you okay?"

"Ohhhh, Lordy." Esther moaned. "I think I twisted my ankle."

Blix watched a vein throb in Esther's neck and helped her hobble back to dry land. "Just be still for a minute, Esther, and catch your breath." Blix looked at the Jeep and weighed her options. The deepest area she had walked through was up to her thighs. If she tried to drive across and got in a deep place, the Jeep's engine might conk out and die, and they'd really be in a fix. Blix looked at Esther, who wasn't that large, and tried to remember her Red Cross training. She could pick Esther up and carry her, or could she? She had been going hard all day and wasn't sure she had the strength.

I have cancer.

The thought almost knocked her over. She'd been so busy she hadn't thought about her illness for hours. "I think the safest thing for us to do is go back to your house and wait it out. It will be dark soon. The wind is picking up, and I don't want us to be stuck on the road somewhere between here and your church."

"They'll be worried, won't they?"

"Shh... shh. Don't you worry." Blix pictured the inside of the Jeep. "There's a towel in my car. We'll use it like a sled or something."

Esther considered this. "I rode a sled once on a golf course in Atlanta. It like to scared me to death!"

"Well, I won't be going fast enough to scare you, I promise. You sit tight. I'll be right back. Now don't go anywhere." Blix sounded a lot funnier than she felt. There was always an emergency aspirin in her wallet. She went to the Jeep and got the aspirin, a towel, and the real-estate "Open House" sign that she and Abbey had peppered with bullets at the firing range.

When she got back to Esther, she told her to chew the aspirin to get it into her system faster. Blix placed the sign on the ground with the smooth side up, then helped Esther scoot herself squarely onto the middle. She looped the towel over a small horizontal bar between the sign's two thin legs. "It's a good thing you're little," Blix said.

It rained harder.

"Hold on, now." Blix grabbed an end of the towel in each hand and pulled. The going was slow but not that difficult. When they got to the front porch, Blix helped Esther get to all fours. From that position, Esther pulled herself up with the aid of a large low limb and Blix's hand.

"That big old tree is why we wanted this house. That and the creek."

With some doing, they got Esther inside and settled on her sofa. Wind banged the front door. Blix went to close it and looked outside at the rushing creek.

"How high does that creek usually get, Esther?" There had been a wide strip of sand when Blix had arrived; it had narrowed since the tide had come in.

"Not very. I keep my chair on the beach and fish out there, most days."

Blix walked back toward the sofa. They were both so wet now that she couldn't tell if it was rain or perspiration on Esther's face. "I'll get a towel for you. It certainly hasn't gotten any cooler since the sun went down, but I don't want you to catch a chill. I'll get some dry clothes for you, if you want."

"Thank you, Miss Blix. Tell you the truth, the dampness feels pretty good at the moment, though I'd like to dry off my face. Linens are in the hall closet. If you want to light the candles, there are matches in the peanut-butter jar on the hearth. Lordy, I'm sweating like a sprinter."

"Were you a runner?"

"Lord, no. But my husband was. He was fast as all get out."

"Well, that was quite an effort you just made."

When Blix returned, she handed Esther a washcloth and towel, then took off her own shoes and dried off, happy she had on the fast-drying shorts and shirt she had bought for her one and only kayaking adventure. She set about relighting the candles, and in minutes, the meticulous room glowed again.

Esther looked up and smiled when Blix joined her. "What now? No one knows we're stuck. Who will come for us?"

"Let's not worry about that just yet. I want to look at that ankle." Blix knelt on the floor beside Esther and unlaced her muddy boots. "Let me know when it hurts."

There was no blood, but when Blix pressed the already puffy ankle, Esther's foot jumped, and she grimaced. To give Esther a minute, Blix knee-walked the boots to the hearth, then scuttled back. A tear glistened on Esther's cheek. Blix wiped it away with the washcloth, then took Esther's hand in hers.

"I'm sorry that hurt. I'll ice it to keep the swelling down."

"All the ice trays are full, and they're going to melt. Might as well use them. There are tea towels in the drawer to the left of the sink."

Blix brought back a handful of ice cubes in a towel and applied the cold bundle to Esther's ankle. "That ought to help."

Esther sighed. "Just give me a minute or two to catch my breath."

Blix studied her patient. "When did you last see your doctor, Esther?"

Esther looked shamefaced. "Last week." She stared at her ankle.

"And... what did he say?"

"He said..." Esther's eyes watered when she looked at Blix.

"It's your heart, isn't it?"

Esther nodded. "Congestive heart failure."

"I'm glad I'm here with you, Esther. Don't worry. You'll be fine."

"I know I will. I'm glad you're with me, though. I get scared sometimes when I hear lots of wind. It sounds like it's picking up out there."

CHAPTER 23

Darkness, hungry and mean, came over Kings Bluff earlier than usual that night. Wind caterwauled through the trees with eerie sounds, one moment low, menacing growls and desperate howls, and the next, hair-raising high-pitched screams. Broken limbs, sand, and sweetgum balls bombed the cottage's wooden siding. Abbey peered out through a gap in the boarded-up kitchen window with a hopeful look, like a child who gazed out and wished for snow, but her Jeep's headlights refused to appear on the road that would lead her friend back. The realistic part of her brain knew full well that Blix would not attempt to drive on an unfamiliar road in the dark and in the rain. Abbey hoped that wherever Blix had ended up was a voluntary decision and that she was not stuck somewhere in a ditch on the side of a muddy road.

Tom was still on the porch, fiddling with the kerosene lanterns like a kid with a new toy. He was eager to light them, put them to their intended use, and relieve them of their decorative conversation-piece status. It was good to see him deal with difficult situations like the impending storm and Blix's absence. He rarely complained and didn't make excuses; he just dealt with whatever came along, though, as Abbey had learned recently, personal issues took longer to tackle than others. She went back to see how he was making out, moved a small wooden table out from the living room, and said, "Why don't you light one of those so we can sit out here. It's stifling inside. At least the air moves out here."

"Suits me." Tom set down the lantern. "I need to see a man about a horse. I'm grabbing a beer. Want one?"

Abbey's wooden rocker rail bumped on the uneven floorboards, the sound familiar and comforting against the disquiet of the increasing wind. "I'd love one. Maybe it'll help me nod off later." *There has been way too much going on today for me to sleep.*

Tom grabbed his flashlight. He returned with two dripping bottles. "We weren't thinking earlier. We should have invited everyone over here after the potluck. We're all sitting around waiting for something to happen, and we could have done it together—had a hurricane party."

"Please don't jinx us by saying that word. St. Augustine, Jacksonville, and Fernandina could be getting hammered right now, and here we sit, fat, dumb, and happy, like two college kids. All this waiting is the pits."

"Relax. You're just worried about Blix."

"Well, aren't you?"

Tom shrugged. "Sure. But there's nothing we can do about it." He took a sip. "Try to distract yourself. Think of something funny you have done in the dark."

Damn man. Still scared to talk about anything serious, but at least he's here. And he's talking. I'll let him set the pace to grease the wheels. Abbey thought for several seconds. "When I was in sixth or seventh grade, we had sleepovers—you know, spend-the-night parties."

"Spend-the-night parties? Girls do weird stuff."

"They were fun. That's how we celebrated birthdays when we were teenagers but not driving yet. There'd be eight or ten of us." Her finger followed a drip on her bottle. "We'd chow down on chips with sour-cream-and-onion dip. Yuck. And there were always bowls of M&M's."

"You ate junk food?"

"Yes, me. The thought of it makes me want to throw up, but I did it back then."

"I could go for some chips and dip right now," Tom said. "So, what else did you do besides eat at these girl parties?"

"We'd darken the room, and one girl would lie down on the floor. The rest of us would split up, four to a side, and we'd put our index and middle fingers under her head, shoulders, hips, and calves, and on the count of three, we'd lift her off the floor like she was nothing."

Tom stared at her and shook his head. "Right. You young girls lifted a friend with your fingers."

His doubt rankled Abbey. Ordinarily, she would shuck it off for what it was—a tease—but she wasn't willing to treat him as usual because he hadn't been usual lately, so she took it as an opportunity to make a point. "Yes, it was a silly party game where a bunch of girls put their trust in one another."

"Huh," he said. He took a pull on his beer but didn't question the trust angle.

The humming sound of rubber on asphalt interrupted the ensuing silence. Abbey set down her beer and grabbed her flashlight.

SEVERAL MINUTES LATER, she returned. Tom stood at the screen, staring out into the darkness. Without a word, Abbey sat.

Finally, Tom turned toward her. "I take it that wasn't Blix."

"No. It was Snag, patrolling."

A gust of wind blew the riverside screens inward. "The wind just changed," Tom said.

"Something must be coming," Abbey said.

The strong odors of rotting spartina grass and dead shellfish whiffed by, and then came the fresh smell of rain. She inhaled deeply. *There it is. I love that smell.* Wet drops spattered the front edge of the porch. Tom went inside. Determined to give him space, Abbey rocked slowly, focused on the different sounds of rain: it thumped the ground, pattered the leaves, pinged the tin roof, and tapped the front of the porch, all soothing and individual, familiar sounds. Soon, it blew in on her feet and became the raucous sound of millions of BBs dropped on the roof from the treetops. She shivered, turned on her flashlight, and went inside. Tom sat on the sofa in the dark. A fresh beer bottle dripped in his hand.

"Tom..." Abbey said, extinguishing her light when she was near him.

"No, let me explain, or try to. Come sit by me. Please."

She sat.

"You're shivering. Are you sick?" He ran his palm across the top of her head. "How can you be cold? It's hotter than Hell in here."

"I got sprinkled on out there and got a little chill is all. I needed to cool off anyway." She refrained from looking at her watch. She didn't want to distract Tom. *I really hope Blix is okay.*

"She wouldn't drive in the rain and pitch dark, would she?" Tom asked.

Abbey pulled at a thread on the knee of her frayed Levis. "We always know what the other one is thinking."

"I know. It's odd, but nice, too," Tom said. "Neither of us can get away with anything." Abbey didn't know whether to laugh or punch him, but his tone told her he might be teasing to pave the way for a serious talk.

"I'm almost positive she wouldn't drive in this," she said. "You know how you remember how to get places if you drive there yourself, but if someone else drives you, you're clueless?"

He nodded.

"I drove her to Brunswick today. She might have paid attention, but it's not a familiar area. Plus, the rain. So no, I don't think she'd try it." She dropped the thread onto the sofa. "I hope not, anyway." She felt the deep inhale and exhale of Tom's chest. He took a long pull on his beer.

"You know Benjamin called," Tom said.

"Yes."

"He's helping me with something."

She waited, having learned to hold off on saying anything while Tom formulated what he wanted to say and how. He tended to hold things in. When something really bothered him, he tried to sort it out on his own. He was also a thinker, considered every angle—a trait that served him well in law but made their relationship difficult, because she was a talker, hated to hold anything in. If she felt it or thought it, she said it. Tom thought it was a sign of weakness if he couldn't fix things on his own. He had difficulty talking about a problem to get her opinion. *Opposites attract.*

"That letter that came to the house this week," Tom said.

Abbey took a deep breath and held it.

"I met this woman when I was in law school. We went out a couple of times." He glanced at her. "I know this is going to sound trite, but she didn't mean anything to me."

Abbey let out her breath. "I guess that means you slept with her."

This time, Tom took the deep breath. "I won't lie to you, Abbey. Ever. Yes. Once. She was a real party girl—not in the sense that she was a girl who was fun and drank and partied and was friends with everyone, including the guys, but in the sense that she drank a lot and hit on all the guys all the time. She showed up at a few of our parties, and I was flattered when she came onto me. She was attractive, fun, and..."

"Easy," Abbey finished for him.

"Yes." He took another long pull on his beer. "Our second date was a party at the house I shared with some law-school friends. She got really drunk, and after a while, I figured out she was working the group, looking for an easy mark, while I was busy making sure everybody had a beer."

"Working how?"

"Trying to hook up with my friends. It was obvious after I realized what was going on. I'm such a dope. At some point, I realized I hadn't seen her for a while, so I went looking and walked in on her in my bed with some guy."

"Oh." Abbey grabbed Tom's arm. "Gross. I hope you threw away those sheets." *Where is this going? Just let him talk.*

Tom shook his head. "It gets better. My friends and I cut her off after that. I never saw her again until she appeared at my office several months ago."

Abbey huffed. "Oh great."

Tom said, "She had moved to Atlanta and wanted to get together. I told her that would be inappropriate, that I was married and had children, and she left. Then I would be eating lunch out, or several of us would be having a drink downtown after work, and there she was. She'd watch us while she ate or drank or whatever-in-the-hell she was doing, and she'd wave at me like we were friends or something. It was very strange." He drank again. "Then the damned letters."

"Letters?"

"Yes. I got two at work, and when I didn't respond to those, I think she sent the one to the house."

"And the hang-ups?"

"Probably her. What freaks me out is that she does it when she knows I'm probably not at home. I think that's her new strategy. She wasn't able to get my attention, so she's trying to get yours, and that really pisses me off. This whole thing is starting to feel like that Eastwood movie *Play Misty for Me.*"

"And Benjamin is helping."

"Yes. That's what all the calls have been about. He has been checking up on her. When I talked to him yesterday, he said he might have a lead. It looks like she has a history of doing this."

Abbey said, "You said you called him today."

"Yeah," Tom said. "You know that yellow car you said was checking out our house the other day?" She nodded. "She drives a yellow Ford."

This is too bizarre. "Tom, we have all dated creeps. Remember my ex? And yours? Sickos are out there, and they prey on people like us. Everybody I know has been suckered by one at least once." This time, she took a healthy draw from her beer and thought about what Tom had said. He was right. His encounter rang of *Play Misty for Me.* She wondered if he was totally blameless. He was good-looking, flirty in a low-key, sexy way, and successful. What woman wouldn't make a play for him? "I'm sorry you didn't tell me before. I've been worried."

"I know. I'm sorry. I didn't know what to do. I wish you had said something about the hang-ups. And the damned yellow car."

Is he trying to shift the blame here? "Come on, Tom. Everybody gets hang-ups and wrong numbers." Abbey's voice had an edge to it. "I have never had any reason to think it was some woman stalking you."

"I know. I should have told you."

"You're damn straight. When did she show up? Beginning of July?"

Tom thought. "About then. How'd you know?"

"That's when you started to pull away. And I saw you having a serious conversation with Benjamin at the club while the boys and I watched fireworks on the Fourth."

"Damn. I am so sorry. How did I ever think I could get anything by you? My wife. The sleuth."

"That's why you asked me to be your partner, remember?" She patted him on the thigh. "Want a glass of water or iced tea? Beer fills me up."

"Tea, please. Only if there's some already made."

Abbey went to the kitchen and got drinks. On the way back, she pointed her light at the barometer. "Huh. This might not be good."

"What?"

"The barometric pressure. It's just below the thirty mark, so I think that means the weather has really changed."

She handed him a glass then sat beside him. Wind shook the cottage and battered its exterior with what sounded like small bits of things it had picked up.

"I wonder what that is," Tom said.

"Sand, probably blowing up from the road. There's sand mixed in with the layer of shells out there."

"Makes sense."

"It's nerve-racking sitting around waiting for something to happen. You've been told it's out there building by the minute, but you can't see it or touch it, and there's nothing you can do about it anyway." Abbey shook her head. "It's like Blix's cancer, sort of, but she knows where the cancer is and can do something about it if she wants to. Hell, that's a dumb analogy. I have no idea what I would do if I were in her shoes."

She picked at a callus on her palm. "I hate to even say the 'C' word, much less think about having it, knock on wood." She tapped the table beside her.

Tom yawned. "Bedtime, I guess. If this thing turns ugly, we'll need to be ready." He took her hand. "I'm sorry I didn't tell you about my mess earlier. No wonder you have been short with me lately."

"You think?" She punched him in the thigh. "The night before I left, you were on the phone when I got out of the shower. Was that part of this?"

"It was Benjamin. Damn." He shook his head. "I should have said something then, but I thought I could handle it and you'd never have to know."

"Tom, you weren't normal. I knew something was up. You dropped all kinds of hints."

Tom shrugged. "I would never do that to you." He pulled her to her feet. "I have missed you."

"Likewise."

Tom said, "'Come into my parlor,' said the spider to the fly." Her led her down the hall.

Abbey's eyebrows raised. "What? I married a poet. How sweet."

He pulled her into their bedroom.

"But hold on a minute," she said. "Don't cunning spiders eat the legs and wings off poor, unsuspecting flies?"

"Aha. She's onto me."

Part of her wanted to resist his charm and affection until she was absolutely certain he had been straight with her. Another part wanted their lives to get back to normal. They climbed into bed.

In a gravelly voice, inches from her face, Tom said, "I think this is where I'm supposed to whisper sweet nothings in your ear."

"Shut up," Abbey said. "Spiders don't talk."

***

THIRTY MINUTES LATER, persistent rattling sounds made any thought of sleep impossible. The house was so crooked that open doors needed help to keep them from rapping against walls. Abbey got up and put needlepoint-covered bricks, one of Boonks's additions, at the bottoms of several doors to snug them up against walls. She made her way back to bed. "I feel awful lying here all nice and snuggly when there's no telling where Blix is sleeping."

No response.

"Tom?" She turned her head toward him, but his deep, steady breaths told her he was already out. *Romeo to Rip Van Winkle, just like that.* She caressed the top of his head. "Good night, darlin'. Sweet dreams. I love you." Her whisper was drowned by the sounds outside. For several minutes, she listened to his breathing and inhaled his fragrance. Their love-making had been intense, yet honest and sweet, without a trace of guilt. *Yet once in doubt, forever cautious? Or will that feeling eventually go away?*

Her head dropped to the pillow. *Breathe deeply.* She closed her eyes and imagined what the storm looked like from above the clouds. She punched the light on her sports watch. Eleven o'clock. Relieved that she and Tom had finally talked, she thought about her boys: Walt, her little red-headed, blue-eyed spitfire, and patient James, his protective older brother with those snapping brown eyes. She imagined them with her mother, eating watermelon in the cold, tumbling mountain stream.

CHAPTER 24

After none of her go-to-sleep tricks worked, Abbey grabbed her book and flashlight and went to the living room. She had just settled in when she heard a light knock and shined her light around the room. Tom had been sleeping soundly when she'd left the bed. She had never been frightened when alone at the cottage and wasn't now, though maybe she was a little on edge. She closed her book and listened. Outside, the wind howled, but below that was an insistent, rhythmic sound. When Abbey stood, her feet crunched on grit. No matter how often the wood floors were swept, there was always sand. The cottage gave voice to its age with creaks, sighs, and the occasional shudder.

She followed the sound to a window in one of the unoccupied bedrooms. She pressed her fingers to the glass in the lower sash, and the noise stopped. *It's just the wind.* She doused her light and tiptoed back into the bedroom where Tom still slept soundly. Abbey felt around the spare bed for her shorts and T-shirt and slipped them on, then grabbed her watch from the bedside table. She felt her way in the dark with her feet and hands and made her way to the porch, then turned on her flashlight. Five-by-eight sections of screen had torn from their restraining tacks and billowed like full skirts on a windy day. The uneven shell road in front of the cottage made the approaching headlights undulate in the steady rain.

Clumps of Spanish moss and broken limb tips had been blown everywhere. Abbey slipped on the flip-flops jammed under the screen door, walked out to the front stoop, and waved her light up and down. The truck slowed then drove across the yard and stopped inches from her. The passenger-side window went down.

"Hey," Snag said. "What are you doing out here in the middle of the night, crazy woman? You might blow away."

"Windows in the cottage are as old as Methuselah. They rattle when you walk across the room, and tonight, they sound like a mariachi band. Anyway, I had trouble sleeping. I had just gone on the porch with my book when I saw your headlights."

"I think you're fixing to get real wet. Hop in and go ride with me."

THIRTY MINUTES LATER, after they had cruised the bluff, they drove up in front of the cottage. Abbey said, "If I remember fifth-grade science at all, if the wind continues to circle, it'll heat up, rise, and pull up moist air with it. That can form a cyclone or a tornado. Whatever you want to call it, it's not good."

"Hurricane, maybe," Snag said.

"I'm not wild about any of those," Abbey said.

A bright white light moved across the screened porch. "Uh-oh. He's up," Snag said. "We've been caught red-handed."

"He'll get over it," Abbey said. "He's not the worrying kind. He must have heard us leave."

Snag pulled up as close to the porch as he could and rolled his window down partway. "I found this little lady standing out here a while ago, and I was afraid she was going to get wet, so we went for a ride. I hope you weren't worried."

Tom stood at the top of the steps. "Not at all. She can take care of herself."

"You can tell how worried he was," Abbey said as she hopped out of the truck.

"It's so noisy under this tin roof, I couldn't have heard you anyway, Snag. Y'all see anything interesting?"

Abbey joined Tom at the top of the steps and said, "Just high water."

"Want me to spell you for a while, Snag?" Tom asked. "I'm happy to keep an eye on things."

"No. Y'all get some sleep. I reckon if it's going to do anything, we'll know it soon enough. Wind's changing like it's been doing all night, so I reckon something's on the way."

Abbey hooked a finger through one of Tom's belt loops. "Thanks for the ride, Snag. Go home and get some rest. We'll see you in the morning."

As Snag drove off, Tom hung an arm around Abbey's shoulders and gave her a squeeze. "We'll have our hands full in the morning cleaning up the yard," he said.

She yawned. "If you don't mind getting wet, walk with me to the dock. I've never seen the river like this."

They made it as far as the walkway to the dock. Their lights swept across churning whitecaps. "The grasses are totally covered," Tom said. "Tide's been going out for a while."

The drizzle grew harder. "Come on," Abbey said. "It's coming." They trotted back to the cottage.

In minutes, rain blew onto the porch and pounded the tin roof so hard they couldn't hear each other talk. They dropped their wet clothes into a heap on the porch, dried off, and crawled back into bed. Soon, they were propped up in bed with pillows behind their backs and beams of light on their books. Abbey said, "I love to listen to the rain. This is perfect."

"Uh-huh," Tom mumbled. "Are you still worried about Blix?"

"Not now. She wouldn't think of driving in this. Wherever she is, she's staying put."

"You sure?"

"Positive. She'd never endanger anyone else on the road. Now go to sleep."

Moments later, Tom's paperback slapped the linoleum floor. Abbey reached over and turned off his flashlight.

At the end of her chapter, she put her book on her bedside table and turned off her own flashlight. She imagined Blix safe and dry, comforting one of the reverend's flock. *Goodnight, Blix. Stay safe.*

CHAPTER 25

The bed shook. Abbey bolted upright, both hands flattened on the mattress beside her hips. Lightning strobed beyond the windows in frantic bursts. Thunder vibrated the walls. She pressed gently on Tom's chest and gave him a shake. "Tom."

He grumbled.

"Wake up."

"Why? What's going on?" He sat up and grabbed her hand.

"Something's happening. I think the storm is on top of us. The cottage just shook me out of a dead sleep."

"What?" he asked. Bright light flashed through the windows. An ear-splitting crack followed. "Damn." He yawned and gave his head a vigorous scratch. "The hair just stood up on my head."

The house groaned and creaked. Doors bumped against walls. Tom tossed the sheet aside.

"Come on," he said. "Bring your flashlight."

Naked as two jaybirds, they stood in the bedroom doorway to the screened porch. Water pooled all over the porch floor. Abbey aimed her light beam outside. Grass was barely visible beneath the blanket of limbs and moss. "It's a mess out there."

"What time is it?" Tom asked.

Abbey checked her watch. "One-thirty. Happy Labor Day."

Tom's light zigzagged over hers. "Damn. When's high tide?"

"Around nine this morning. I checked it yesterday, so I'm pretty sure that's right."

"Which means it'll turn around three and might get to the road by five or six. It's a good thing this little house is up on sturdy pilings."

The wind's howl grew louder. Limbs snapped. The ground bounced as trees toppled. Torn, fibrous insides of cedars expelled fragrant scents. A sudden crack to the left made both Tom and Abbey jump.

"Okay, Tom, it's here. Now what?"

Tom was already on the move. "Come on." He grabbed her free hand. "Bathtub's our best bet. Get dressed. Fast."

They scrambled into clothes. Abbey snatched their pillows and bedspread. Their route to the bathroom went through Blix's room. Her light hesitated on Blix's hairdryer. *Be safe.*

She folded the bedspread several times, then arranged it on the bottom of the clawfoot tub and put down pillows for backrests. "This'll be snug."

Tom hesitated. "I'll get our shoes."

"Good thinking. And grab some cups. We can get water from the sink." When he left, Abbey darted to the living room and put her light on the barometer. *Damn. Pressure's down. A lot.* She scrambled back to the bathroom.

Tom returned several minutes later with both hands full. Abbey worked out ridges in the bedspread, then stepped into the tub and squirmed into her space. Tom stashed things around the claw feet. Abbey looked up when something crinkled. Tom held a large bag of barbecue potato chips.

She frowned. "Chips?"

"Oh, come on. We never eat this stuff at home. It's a storm. We're allowed." He stepped into the tub, then nestled in behind her and stretched out his legs beside hers. "How's that?"

"Got a shoehorn?" She held her light on the bag in his hand. "Are you going to open those things or hold them until breakfast?"

He opened the bag and grabbed a handful of chips, then dropped it into her lap.

She said, "Wish I had an ice-cold Coca-Cola."

"Oh, ye of little faith." Tom reached under the tub; ice rattled. He pulled up a Diet Coke and a Heineken.

"Way to go, Tom. You know, things go better with Coke."

He groaned, then said, "If I only had a camera, we could make a fortune. Next Super Bowl, they would run our ad: you in a clawfoot tub drinking a Coke with all hell breaking loose outside and you saying things go better with Coke. It'd be great."

"Sorry, Blix has the camera." Abbey crunched on a chip. "These things are so damned good."

"Yep." For several minutes, the predominant sounds were crunching chips and howling wind.

"I hope Momma isn't too worried. Lord only knows what she's heard about this thing up in the mountains, though I know they get the Atlanta paper in Highlands."

"It's just as well. Her worrying wouldn't change a thing, and she has enough on her hands with the boys. You know they're having fun."

"*Burros*. Now they want *burros*." She sipped. "By the way, I looked at the barometer. Pressure's way down."

"That fits. Pressure drops right before a storm hits. Brunswick is supposed to get the brunt of it, so we should be just on its leading edge." He took another handful of chips. "Of course Boonks is worried. Wouldn't you be? We'll run over to Brunswick tomorrow and call her and my office."

"Good. Maybe you can talk to Detective Benjamin."

"Don't worry. He's on it like a dog on a bone," Tom said.

"What are the odds this thing will hit Kings Bluff instead of Brunswick?" Abbey asked.

He hesitated, then squeezed her thigh. "My money is on Brunswick, because that's what the experts say."

"Are you sorry we didn't leave, Tom?"

"Well, I'm trying to be very Presbyterian about all of this, honey."

"What? That you, Blix, and I were supposed to end up right in the bullseye?"

"Blix was sure convinced," Tom said. "Maybe we don't even know yet why we're supposed to be here. I mean, I left and came back, for crying out loud. All I know is I'm not worried. Things will work out the way they're supposed to."

"You sound just like my mother," Abbey said. "I was raised Methodist, so I don't quite know what I think about your predestination thing, but I agree. We have already helped people, and maybe we have more to do." She took a sip. "Of course, I could be fooling myself, since I got you and Blix into this. Faith. Momma would say to have faith, so I think I will." They clinked drinks.

Powerful gusts whistled through gaps in old tongue-and-groove walls. The white eyelet curtain in the bathroom's only window fluttered. Because the cottage was off the ground, supported on concrete pilings, objects whipped beneath it and scudded and bumped against its underside.

"What on Earth do you suppose that is?" asked Abbey. "Sweetgum balls and hickory nuts, I imagine."

Tom asked, "Are you scared?"

"Not really, and I'm not sure why. Probably because you're here with me." She squeezed his calf. "It would have been different if you hadn't come back and we hadn't talked. That wouldn't have been so good. I'd be scared to death if I was sitting here by myself."

"I'm so sorry. I should have known better than to try to keep something from you."

"Maybe you're a little buttheaded?" She twisted her head on his chest and looked up. Though she couldn't see him in the dark, she felt his breath on her face.

"I stand accused," he said. "But it takes one to know one."

She punched him. "You know, Tom, if the boys had been with us, we probably would have high-tailed it out of here at the first hint of a problem."

"Yep. We'd be home watching a baseball game instead of sitting in this bathtub."

"That's for sure. I need to powder my nose." She stepped out and headed to the hall bathroom.

"Do you really powder your nose?"

"No," Abbey called back, "it just sounds nicer than the alternatives."

When she got back, they rearranged.

"What time is it now, honey?"

"Two-thirty," she said. "Two-and-a-half hours, and it'll be legal for us to get up."

Thunder rolled all around them, and the wind continued to howl. Damp earth and rotting-leaf aromas scented the moisture-laden air. "This is kind of cozy and pretty romantic," Abbey said. Tom kissed the top of her head. Their breathing slowed, and their bodies relaxed on the cool porcelain of the tub.

CHAPTER 26

Tom's groggy brain tried to put a name to the labored groan. He saw only darkness. Sensing danger, he tensed, his body achy in its cramped bathtub position. Abbey's arms rested on his thighs. He pressed the light button on her watch. Four o'clock. Still hours until sunrise. The unsettling noise came again, this time followed by a loud crack, like a hardball whacking a bat, only louder. The crash that followed was no more than seven feet overhead. Tom's hands flew to his face; his shoulders hunched. The impact obliterated drywall and shattered glass. Nails and screws long settled in walls squealed as they were pried away. Abbey groaned. Misty rain drizzled through the space where the ceiling had been. Crumbled bits of wallboard peppered Tom's hair and eyelashes and instantly dissolved into pasty-white streaks that drizzled down his face. Then all went quiet, save for the incessant wind.

Shaken, it took Tom several seconds to investigate something that tickled his ear. *Blood?* He felt, but his ear was dry. Reaching out, he touched a leaf attached to a branch. He groped the floor beneath him for the flashlight he'd left there. He pointed the beam upward and saw a tree with the girth of a horse. Beyond the tree was only air, black as pitch.

"Abbey, there's a..." He lowered the flashlight and looked down. Red splotched the front of his white T-shirt. "What the..." He felt all around his face, then pointed the light at Abbey's. A red drip hesitated on the tip of her nose. He thumbed it away, wiped it on his shirt, then felt around her head and found an open gash.

"Oh my God." He tried to move. His knees, locked in their cramped position, screamed in pain. "Abbey, honey, say something. Talk to me. Please."

He put his hand on her chest and felt movement. "You're breathing." He struggled to a sitting position, then worked his leg over the side of the tub and stretched his foot to the floor. Inching himself out from under Abbey, Tom gently lowered her head to his pillow in the bottom of the tub and stood as best he could. Hunched over, he felt her face and stomach, then ran his hand down her legs. His light went back to her head. The angle of her neck looked all wrong. *Oh, come on, come on, come on. Think.* He racked his brain for any tidbits of first aid he'd learned in Scouts or the Army. He remembered not to move her, lest she have a break or concussion. Blood streamed from the wound. *Ice stops blood flow. I need ice.*

He took a deep breath to force himself to calm down. Foolish reactions wouldn't do anyone any good. He looked around the destroyed room, and his eyes lighted on the wooden medicine cabinet that had been suspended on the wall above the sink at the head of the tub. Its eighty-some-odd-year-old nails had been no match for the downward thrust of the limb; it now lay on the floor at the end of the tub with a bloody red smear on a corner. Tom counted seconds as the small alligator emblem on the front of Abbey's shirt rose and fell. *I'll give her a minute to come around.*

"Five, six, seven…" Heat and the closeness of leaves and limbs were suffocating. Tom dropped his head back and sucked in fresh air as he counted. At sixty, he said, "Abbey. Talk to me, honey. Come on. Wake up." He jiggled her toe.

Her body slumped in the tub like a sack of wet sand. What-ifs flooded his brain. *No. Stop it.* He pushed those thoughts from his head. *Move, man. Do something.* Trapped by the tree, he snapped off small nearby branches until he had cleared a space in which he could move. He tossed the medicine cabinet out of the way and continued to talk to Abbey until he had cleared an area large enough to hoist himself through. He grabbed a towel from a hook on the door that had been torn off its hinges and now leaned against a wall. There was still ice in the cooler under the tub. He grabbed a handful of cubes, put them into the towel, and held the cold compress to Abbey's wound.

Several seconds later, her eyelids fluttered; her fingers clenched into fists, then relaxed.

"That's it, honey. Come on now, Abbey. Take a deep breath. You're okay."

She grabbed the sides of the tub. Her eyes opened wide. She lurched up, then slumped back with a moan. "Ouch." Her right hand went to the gash in her head and came away bloody. "Gross. What happened?"

"Slow down, honey. You're fine. Something ran into that hard head of yours and knocked you out cold."

"I was out?"

"Like George Foreman after an Ali punch. You were conked on the head by the medicine cabinet that used to hang over the sink."

"By what?"

Tom pointed his light at the medicine cabinet, which lay on its side by the toilet.

"It feels like I was beaned by a damn two-by-four."

"You were lucky it wasn't worse."

"Damn." She poked around the wound. "It hurts. What made it fall?"

"That." Tom aimed his light and shook a branch.

Abbey peered around the bathroom. "Holy smoke. Is that the whole tree?"

"Can't tell yet. Might just be a huge branch. It just happened. I've been waiting for you to come around, so I haven't been outside to see the damage."

"Well, shoot. Help me out of here. Has it stopped blowing yet?"

"Sounds like it's calming down. Here. Grab my hand. And take it slowly."

They retrieved their shoes and climbed through branches until they got to what had been the living room. Both exterior walls were gone, obliterated by the giant sweetgum tree that now occupied the living room and the bathroom. They worked their way along the tree to what was left of the old entry: a set of brick steps. Abbey laughed. "Remember the song 'Stairway to Heaven'? I don't think this is what Zeppelin had in mind."

"I doubt it."

They picked their way around the debris-strewn yard and walked to the road. From what they could see by flashlight, the neighbor's property looked just as bad.

"Hey! Y'all all right?" They both turned. Snag stopped his truck.

"Abbey had a run-in with a medicine cabinet."

"Oh yeah. I see. You'll have one big goose-egg, there, darlin'."

"Already do." She touched her head. "One of those old sweetgums took out the middle of the house."

Snag threw his truck into park and stepped out. "Let's take a look. I have a saw in back." He grabbed a chainsaw and a major flashlight from the back of his truck.

The three climbed back into the living room. "Dang," Snag said. "Where were y'all when this thing came down?"

"In the clawfoot tub," Tom said.

"That's cozy, but good and sturdy, I reckon. We did the same thing up at my house when all them trees started coming down. My wife claimed the big soaker tub in the master, and I got the little one in the guest room. You two fit in one tub?"

"Yep," Tom said. The two men exchanged a look and grinned. "Cozy. It wasn't bad at all."

Abbey shook her head, immediately regretted having done so, and then rubbed her forehead with the tips of her fingers. "You men."

Snag cranked the chainsaw and cut limbs into manageable pieces. Tom passed them to Abbey, and she pitched them outside. Ten minutes later, they were at the bathroom doorway.

"This is where we were pinned in," Tom said.

"Dang big limb," Snag said. His saw chewed on section by section. When he'd cleared the bathroom, he grabbed the offending medicine cabinet. "This'll make good firewood, unless you want to put it back up for old times' sake."

Tom wiped sweat from his face with the corner of his T-shirt. "Pitch it."

"Oh, come on," Abbey said. "That's an antique." She opened the cabinet door and removed a small tube of toothpaste, a comb, and a worn orange emery board and dropped them in the trash can under the sink.

"You can go get it later, if you want it," Tom said. "Pitch it." Snag tossed it into the yard.

"I might just," Abbey said. "It goes so nicely with this room."

"Room's hardly there anymore, honey."

"Let me think about it."

"You two cut it out," Snag said. "We're all pretty lucky is all I have to say."

Abbey grabbed Tom's arm. "Okay, I'm out of here."

"Where do you think you're going?" Tom asked.

"To get Blix. I've got to get to Brunswick."

"Ain't no way," Snag said.

"What do you mean?"

"Hell, you wouldn't even make it down Kings Bluff Road, Abbey. I tried. It'll take days to clear enough debris so you can even get to the highway. Tide's coming in, and you sure as heck don't want to get stuck on that paved road when it floods, which it will when the tide's in full. That road's a lot lower than we are here on this bluff."

"Honey, we need to make sure everybody's okay here first," Tom said. "You can't just light out like it's a normal day. People need help."

Abbey stared at the ground and clicked her flashlight off and on. "You're right. How is everybody else?" She probed around her wound.

"Couple of trees on houses and busted windowpanes. About like yours."

They walked through the house. Other than some lost windows, the walls were mostly intact in the rest of the house, and the bedrooms, kitchen, and dining room were usable. Chainsaws were already hard at work up and down the bluff, and the new day had barely broken.

"As soon as we're sure no one needs us here," Abbey said, "I'm going to Brunswick." She looked right at Tom. "Even if I have to fly."

CHAPTER 27

Moving steadily northward and gaining strength, the hurricane wind and thundering rain all but drowned out the muffled whimpers inside the darkened AME church. Low voices recited Bible verses with a familiarity gained from repeated readings over the years and spoke with hope born of love, trust, and faith. Most asked for strength to endure yet another of life's challenges. Trying times did that to people, made them turn to the Lord when they had nowhere else to go and all else had failed.

Gusts of wind roared one minute, screamed the next—pummeled doors and wracked windows like the Devil himself doing his best to get inside where it was quiet and dry and full of prospects. Otis sat on one corner of a thick pallet of blankets, his back flattened against a wall. He kept an eye on the front door to make sure it remained barred against the fearsome elements outside while, at the same time, he kept an eye on Granny and his siblings, all huddled together like a litter of pups. He'd been so busy that he hadn't thought about his momma until that moment. He wondered where she was, where she'd been, if she was the least bit worried about her family. *Did she leave town without us?*

Latisha watched him from the opposite corner of the blanket, an open storybook and a lit flashlight on her lap. Joseph lay beside her on his back, blowing spit bubbles and fingering his toes. Now and then, he clapped his hands over his ears and looked around wide-eyed for the howling boogeyman who threatened to come inside.

Otis had scavenged scrap lumber from a nearby construction site the day before. He and Reverend Isaiah had nailed odd-sized boards over the church's windows like Blix had told them they had done at Kings Bluff.

Otis grabbed the large light he'd brought from the kitchen and crawled to Granny. "Are you okay? Need water or anything? You hungry?"

"No, honey." She patted his hand. "I have my water here. Later, maybe we can make a pot of coffee. I know there's some instant in the pantry. Thank goodness the stove's gas."

"Yes, ma'am. The children okay?"

"They're sleeping. They're plum wore out."

He looked at his brothers and sister and thought how lucky they were to have their granny. "I'll see to that coffee soon as I check out front and see what's going on."

"You watch yourself," Granny said. Her fingertips brushed his back as he walked away. Otis knew she depended on him, being the oldest grandchild and all, and he knew she knew he wasn't immune to mischief, but he appreciated how she gave him credit when credit was due. He looked back at her, all old and gray and still looking after little children. He wondered if his momma ever felt ashamed about her ways.

As Otis passed by, an old man said, "Tell us what's happening, son."

At the front of the church, Otis grabbed the back of the pew that he had secured against the front door the night before and dragged it several inches across the floor. A gust slammed the door against the pew and knocked him backward, allowing only a fraction of a second to glimpse outside. Sheets of rain blew sideways and pelted waves that rolled as though headed to a stretch of sandy beach instead of the flooded front lawn. Otis scrambled to regain his footing and muttered, "Lord help us," then leaned his weight into the sturdy back of the pew and pushed it against the door, like he had done the sled at football practice.

The door inched into its frame; the hardware clicked into place. Otis rested with his hands on the back of the pew and caught his breath while he pictured what was happening outside. In a low voice, he said, "Excuse me, everybody." Several looked up. "I need for y'all to listen for a minute." He made eye contact with the pastor. There was a new sound, like overflow from a rain gutter slapping concrete. Heads turned to those close to them. Murmurs rose.

"Oh, sweet Jesus" came from someone at the front of the church. "That sounds like water. We're gonna drown."

Otis went to the nearest window at the front and shined his light through a gap in the boards. Waves crashed over the front steps and entryway. What had been a familiar landscape of parking lot and trees and shrubs the previous day was now covered by a skim of water that reflected splashes of intermittent moonglow. *How deep?* No matter. The church had become an island. Otis crossed to the other side of the sanctuary and looked out. He barely made out Latisha's house. Moonlight glinted off her porch swing as it banged crazily back and forth. Transfixed, Otis turned his head toward Latisha and said, loud enough for everyone to hear, "I think everybody'd better go on and get up."

Reverend Isaiah joined him and bent down to look outside. "Unh, unh, unh." He patted Otis on the shoulder. "I've never seen it like this before. You know, Brunswick's real low. That can't be just rainwater."

"No, sir. I don't believe it is." Otis felt something touch his leg. He looked down. Joseph's fat little fist clutched a handful of the hem of his shorts; the little boy's big brown eyes stared at him, questioning. Otis hoisted the boy to his hip.

Latisha joined them. "What's going on?"

Otis stepped back and handed her his flashlight.

"Oh my God." Her hand went to her mouth. "What will we do?"

Otis glanced at the ceiling, then back at the pastor. "Is there an attic with a floor up there?"

"There is. We use it to store Christmas and Easter decorations, items we only use once a year or so."

"We'd better take a look," Otis said. He handed Joseph to Latisha while Reverend Isaiah spoke to Sam and Franklin.

Flashlights lit the path to the kitchen, where, save for the wind, it was quiet. Otis moved his light around the room. A pile of rope and chain lay around the feet of the stove. "White Boy done run off." *There was only one thing he came here for.*

"We'll worry about him later," Reverend Isaiah said.

They went to the storage room off the kitchen; Otis glanced at the truck through the busted doorframe. The hood was up. *He done run off with all of them jewels. Good.*

A retractable ladder's pull cord dangled from the ceiling. Otis lowered the ladder. He and Reverend Isaiah went up, and Sam and Franklin waited at the bottom. A dusty plastic Christmas tree in a stand stood at the top of the stairs. A handmade star coated with glued-on silver glitter still adorned the top. "I intended to put that tree out in the trash first of the year," the pastor said when they were both able to stand. "Church ought to have a real tree."

If it felt uncomfortably warm downstairs, the people would feel like they were going to suffocate before they sweated to death in the attic. Boxes labeled "CHRISTMAS," "EASTER," and "NEW YEAR" were stacked against the walls. Extra-large black plastic leaf bags filled with who-knew-what were crammed into low-ceilinged spaces.

"Let's get some air in here," Otis said. He raised the window in the front gable. "There might be enough room if we clear out all of this stuff." He scratched his head. Perspiration prickled his scalp beneath tight black curls.

"Course, the ladies will pitch a hissy fit if we toss it all out," Reverend Isaiah said. He thought for several seconds. "It's just stuff. I bet we haven't used most of it in twenty years."

"So, pitch it?"

Reverend Isaiah hesitated, then said, "Tell you what. Let's make an executive decision here."

Otis grinned at the notion of being an executive.

The preacher said, "Things that are closest to the ladder and marked 'Christmas' and 'Easter,' let's pass down the ladder. This will give folks downstairs something to do. Then, what's stuffed way back under the eaves, let's pitch. I know that stuff hasn't been looked at for years, and we need the room."

Otis nodded. The pastor called down to Sam and Franklin and explained what he wanted them to do while Otis collected black trash bags from under the eaves and dragged them to the open window. One hour later, the space was empty.

The reverend asked, "You want to direct traffic down there or up here?"

"I'll go down so I can help them up the ladder, sir, and you meet them at the top and give them a hand."

"Good idea, Otis. Once everyone is up here, they can have a look out a window to see what's going on before they get settled."

Otis went down to explain what everyone needed to do, and then he helped the elders move their hands from rung to rung and offered encouragement. After the seniors were safely situated, the children giggled and teased and scrabbled on up to their new hideout. Latisha handed blankets, bedrolls, and jugs of water to Otis, who passed them up to Reverend Isaiah. By the time Otis and Latisha went up, everyone had a space and a soft pad on which to camp.

Otis peered out the window toward the street. He motioned to Latisha and said in a low voice, "Water's already completely over the turn-around in front of the church. And that's just since we started to move everybody up here. High tide's not 'til nine o'clock this morning. Water's gonna keep on rising."

Latisha craned her neck to look down the street. "It'll go up the steps to my house. What'll we do if it keeps on coming, Otis?"

"We've done about all we can. Hopefully, somebody'll come looking for us before too long. It's rising while I'm looking at it."

A percussive thump made them jump. A huge tree had fallen across the sidewalk between the church and Latisha's home. Below them, a wood-splintering crash jarred the building.

"Front door, probably," Otis said. Latisha grabbed his hand and pulled him to where Granny entertained Joseph with patty cake, patty cake. The church shimmied. Objects careened into its wooden siding. Glass shattered.

"Momma?" Joseph whimpered. His tiny hands and feet squirmed as though they wanted to go somewhere to hide.

"It's okay, baby." Latisha picked him up and rocked him back and forth on her hip as she murmured in his ear. Her wet eyes found Otis's.

He shrugged, then walked over to the pastor and whispered, "We need to make a plan to get out of here if that water keeps on." Reverend Isaiah nodded.

"Listen up, folks," the preacher said. "You all know how the tides work around here." There were "uh-huh"s and nods. "We haven't even hit high tide yet."

Otis climbed down the ladder. Earlier, he'd seen an axe in the storage room. He went right to it. The discussion was still going strong when he returned to the attic.

"Where'd it all come from?" Gracie asked. "It's supposed to be in the river, not up here in the yard."

The preacher said, "It came from the rain and the river, and it's about to come from the ocean, when high tide gets here. Now we all chose to stay in town, but a lot of folks left. They warned us there wouldn't be rescue people around, so we're on our own. I'm not trying to scare you, but that water's probably coming into the church before too long." Some gasped, and others shook their heads. "There's nothing we can do about rising water except decide on a course of action. If it comes up into the church and looks to be still rising, we'll have to cut a hole in the ceiling and get up on the roof."

"How we gonna cut a hole?" Franklin asked.

Otis, with axe in hand, joined the preacher and held up the tool for all to see.

"Where'd you get that?" Sam asked.

"Storage room."

Sam said, "Maybe after a while, we can start pulling up floorboards up here. We can use them like rafts. This is good old wood, and it'll float like a boat. All you have to do is stay on top of it, or at least hang onto it."

"Sit down here, boy," Granny said. "Rest." Otis nodded and sat beside her, the axe at his side.

No one wasted energy moving about in the sweltering heat. Even the youngsters seemed doped, limp as wet bath towels. Clusters of adults talked among themselves—no need to whisper, because it was difficult to hear over the clamor of the wind and the crashing of limbs and flying debris. Suddenly, there was a new noise, a gentle sound almost indistinguishable from that created by old creaking boards asked to withstand forces they hadn't encountered since they'd had roots in the ground. At first, it was almost familiar, like the slow drip of a faucet or the tap of a loose shutter. Then it multiplied, its staccato beats closer and closer together. Otis stood and peered through a window. He looked back at Reverend Isaiah, who was talking to Sam and Franklin, and gave him a nod. Otis looked out again and watched asphalt roof shingles flip through the air like a covey of flushed quail.

The pastor came up beside him, and Otis pointed to the flurry of sailing shingles. "Roof's going."

"Sure is, son. There goes the decking. We'd best tell everybody."

They went back to the center of the room and told everyone to cover up. Moments later, loud gunfire-like pops sounded above them. There was a loud screech, then a gut-wrenching tear as wood cracked and splintered. A corner of the roof pried up, and then a large section of it tore away and was swallowed by dark, angry sky. All eyes stared up into the boiling maw of dawn. Groans escalated to screams when the floor beneath them swayed.

CHAPTER 28

On the sofa where she'd dozed off and on, Blix awakened fully when she heard a slow, agonized crack. A deafening screech sent her diving to the floor as a massive limb crashed through the roof and thudded to rest across the house. Rain plinked into the two muddy boots on the hearth beside her head. Wind played the gaping hole in the roof like the wood-wind section in an orchestra. Blix lay there for a moment, then pushed herself up and looked around. *Oh my God.* She had left Esther asleep in her bedroom. Scrambling to her feet, she said, "Esther, are you okay?"

She grabbed one of the tealights in a holder and the jar of matches from the hearth. The tree had fallen across the front of the house. Crunching broken glass and bits of sheetrock under her feet, Blix worked her way to the hall and back to the bedrooms. The tree's trunk and limbs occupied the front bedroom like an uninvited guest. The exterior wall on that end of the house was no longer there. Esther lay perfectly still in her bed, her eyes wide open. Blix put the candle on the bedside table, then put her hand on the older woman's arm. "You're okay, Esther. A tree fell."

"I thought I was dreaming," Esther said. "What's that noise?"

"You weren't dreaming. That noise is the wind."

"It's drafty in here. I guess that's 'cause of the wind."

"Esther, a tree fell on your house. You lost a wall or two. One in here. We should get you to the living room, but I need a tarp or some sort of cover to put over us, because there's a big hole in the roof." Blix helped Esther sit up.

The older woman looked around and gasped. "What happened to the wall?"

Blix said, "It was a very large limb."

"Goodness." Esther found a small flashlight in the drawer of the bedside table and handed it to Blix, then directed her to the front bedroom.

Just inside the door, Blix found a camelback trunk. She ran her hand over its top. *This is gorgeous.* There was a squeak. Blix braced herself. The limb settled. She stood stock still for a moment, then shined her light around the destroyed room. The wall on that end of the house was gone; what remained of a lovely old lamp was nothing but sharp fragments and a crushed lampshade on the floor. A sodden quilt clung to the foot of the bed that was barely visible beneath the tree. *Poor Esther.* Blix raised the top of the trunk. Inside was Esther's husband's military paraphernalia. Blix took out a carefully folded parachute, two hand-knitted Army-green woolen vests, an Army-issue canteen, and two pairs of heavy green wool socks. She took the items back to Esther and sat on the bed beside her.

Esther took the vests and laid them in her lap. She ran her hand across the scratchy wool. "I can't tell you how many of these I knitted during the war. Us young wives got together at church and knitted these for our boys."

Blix watched the rabbit-like flutter of Esther's carotid artery. *Congestive heart failure. Keep her warm, dry, and hydrated.* "I know this has a history, Esther," she said, offering the parachute.

"Oh yes," Esther said. Her hands left the vests and rested on the carefully bundled parachute. "That belonged to my husband's best friend, a white farm boy from North Carolina. They didn't know each other very long, but long enough to pray together. My husband pulled that boy and this parachute out of a tree." She patted the bundle. "My husband held that poor boy's hands until he died." Esther patted the bundle again and sighed.

"Esther, may I use the parachute to shelter us? Keep us out of the rain?"

Esther smiled. "Why certainly, sweetie. That would please me."

Blix helped Esther hop to the living room and settled her on what remained of the sofa, and then she retrieved the parachute. Using the limb as a ridgepole, Blix draped the parachute across it and then padded the floor with sofa cushions, on which she layered folded wool Army blankets and foul-weather gear from the trunk. After the two women squirreled inside their makeshift tent, Esther said, "I can see you have been through some bad times, but I think you don't want to burden anyone with your pain. Pain is easier when it's shared. You have been a blessing to me. I hope you feel you can unburden your heart with me."

SOMETIME LATER, BLIX stirred. Beyond Esther's soft puffing snore, she heard the wind's aggressive push and shove. She pulled aside a portion of the chute and crawled out and aimed her light toward the destroyed ceiling. She recalled different sensations from when she'd been resting on the sofa earlier. There had been the crack followed by the limb crashing into the living room, and there had been a thud that had reverberated through the house like a shockwave. It was too dark to see much outside, but she had to know if they were in danger of the limb dislodging from where it now rested and crushing them to death. Illuminated by her flashlight, Blix trailed her fingers along the ridges and deep valleys of the centuries-old limb and imagined it as the disembodied tail of a great tyrannosaurus rex. She wondered who else this great live oak had protected: an Indian family, or the territory-seeking soldiers of Spain, France, and England? Perhaps there had been a Confederate boy who'd rather climb the tree to spy on hatchlings in nests than carry his side's flag into the next battle.

Blix's reverie was broken by Esther's voice. "What do you see out there?"

"Not much. It's too dark, but at least the rain has stopped. How's your ankle?"

After a moment, Esther said, "Another aspirin wouldn't hurt."

"Are they in the bathroom medicine cabinet?" *The bathroom without a back wall?*

"Yes."

Eager to move around, Blix took her time as she went down the hall. The limb had cut clean through the ceiling but left some interior walls standing. Though it was now lying outside on the ground, the bathroom's far wall was pretty much whole, both medicine cabinet and sink still attached. Blix dropped several feet to the ground. Leaves and sand pelted her as she searched through the jumble of bottles inside the cabinet and found the aspirin. A crushed, rust-colored chrysanthemum peeked out from beneath the wall. Small boxwoods encircled the area where the wall lay. *I'm in her flower garden.* A small shed sat farther back, with a shelf attached that was filled with clay pots of various sizes stacked one atop the other, all totally unharmed.

Blix shined her flashlight past the garden and along the rear of the house. The air carried the scent of the cedar she remembered from opening her mother's old blanket chest. A tangle of downed branches at the end of the house prevented her from seeing farther. She climbed into the open-air bathroom and made her way back to the living room. "The kitchen looks pretty good, Esther."

"Is the cookie jar still there? I'm kind of hungry."

Blix entered the compact room and flashed her light around until she spotted a large, round glass container with a dented gray metal screw-on lid. She had seen that kind of container, with a high price tag attached, in an off-the-beaten-path country store. This one was filled to the brim with irregularly shaped cookies, obviously homemade. "I found the cookie jar. I'm on my way."

As she passed the refrigerator, she looked inside and grabbed an old-fashioned glass water bottle with a flapper lid, then took two small juice glasses from the drying rack by the sink and held the cookie jar to her belly with crossed forearms. She went back to the living room and set her things down on the floor beside Esther, who sat with her back braced against the sofa.

"It will be a little while before it gets light, Esther, but maybe we can move around some, stretch our legs. I bet you're tired of sitting."

"Sure am." Esther removed the lid of the cookie jar, took out two large cookies, and handed one to Blix. They devoured them. "Want another?"

"Not yet, thank you. That's just what I needed." Blix handed the aspirin and a glass of water to Esther. "Is this well water? It's very good."

"Artesian," Esther said. "Best water in the world."

Blix sipped and nodded. "Excellent. My friend at Kings Bluff gets her water from a huge aquifer." She drank again.

"After you get this down, we'll consider our options. You hang on there for just a minute while I go see what the creek looks like." She hesitated. "Esther, do you swim?"

"Swim? Why, no, Miss Blix... why do I have to swim?" She was silent while Blix made her way under the limb and to the front door. Then Esther said, "I guess you can tell me how to do it. I had a dog once. That sweet boy loved to swim in that creek out there. I imagine I can do like he did. Didn't look too hard the way he did it, paddling his little feet like that, keeping his head above the water." She thought for several seconds. "That's the main thing, keeping my head above the water."

"I hope it won't come to that," Blix said. "If it does, we'll be fine. Don't worry."

Portions of the front wall of the house had been splintered. Blix stepped down from the living-room floor to the front porch and went ankle-deep into the water. She tried to remember what Abbey had told her about tides during storms—something about the storm pushing extra water behind the high tide. They'd been concerned about flooding. *Tide surge. That's what it was. She said that's when people drown. What if we have one of those surges?*

Blix and her siblings and parents had spent vacations in Florida, where beach houses were built high off the ground on columns and everyone parked their cars underneath. Esther's house reminded her of those beach cottages, though, unlike them, Esther's river house was supported on low pillars no more than two feet high. *They might hold for a little while.* Shining her light on the huge oak tree, Blix made a mental note of the height of the water in relation to a series of short boards nailed at intervals into the trunk of the oak—a ladder to some child's treehouse.

Running her hand along the limb for support, Blix waded to the end of the porch and shined her light around the surrounding area. A leaning cedar threatened Esther's kitchen. Blix calculated the location of the cedar's trunk and its distance from the living room. The tree was massive, easily four feet around at its base. Her light followed the length of the tree across the road to where it had snapped. *If that tree hadn't deflected off the live oak, it would have landed right on top of us.* She put that possibility to rest and went back inside to Esther.

"Just to be safe, I think we should get to higher ground."

Esther's eyes widened. "We're leaving here, now? Where are we going?"

Blix thought for several seconds. "Do you know what time high tide is?"

Esther closed her eyes. "Let me see. It was around eight yesterday morning, I believe. I'd been up for a while and gotten all my chores done and—that's right—I walked out to the creek with my second cup of coffee. It was mid-morning."

"It's rising now. Quickly. I think our best bet is to get up in that old oak tree of yours somehow. Did your children have a treehouse up there?"

"Of course they did. Some of it's still up there, just not giving up. I reckon its waiting for another little boy. You can still see the boards they used to climb up to it."

"That tree has been your friend for a long time. I think it saved us from the big cedar across the road."

"What, it's gone?"

"Afraid so."

"That cedar's always breaking limbs in storms." Esther looked at the oak limb. "We're going to climb that tree. Now how we doing that?"

Blix's light moved around the room. "I'm not sure, but we'll figure it out as we go."

Several minutes passed in silence while Blix paced and thought. Then, Esther said, "Miss Blix, I was just thinking. I always clean my fish on the back porch. Isn't any porch, really—it's just out the back door through the kitchen, but it has a sink and a counter with a metal cover on it. I keep a supply of ice picks back there for when crabs try to get away and for skinning catfish, that kind of thing. You think one of those picks would help me grab hold to that limb? I saw these mountain climbers on the television one time, and they had things they dug into ice and rocks to help them climb."

"If it makes you feel better, I guess it can't hurt." Blix went to the back porch and found an assortment of ice picks stuck in a post. She grabbed two of the picks with sturdy handles and took them back inside. "Let's get your boots back on." She dropped the picks on the floor, then collected the boots from the hearth, brushed them off, and emptied them of water. She looked out front to see how high the creek had risen on the tree. It now approached the bottom rung of the ladder. Water was on the rise.

CHAPTER 29

Dawn's first light was of little comfort to the group in the church's attic and only served to make the danger of their predicament more obvious. Earlier, the noise of things blowing apart and hurtling into other objects had unnerved even those who had seemed cool under pressure. As exhausted as he was, Joseph refused to sleep. His eyes darted from the gaping hole in the roof to his mother and to Otis. The church creaked like an old body's bones. Otis shot to his feet and was immediately unsteadied by the unrestrained wind. He looked up. The live oak against which the church now leaned had stood its ground and kept the church from toppling. Otis stepped carefully across the floor. The attic's walls still refused to give in.

Otis felt Reverend Isaiah's eyes on him and wondered what the preacher thought about his sudden interest in the church. He'd never been a regular member of the congregation, but he always went with Granny and his siblings to Christmas and Easter services, and that was about it. He had to admit he felt good about showing up for this storm. He knew he'd been a big help. Latisha had told him Reverend Isaiah had asked about him and she'd filled him in on what she knew. He was curious about what she might have said. Though they lived in the same neighborhood, it wasn't like they had ever hung out together or anything. She was a married woman with a child. And her husband was dead. As though he were reading Otis's thoughts, the pastor pushed up from the floor and joined him. The reverend seemed to study the situation, and then he leaned in close, his mouth to Otis's ear, and said, "Water's come on up since we moved up here."

"Yessir. Sure has."

Low whitecaps washed across what had been the wide-open parking area. The truck where Otis and White Boy had stashed their goods from the jewelry store looked in danger of washing away. Otis wished it would. Thinking about events the night of the robbery had kept him on edge ever since. Now he knew that what he should have done was stay home that night or come here to the church to help Latisha and the reverend prepare. *Damn. Why'd I ever listen to that no-count White Boy? It's like Granny says. That fool's nothing but an accident waiting to happen.* The hood of the truck was now gone, as were the two white pillowcases he and White Boy had stashed there for safekeeping. *He probably took them after he broke loose. Damn.* What did any of that matter now? What did anything matter now? *We're probably all going to die unless we get help. I got to do something for us. Anything.*

Reverend Isaiah patted him on the back and turned to take his leave.

"Yessir, Reverend. It's all the way up to the bed of your truck."

"That's a good couple of feet, son."

From the church's attic, Otis had a clear view all the way to the Brunswick River, though everything looked like the river now. There were no banks anymore, nothing to hold the river back from the land, nothing to prevent that water from taking over everything in sight. Downtown looked like rows of boathouses perched along a roaring, ravenous monster.

Above the whir of the wind, a deafening shriek pierced the air. Both men went bent-kneed as their eyes searched for and found the sound's source. A telephone tower downtown had begun to bend. The top half leaned at an odd angle for several seconds, then dropped and disappeared into the rushing water. Boats left in the river had dragged their bottom-mounted mooring floats with them and careened into other boats as they were swept along in the churning current. Boats on trailers crashed into other trailers; the whole lot rode the powerful water toward buildings, trees, anything that stood in the way. Though it was difficult to distinguish individual noises over the whipping wind, the combined sounds of chaos were gut-wrenching.

Otis turned toward a different sound close by: a prolonged crack that refused to give. There was an explosive *pop*. "There." Otis guided the pastor's gaze with a pointed finger. "Look." A house several doors down rocked. Its roof lifted off like a bird and somersaulted into the sky. Its beams broke, walls collapsed; remnants scattered in the wind like a tossed deck of cards.

"How could that happen?" asked Reverend Isaiah.

Otis stared at the empty lot. "All that water rushing underneath. Look at the pilings. That one's getting ready to topple over. See there?" He pointed again. "Water's running over that one that's already on the ground. Water gouged out the pilings. After that, there wasn't nothing there to support the house."

Reverend Isaiah stared at the swirling, lapping water that seemed intent on destroying the concrete pyramids on which the house had stood. "Water will have to get pretty doggone high to get to us up here." He wiped sweat from his brow. "Only thing we have going for us besides our prayers is that this church was built out of heart pine. It's solid. I know. If you'd ever tried to drive a nail to hang a picture downstairs, you'd know, too."

"That old oak's helping," Otis said.

Just then, a little round Volkswagen Beetle bobbed by, nicked a crepe-myrtle tree, and swirled along slowly, making complete circles like a drunken bug.

"What're you looking at, Otis?" Latisha asked from behind him.

"Hang on. We're deciding what to do."

"But what do you two see that's so interesting?"

The lid of a Weber grill was caught in a swirl in front of the hoodless truck. Otis looked several doors down to his grandmother's house. Sheets that he'd seen her hang on the line to dry the morning before flapped in shredded strips from the broken limbs of the mimosa tree she'd loved. He pictured the tender marijuana plants that had been in his garden, knowing they had been destroyed along with everything else. He was relieved. The swollen carcass of a dog floated by. It looked like the noisy beagle that barked at him every time he passed its fenced yard. He swallowed, then cleared his throat. "Nothing but an old grill top. That's about all."

"Otis, baby, tell us what's happening," Granny called out from her spot. She sounded worried. Otis left Latisha with the pastor and went to his granny. His brothers and sister were clustered around her like spat on an oyster rake. Otis sat on the floor beside his family and took the old woman's hand in his and stared at it. He'd seen the small diamond ring and gold band on her ring finger and the tiny ruby ring on her baby finger many times before, but for some reason, he'd never paid them much attention.

"They're pretty," Otis said. Their eyes met. "You know I love you, Granny. And I appreciate what you do for me and them." His eyes moved over each of the small children gathered around her and then to the window. Not far away, glass shattered and roofs whirled through the air like slashing samurai swords. The church shuddered against the brutal wall of water that grew as it surged, full-force and unforgiving, across the lowland that was Brunswick.

CHAPTER 30

Throughout the morning, while the storm moved farther north, the sounds of chainsaws at Kings Bluff sounded more like a lumberyard than the usual sounds of outboard motors headed out to fishermen's favorite spots. Long forgotten were the raft race and fishing tournament. The first Monday of this September was all about clearing the club's acreage of storm debris caused by wind gusts that had reached upward of one hundred twenty miles-per-hour in the pre-dawn hours. It would take several days to make a dent.

Snag left his chainsaw with Tom so he could clear some of the more manageable limbs on the property. Abbey had a different idea. She rummaged around in a kitchen drawer and found several pairs of worn cotton work gloves on top of the oyster knives. Cold weather and oyster roasts over open fires were a mere wishful thought in that morning's stifling heat.

"Tom, put these on." Abbey tossed him a pair of gloves. "Let's go see what the paved road looks like."

He shook his head. "Honey, you heard what Snag said. There's no way we can tackle that road."

"I've got to try to get to Brunswick, Tom. This mess isn't going anywhere. I have got to know one way or the other if Blix is okay." She headed for the paved road with a pitchfork and a shovel.

An hour into moving marsh canes and limbs from the road, Abbey went for water and came back with two cups. "Drink this before you pass out. You're sweating like a racehorse."

"Thanks." Tom took two gulps, then wiped his brow. "Racehorse. I feel like I just did a mile."

"Studly. You're a real thoroughbred."

"Could have been a pig, I guess." He laughed then drained the cup. "Where'd you get this?" He handed her the empty cup. "It's good and cold. I could use another, but I'll get it."

"All our water is from an aquifer, so it's always good and cold. Like the pool. There are big metal containers of it in the clubhouse. And there's food. Folks brought lunch."

"Are you feeling okay?"

Abbey touched the swelling on her head. "I'm fine."

"Figures," Tom said. Then he mumbled under his breath, "Hard-head."

A black Dodge diesel truck pulled up to them with a driver neither of them recognized. Snag leaned out of the passenger-side window and said, "We just checked on Roosevelt."

"Is he okay?" Abbey walked up to the truck.

"He's got trees down like everybody else, but he's worried about Hongry—said he had a bad feeling. If y'all want to take a little break and go see what's up, hop on the tailgate. I'm afraid you're fighting a losing proposition there. It gets much worse down the road a piece." He eyed the chainsaw in Tom's hand and nodded. "And bring that."

Tom looked at Abbey. "We agreed we would make sure everybody was safe here before we tried to go to Brunswick."

"I know." She sighed, then threw her tools into the bed of the truck. Tom let down the tailgate and they hopped on.

All along the road, individual pines had been knocked over as though swatted by ornery giants. Uprooted hardwoods lay helpless on their sides, their tangled roots clumped with earth and oyster shells. Farther on, the road was impassable to anything but a four-wheel-drive vehicle. *How will I even get to her?*

Minutes later, the truck turned and bounced onto dirt. An old green pickup truck was pulled over in the rough. Everyone knew Roosevelt's truck. The old man was nowhere to be seen. Abbey poked Tom's thigh. "He must have walked to Hongry's. He's been stuck in that truck enough times to know what it can and can't handle."

The four-wheel-drive Dodge dug into the road's sloppy surface. Wet sand pelted the backs of Abbey's calves and stung her ankles. As she held up a leg and wiped off the grit, the truck fishtailed and knocked her into Tom's shoulder, then found the ruts again and gained traction. Twenty or so feet later, they stopped. Tom grabbed the chainsaw, and they followed Snag and the driver.

Several trees blocked the road, so they jumped a ditch to get around the base of one of them, only to have to get around another and another. "That there's the problem." Snag pointed to the right.

Across from Hongry's little house lay a field with piles of mounded scrap wood from the most recent tree harvest. "There's nothing there to stop the wind. Hongry's place might not even be there anymore. Dang. I hate to see all this." Snag ambled on at his turtle pace, but after his last comment, Tom and Abbey sped up.

Several minutes later, Tom said over his shoulder, "There's Roosevelt." He called out, "Roosevelt. Hold on."

The old man turned from the sapling gripped in both his hands. His shirt and cotton Braves cap were wet with perspiration. Blood from small scrapes tinged the sweat that streamed down his arms. A red streak in his frosty white hair dribbled blood down his forehead. A pile of busted limbs lay within tossing distance of his feet. "I think I hear somebody talking in there, Miss Abbey. We got to move these trees."

Abbey walked up beside Roosevelt, and Tom put a hand on the man's arm to still him. Abbey knew her husband didn't do things without first thinking them through. He assessed the situation, then motioned with the chainsaw hand. "We have to be very careful where we start to cut, Roosevelt."

Snag and the other man appeared. "Everybody, this here's Ed," Snag said. "He works for a feller in Brunswick who has a tree-removal business. Lucky for us, he lives down Kings Bluff Road." Ed held a chainsaw that made Tom's look like a nose-hair clipper.

Ed circled Hongry's house. Now and then, his saw chattered. Several minutes later, he reappeared and spoke quietly to Tom, whom he dwarfed by a good three or four inches. Ed looked like he could handle any tree he encountered. With his chainsaw, he motioned to the offending cedar limb that was sandwiched through Hongry's roof like a hot dog in a bun. "The rest of the tree is over there on the far side of the house. I figure between it and a big oak back there, I might be able to get close enough to that limb to get rid of it. I just need to run back to my truck for a few things." And Ed was off.

Snag said, "Ed told me if we want to do something, we can gather the crab traps, cast nets, buckets, and garden stuff and put it off to the side so it doesn't get in the way or get crushed." He shrugged when Abbey pouted. "Well, that's what he said, and he knows what he's doing."

"I know where Hongry keeps everything," Roosevelt said. He picked his way past fallen trees to the rear of the lot; Snag followed him to a small shed.

Abbey grabbed Tom's arm and steered him toward Hongry's garden. "I've seen him lean his garden tools over here." They lifted limbs from the crushed fence and tossed aside what had been a gate. Abbey spotted a wooden handle lying in a furrow. "He wants to keep us out from underfoot." She grabbed the handle and shook dirt from the hoe.

By the time the B-team had done its job and piled everything out of the way, Ed was back with a bow saw and several loops of rope. "Tom, Snag, y'all come with me." He disappeared again, and they followed.

Abbey spotted a log away from the action that offered a good view. "Roosevelt, we'll only be in the way. Let's have a seat over here and watch from the peanut gallery."

Roosevelt let out a deep breath. "I wish there was something I could do."

"I know, but Ed is a professional. Let him do his work."

Roosevelt glanced at the crushed little house, then joined her on her perch.

For the next forty minutes, Snag and Tom did what Ed told them to do, and Abbey and Roosevelt watched from the sidelines. Section by section, the fallen trees were lifted off and away from Hongry's house. Without his usual tree-trimming equipment on hand, Ed gained height from the branches of a giant magnolia that had escaped the storm relatively unscathed. He secured ropes in the tree like a web-spinning spider, then directed Tom and Snag to where he wanted them to stand and proceeded to pitch coiled sections of the secured ropes to them. Each rope landed at its receiver's feet.

"He must have played ball somewhere," Abbey said to Roosevelt. "Why don't we move sections as they cut them?"

Roosevelt hopped up. "Good idea."

Most of the logs were too heavy for them to pick up, so they rolled them out of the way. Roosevelt was quiet and kept glancing over at Hongry's house; Abbey made conversation to distract him. There was no telling how long Hongry had been barricaded inside. In a moment of silence, when no one talked and the saw was quiet, Abbey heard a muffled voice inside the house. "Someone is talking in there, Roosevelt," she said.

"I knew I heard something, Miss Abbey."

When the last length of limb was lifted from the roof, Abbey and Roosevelt cleared enough from the walkway so they could see the Airstream logo on what served as Hongry's front door. Though slightly crushed, the trash-picked treasure still walled off the interior of the house from the outdoors. Roosevelt grabbed the door handle and pulled. Nothing. "Anybody got a screwdriver?"

"I do," Ed said, so near Abbey that she jumped.

"Oh," she said. "You sure got down fast."

"Time's money," Ed said. He pulled a screwdriver from his work belt and attacked the rusty hinges. Within minutes, they lifted the door from its frame.

Roosevelt entered while the other four crowded the opening and peered in. They would have taken up too much room in the tight quarters, had they tried to go farther. There was laughter inside. The four moved away from the door as Roosevelt exited with a grin on his face. Close on his heels came Hongry. When his eyes met those of his rescuers, the little man broke out in a wrinkly-faced giggle.

"I know what you told me other day, Miss Abbey." He shook his head. "That storm come on in the middle of the night, and I didn't want to just show up at your house. I would have scared you and Mr. Tom plum to death, and I done seen you at the firing range. I know you can shoot."

That was about as many words strung together in one effort as Abbey had ever heard him say. "Lord, Hongry, I'm just glad you're okay. Who were you talking to in there?"

"Him." Hongry pointed to his chest. Tiny paws grasped the top of the pocket of his red flannel shirt; the small squirrel's black eyes blinked. Hongry looked at Tom and said, "His nest blew out of a tree. I'll turn him loose when he's able."

Tom nodded. "I'm sure you'll take good care of him until then." Years earlier, soon after the death of Tom's first wife, Hongry had rescued a wounded eagle and Tom had teased him about keeping it as a pet, which he'd had no intention of doing. Since then, the two had enjoyed an unusual friendship. "If it rains again, your house is going to leak, Hongry. Where will you sleep?"

"My house," Roosevelt said. "I got plenty of room."

Ed had already headed to his truck. The others joined him. The truck's radio was on by the time they got there. What was now being called a Category 4 hurricane had dealt the coastline from St. Marys on up a glancing blow. By the time it had spun past Kings Bluff in Waverly, Georgia, it had whipped around and had come back at Brunswick head-on with everything it had had.

Abbey leaned into Tom. "Somehow, I've got to get to Brunswick."

CHAPTER 31

Otis Simmons was awakened by a child's voice. *Oh Lord. I guess I ain't dead. Not yet, anyway.* His muscles reminded him that the only thing between him and the attic's wood floor was one of his granny's thin handmade quilts. Images of the past several days played through his mind, along with reminders of the drug dealer he'd thought he wanted to be—an image he now dismissed as nothing but a foolish clown-boy trying to be what he wasn't. He was through with all that nonsense. Over this short period of time, he'd noticed a change in himself. Now he knew what it felt like to be a man. He lay there and thought about his little family, how he liked looking out for them, being the responsible big brother. *What would Momma think about me taking care of everybody, being responsible? Damn red shoes. Where the heck is she when she ought to be here looking after us?*

He thought about Joseph and Latisha and what they'd all been through. He pushed aside the silver tarpaulin that had covered him and his family overnight. It had held off the rain, for the most part. Gray-blue sky filled the space where a roof had been not so many hours earlier. Everything had happened so quickly. Nearby, Joseph stood on stumpy legs and tugged at the tarp draped over his mother. "Up, Ma-ma. Up. Up."

"Hey, Little Man," Otis said softly. "Look at you, standing up like that." The child smiled, pumped up and down on bended knees, and giggled. "That's right. You keep working them muscles. You be running before too long. We get out of this, and I'll get you a little football—teach you and my brothers how to pass." Otis stretched his limbs straight out in front of him, then got slowly to his feet. "Let's go see what's going on outside."

People stirred as he stepped around legs and feet and made his way to the window where he and Reverend Isaiah had made executive choices. He spent a moment enjoying that thought. Below, the parking-lot-turned-lake was calm, save for innocent ripples that ferried along bits of small unidentifiable objects.

"Dang, Little Man. It looks like the river done left where it used to be and come to us. There's a story in the Bible about this man named Noah. God told Noah to build a boat, so he did. He built a big old boat—called it an ark. He saved his family and a male and a female of each animal in the world from drowning. We might have to build us an ark to get out of here today."

"You telling my baby Bible stories?" Otis turned. Latisha walked up and stood by him. She looked through the windowless space. "Oh my Lord. What are we going to do? How much higher is that water coming?"

"It ought to be done soon, Latisha. Watch the stuff floating by. Tide will turn and take it all in the other direction before too long."

"I know about the tides, Otis Simmons. I live here. Remember?" She smiled. He handed Joseph back to her and walked to the folded drop-down ladder. Reverend Isaiah joined him.

"Do you think it's safe to go down there and take a look?" the pastor asked.

Franklin and Sam appeared.

"Only one way to find out," Otis said.

"Sam, Franklin, help us push this thing down," Reverend Isaiah said.

The four men knelt on either side of the collapsible ladder and pushed on it.

"Seeing as I'm the youngest, I'll go first and check it out." Otis's legs dangled through the hole. "I wouldn't want any of you old men to get hurt or nothing." He cracked a smile and cut his eyes toward Latisha, who grinned and shook her head.

"I think he trying to impress somebody, Joseph." Latisha rocked her baby back and forth on her hip. "What do you think?"

"Uh-huh," Franklin said as he glanced at the pretty young woman and then back at Otis. "Get on with it, young-un."

Otis lifted the folded bottom section of the ladder with his toes, then descended on rungs until his feet touched water. He stepped into the storage room. Hanging on a peg to his left was the preacher's sport coat; below it, in a cubby hole, sat a shiny pair of black dress shoes. Otis glanced around. Everyone else was still in the attic. The shoes were fine ones and smelled of shoe polish and leather. Several days ago, he had wanted to get rich and had thought selling drugs would get him there fast. Then he'd gone with that damned no-good white son-of-a-bitch to rob a jewelry store. A lot had happened since then. He picked up a shoe and peered inside. *Size thirteen. Wing tips. Nice.* He ran his finger along the smooth leather and the single row of small perforations. He'd tried on a similar pair at the Salvation Army once, and the salesperson had asked him where he'd planned to go in those "banker's shoes." Lifting his foot, he placed the sole of the leather shoe to the bottom of his worn white Converse. *Perfect.* He replaced the beautiful leather shoe in the cubby and waded into the kitchen.

"You okay?" Sam called down from above. "What do you see down there?"

"Looks like all the windows is gone, and..." Otis stopped talking. A well-fed snake lay across the island in the middle of the kitchen. It had taken note of Otis's arrival. *Shit.* "Uh, Sam, you still got that white lady's, uh—her hardware?"

Sam said, "Uh-huh. Sure do."

Otis's eyes never veered from the snake, as though his stare would hold the reptile in place. "Can you bring it down?" The snake's head moved like it was either listening or taking aim, and its tongue flicked. Otis swallowed. "Sam, now. Fast."

The ladder creaked as Sam descended. "What's going on?" Sam whispered as he crept up beside the frozen Otis with the pistol hanging loosely by his side.

"That." Otis indicated with his chin.

"Oh." Sam whipped the gun up and got off a one-handed shot. A chunk of snake flipped to the floor. There were yelps from the attic.

Otis called up, "Everything's okay now. You can come on down, Reverend."

Sam rummaged around drawers and found two spatulas, with which he lifted the business end of the headless water moccasin.

Reverend Isaiah appeared and said, "Oh, good Lord," just as Sam tossed the snake out the windowless hole over the sink. He went back to retrieve the head and flipped it out the same way. "Now how do you suppose he got up there?"

"I reckon he swam and figured out the rest," said Sam.

"Suppose there are any more?" asked Reverend Isaiah.

"Reckon so," Otis said. "Where else you think them critters done gone?"

"Guess you're right," said Reverend Isaiah. "They've been displaced just like we have. Watch where you put your hands, where you step, and where you sit, fellows."

They filled Franklin in when he joined them. "Where is it?" the old man asked. Sam thumbed toward the window hole.

Otis looked around the room. "How many shells you got left, Sam?"

"We're all right," Reverend Isaiah said. "I brought my pistol and two boxes of thirty-eights." He patted his pocket. "I suggest we stick together while we look around."

The newly formed posse inspected every exposed surface, shelf, and cabinet in the kitchen, then moved out to the sanctuary. Something underwater bumped Otis's leg. "Oh shit." He side-jumped to the top of an upside-down pew.

"Ain't nothing but an old turtle," Sam said. Otis watched the flat black shell glide toward the hole where the front door had been.

The pew where Otis had escaped the turtle moved. "Y'all, something's happening. This here pew I'm standing on just moved."

"Y'all better look out now," Latisha yelled down from the attic. "You'd best get on back up here now, and I ain't fooling. Big things is moving around outside."

The four men waded back to the kitchen. "Tide's coming in," Sam said. "It's gonna be very high, that's for sure. When I killed that snake, the water was only up to the bottom of that island cabinet. Now it's up to the door."

They scrambled up the rickety ladder and gathered at the windows with the others. At that height, they watched an invisible power source move everything in its path. "Tide surge," Franklin said. "That's when things get tore up bad."

"What's a tide surge?" Granny asked.

Franklin said, "It's when you have a real high tide, like the moon tide we've had this weekend, at the same time you have wind and low pressure, like we done had. What happens is we have even more water pushing in here from the ocean behind what's already coming in here because of the moon tide."

Granny looked puzzled but said, "Oh."

"If it comes on up to us, we'll need something to use as floats," Reverend Isaiah said. He looked around the cramped space.

Otis appeared with the axe and a length of rope that he had stashed in a corner. "I'll cut out some boards." He held out the rope. "We can all grab hold to this rope and stay together, but don't knot it around your arm or your body. Just hang onto it. If we get stuck someplace, we need to be able to get away and swim—or paddle on our boards."

Terrified faces stared at him.

He looked hard at his little brothers. "Jessie and Cass, you two stay with May, now. Y'all got to take care of our sister. No matter what. You hear me?" The little boys nodded. Jessie grabbed May's hand.

"We'll all stay together, like a train," Latisha said.

"That's right. Just like a train," Otis said. "We ain't letting this storm lick us. Hang onto your board, no matter what. It'll float until somebody comes to rescue you."

Nearby, there was a noise, like something heavy raking across concrete. Otis looked over at the hole where the pull-down ladder was. A child lay there, staring down below. Otis joined him and asked, "What's going on down there?"

The child said, "It's filling up with water."

Storage cabinets had separated from the wall and were shoving against the bottom section of the ladder. "We got to get this ladder up in a hurry," Otis said. Several men joined him, but it was too late. The ladder snapped.

CHAPTER 32

On their walk back to the trucks, Roosevelt and Hongry took their time and talked. Tom and Abbey sat up front in Ed's crew cab so they could listen to the news. As predicted, Brunswick had received the brunt of the storm. It had rained all night, and that in addition to a high tide and tide surge that morning had inundated the city with sixteen feet of water. Stunned, Abbey stared at the radio. When Ed pulled through the gate at Kings Bluff, Snag directed him to take a right on the river road in front of the cottages. "I want to show y'all what our river frontage looks like. The docks are all busted up and..."

Abbey glanced at Tom. "Snag, I need to get to Brunswick. My friend is stuck over there somewhere, and I have got to go find her."

Tom grabbed her hand and said, "Do y'all think we can even make it to Brunswick?"

"I doubt it," Snag said. "You saw what that paved road out there looks like. Nobody can get in or out of anywhere just yet, leastways not in a car or truck, not even a four-wheel-drive truck."

"How about by boat, then?" Abbey asked.

"Our boat?" Tom asked. Abbey nodded. "I didn't look at it this morning, Abbey, but the boathouse seemed okay. What do you think, Snag? Can we do it?"

"Might be the only way. But you really need to be careful. No telling what's floating around out there. If you do it, you have to go slow."

Abbey tried to read Tom's face. She knew that look. He was figuring out the pros and cons, doing his lawyer thing. He asked, "Will we even be able to trailer our boat to the hoist?"

Snag thought for a minute. "You got that big Grady-White, right? You and her brothers, same one?"

"Same one," Tom said.

"Tell you what. My Carolina Skiff's up yonder at that end of the bluff already. If you hitch up your big sucker and try to weave your way around trees and stuff all the way to the other end, you might get stuck or damage your boat. Take that skiff. It's got a flat bottom, and you'll be able to get where you're going. It's old anyway. If it gets tore up, I'll know it went for a good cause."

Abbey looked at Tom. He shrugged. She let out a big breath. "Thank you, Snag. We'll be extra careful."

"I know you will."

"Well, then, let's get going," Abbey said. "Hoist works okay?"

"Hoist is the only dock that didn't get damaged," Snag said. "Ed has a hitch, so we'll see y'all down there in a few minutes. I use ethanol-free in the boat, Tom. I have it, so I'll fill it up for you."

"Thank you," Abbey said. "Can you think of anything else we should take with us?"

"Drinking water's always a good bet." Snag's eyes went from Abbey's to Tom's. "Take your pistol, just in case. You never know what you might run into."

Abbey nodded without making eye contact with Tom. She already knew what he thought about her hardware.

THIRTY MINUTES LATER, they parked near the hoist. "If you just look at the river," Abbey said, "it's hard to believe what blew through here this morning. Then you look at the docks and the trees, and it looks like a warzone. What did Snag say, trees only hit three cottages?"

"I believe so," Tom said. "We got lucky. No telling what we'll find in Brunswick."

Abbey pulled the cooler she had filled with snacks and drinks from the back of the Wagoneer while the men took care of the boat. Once everything was loaded, Snag handed Tom the key. "She'll treat you right. You can turn on that depth-finder there to help you navigate. Sandbars might have shifted, so I suggest you keep it turned on. Feller down the road said he hoped to have power back here by this afternoon, so call me when you know what's what."

"Will do, Snag," Abbey said. "Thanks a lot. I owe you."

As Tom backed away, Abbey called out, "Hey, Snag." He looked at her and cupped a hand over his ear. "This thing's insured, right?"

He swatted the air like he was shooing a fly. She gave him a thumbs up. He waved.

Tom goosed the throttle. Around the first bend, the first of many commercial crab traps lay on the bank far away from the river, its concrete block anchor now abandoned to the bottom. "Look at that," Abbey said as they neared Taylor's Point. "There's a trap way up where we usually park. The water got that high."

"Do you ever feel odd back here?" Tom asked.

"What, since the drug traffickers?"

"Yeah. I just wondered if all of that spooked you. I know you love it back here. But you and Roosevelt helped nab those guys right here. It must feel a little different."

Abbey thought for a moment. "No. My memories of this place go way back before any of that happened. This was Momma's parents' favorite place to fish. It's named after them.

My memories are of fishing here with Grandmother Taylor and Daddy when I was little, catching fiddler crabs there on the bank, and drinking beers back here when I was in college. That drug bust almost feels like a movie I watched or something. Nope, my memories of here are much older and nicer than that one time." She paused. "I do wonder now and then where those two ever ended up, if they're even still alive. They're off the street, and they can rot in prison, for all I care."

"Good," Tom said. Two docks that belonged to the club were on this back side of the property. One was roofed, and the other was open.

"Which one did you fish with your daddy?" Tom asked.

"The roofless one," Abbey said. She chuckled. "Probably because there was nothing overhead to tangle a line on. One of us kids would make a wild cast now and then." Tom squeezed her shoulder.

As the tide ran out, the dark mud bank began to show. "No telling what we'll see out here this morning, Tom. Let's take it nice and slow so we don't hit anything."

"There's something," Tom said.

Two gray lumps were visible high in the marsh. He slowed when they were close. "Oh, I hate that," Abbey said.

"What is it?"

"A momma dolphin and her calf. They probably got stranded and couldn't work their way back into the water."

Tom scanned the bank, then asked, "Are we near Roosevelt's property?"

"Yes. He's just beyond the ridge of trees there."

"He has Black Angus cows, right?"

Abbey saw what Tom saw. A calf had been trapped between a low-lying limb and a mass of grass. "Poor baby. I hope Roosevelt didn't lose too many of them."

"We'll be in the Intracoastal soon," Tom said. "No telling what we'll see out there. Let's look sharp." They hadn't gone far when he said, "That looks like a section of one of the Bluff docks." They approached it slowly. "It has a hitchhiker."

Abbey squinted. "It does. Don't get too close. I don't want him thinking he can get a ride with us."

Tom took another look. "What is it?"

"Big old rattlesnake."

"It looks like a limb," Tom said. "Damn, that thing's big."

"There's plenty for him to eat around here."

When they moved into the Intracoastal, boards, plastic bottles, and beer cans drifted like stepping stones all around them. Floating ricks of dead spartina grass looked like curious whales suspended on the water's surface. "Watch it, Tom. There's a barrel or something up ahead." They neared the object. "GDOT" was printed in bold black letters on the side of the barrel. "Georgia Department of Transportation," Abbey said. "I bet they have to replace a lot of equipment."

What was normally a long and same-old-same-old trip was anything but that today. If their intent had been to scavenge, they could have made quite a haul, but their mission was singular in purpose. Find Blix Stouver.

Soon, Tom said, "Orient me here. Where am I headed?"

"The first island off to our right when we left Kings Bluff was Cumberland. You and I fished over there with Charlie and Zach when they were first checking you out."

Tom smiled. "I remember. It was obvious what they were doing, but I appreciated it. They showed me some of the landmarks. It would be really easy to get lost out here."

"You have to know the channel markers," Abbey said. "The next island we'll approach will be Jekyll, also on our right. You can always tell Jekyll by the causeway and water towers."

"Okay. I see all that."

"To the left up there is the Sidney Lanier Bridge. U.S. 17 runs over it and takes you into Brunswick. A bit farther, you turn right on a causeway that takes you to St. Simons Island and Sea Island."

"You took me over to St. Simons and Sea Island when we first met. Why haven't we been back?"

"Because we have two little boys who love the Bluff. But just you wait. When I was a teenager, I drove over to the islands all the time to meet up with Atlanta friends."

"For beer parties on the beach?" Tom asked.

"You got it."

He said, "Whoa. What's that?"

"It looks like a towel or a sheet or something. Slow down." Abbey stretched out on her stomach on the bow and hung her head over as close as she could get to the water. "You won't believe this." She hopped up and sat cross-legged on the bow deck.

"Try me."

"Fire ants. I read about it once. When their homes flood, they cling together and make a raft out of their bodies, then drift until they reach land."

"Great. If I have poisoned one of their mounds, I bet I've poisoned a thousand," Tom said.

"Let's not give them anything to crawl up on." Abbey rejoined him at the wheel.

They cruised under the Sidney Lanier Bridge and entered the Brunswick Harbor. On the left, where ships were tied up on a normal day to deliver their load of cars, there were containers scattered helter-skelter from the edge of the river to the parking lot. Tom slowed the boat. Cars looked as though they had been picked up and dropped randomly onto other cars and containers. Down farther, sailboats lay on their sides in the marsh. Neither Abbey nor Tom spoke. They crept up the river to the marina where Tom had helped to secure boats prior to the storm. The parking lot looked like a street-sweeper had pushed everything into a mountainous heap.

Abbey's steepled fingers covered her mouth. "My God, Tom."

"Damn tide surge. You know how difficult it is to get to the dock in your shell when you're working against the tide and the wind? Imagine the force behind millions of gallons of water plus a strong wind."

"I can't," she said.

"Damn. The insurance losses will be huge."

Abbey glanced up and down the riverbank. "Can we find someplace to tie up?"

"You never know what'll hold," Tom said. "Plus, there's no telling what's submerged just under the surface. Let's go back under the bridge. I remember a little park or something that runs along there." They retraced their route and cruised up the small river that ran along the park. Several pilings remained where a tourist overlook dock had been. Tom sidled up to the dock and Abbey looped a rope around the pole and secured the skiff.

"I drove to the church the other day, so I can probably figure out how to get there on foot," she said. They got out of the boat and headed across the park. Abbey clamped a hand over her mouth and pinched her nose. "Oh God." Death clung to the humid air like a fetid fog. Distant specks overhead soared like giant black bats in the blue sky. Jagged tree limbs, glass shards, mud, marsh grass, and various reminders of man, God, and animal peppered the landscape like confetti after a parade.

CHAPTER 33

Abbey grabbed Tom's arm and pulled him toward a metal sign half-buried diagonally in a solid two-foot-high hedge of spartina canes. From beneath the sign, a brown hand protruded, its red-lacquered nails broken, its fingers bent at uncomfortable angles. A bone jutted from the middle finger and pointed skyward, a final gesture of despair and defeat or maybe even defiance.

"This looks like a warzone," Abbey said as she pushed aside mounded stalks of the dead grasses, then grabbed the sign and tugged. "Help me." She pushed and pulled, but the sign stuck fast. The smell that escaped the disturbed soil knocked her back on her heels. "Oh God."

Tom knelt beside her. "Honey, she won't be the only one, I'm afraid."

Abbey looked around her, trying to make sense of this newly ravaged ground. "We have to be sure. I mean, I know she's dead, but I have to—to get her out of this—this stuff. What if Blix... It's not right to leave her here like this." She tore at the grass, each individual shaft hollow and light, but when mounded and pushed by wind and water, a virtual battering ram.

"Slow down, honey." Tom gathered large clumps and cast them aside. "Take your time there. I'll work down here to see if I can find her feet."

Abbey wiped perspiration from her brow; her fingertips paused on the goose egg on top of her head. With the next handful, she stopped. "I think I'm almost down to the body."

"Don't touch it, Abbey."

Odd bits of board had been pushed along with the grass mound. Abbey pulled out a strip of framing wood and used it as a tool to shovel and scrape. Minutes later, a white T-shirt, entangled with a black lace bra, was visible. Both garments had twisted into a rope and cinched beneath the woman's armpits. The turbulent water hadn't stopped its abuse until it had stripped the woman bare.

"Here she is." Abbey lifted a mangled seagull feather from the woman's hair. Startled eyes stared back; an angled jaw held broken, ground-down teeth and a mouthful of mud. The woman's right ear touched her knobby shoulder. Abbey shot an anguished look at Tom. "Maybe we should leave her and get to the church." Frantic images ran through her mind: Blix clinging to a board in a torrent of water, Blix fighting for air beneath boards and drywall in the demolished church, Blix buried under hundreds of pounds of spartina grass.

Tom looked to the sky, where the soaring black dots, nature's garbage brigade, spiraled closer. "We can't. Let's cover her as best we can to protect her from the turkey vultures. There's nothing more the two of us can do." He glanced at the lodged-in sign. Abbey's eyes followed his. Each got a handhold and worked the sign back and forth until it moved.

A four-wheel-drive diesel truck rumbled up beside them. The driver's window lowered. "Y'all okay?"

Abbey recognized the man as the sheriff who often showed up at Kings Bluff and drove around the property in his marked automobile to show trespassers that the posted "NO TRESPASSING" signs were not there for decoration.

"Sheriff Tanner, I'm Abbey Taylor Bunn from Kings Bluff. This is my husband, Tom Clark."

"Oh, sure. How the heck did you get over here from there? I'd have thought the river was a mess. I know you didn't drive."

Abbey said, "Snag Privit down at the club loaned us his Carolina Skiff. That's it tied up over there." She indicated with her head. "I have a friend over here at the AME church. We were on our way to the church on foot to look for my friend when we found a body partially buried under this pile of grass. We were trying to put this sign on the body to protect her."

"Doggone tide surge hit here around mid-morning," the sheriff said as he got out of the truck. "Downtown's a disaster. I've never seen anything like it. I don't know how y'all got over here with everything that's got to be floating around out there."

Tom said, "It wasn't easy. We took it slowly. How high did the water get downtown, Sheriff?"

The sheriff looked at the progress Abbey and Tom had made as he walked around the mound of grass. "I know it was over thirteen feet, judging by marks on buildings downtown. I heard sixteen on the radio."

Abbey said, "I guess even the old Victorians downtown got water to the first floor. What about other houses? They can't have more than eight-foot ceilings." She pictured the inside of the church where she had last seen Blix.

"You got that right. And most of them don't have attics," the sheriff said. "The minute me and some of the guys from the station could get rescue boats in here, we went neighborhood to neighborhood to see how folks were making out. It was a sight, I'll tell you. People, dogs, cats stranded on roofs. They cut holes in ceilings and kept on going as high as they could go, but water just kept on coming. We figured it'd be easier to get them off their roofs when the water was still high than wait and have them try to make it back down through their wrecked houses. Lord, I've never seen so much stuff where it wasn't supposed to be. Heck, I saw a shark belly-side-up on Gloucester Street downtown. I've never seen such a mess. All those poor people's houses are just plain destroyed."

"The storm passed over Kings Bluff around one o'clock this morning. Right, Tom?"

"About then, but we didn't have the surge you did here."

"That's what they're saying," the sheriff said. When he stopped circling, he crossed his arms over his chest and continued to stare at the body. "Of course, Brunswick's lower than you are there on that bluff. That's what really got us here. And what got her." He nodded to the body. "Storm probably hit us around two, then the surge on the high tide finished things off this morning. I was over in Jesup at my sister's house, and we had the TV and radio on, so I knew pretty much what was going on. I came back the minute I felt it was safe. Folks from as far away as Columbus loaded up their jon boats and Zodiacs and headed this way. Most amazing thing I've ever seen—like a reverse evacuation. I don't know what we would have done without all that outside help."

Abbey pointed at the metal sign. "We were trying to cover her up to keep anything from getting to her."

Sheriff Tanner paused for a second or two. "I hate to ask, but we're a little shorthanded around here. I, uh, I have rakes, shovels, gloves, and proper—umm—proper disposal bags."

Tom and Abbey looked at one another. She said, "We're happy to help."

Six hands made quick work of the extraction. Abbey turned her head away and asked, "Do you recognize her?"

The sheriff nodded. "Afraid so. We've had run-ins now and then. Her last name's Simmons. She has a bunch of kids. They all live with her mother." His chin dipped toward the woman. "Word has it she doesn't—rather, didn't—stay home much. Nurse's assistant or something like that, worked for an agency in town, but she had another more lucrative line of work, if you know what I mean."

They helped lift the body bag into the bed of his truck.

"Miss Abbey, you said you have a friend over here."

"Yes, at the AME church. That's where Tom and I were headed when we found her." She nodded toward the body bag.

"You plan to make it back to Kings Bluff today?"

"Yes," Abbey said.

"I better give you a lift to the church, then. You'll need a couple hours to make it back to your place."

A white coroner's van was parked outside the police station. The coroner had stopped by with a large thermos of coffee and his wife's fresh-baked muffins to give the sheriff and his staff a break. They transferred the corpse to the van; the sheriff told the coroner what little he knew about the dead woman.

As they left, they passed power-company cherry-picker trucks headed into town. Tree-company logos on the trucks identified their Georgia, Florida, and North and South Carolina locations. Chainsaws whirred, and huge, open-backed trucks rumbled by, filled to overflowing with limbs and logs. The sheriff picked his way through town. "It's been a long time since we've had one this bad."

"Eighteen ninety-eight is what I heard on the radio," Abbey said.

"That's right. Same deal. Sixteen-foot tide surge with that one. Difference is, there wasn't much of a town here then. That one about wiped out everything that was here, though," the sheriff said.

"I can't imagine having that much water coming at me," Abbey said.

For close to ten minutes, they crept along, and then the sheriff said, "The church is right along here somewhere."

Abbey sat up. Everything had changed. Concrete and brick pilings were all that stood where several houses had been, and the structures that remained had been severely damaged. She looked for the big trees out in front of the clapboard church.

The sheriff braked at a massive live oak just beyond a driveway bib. Abbey peered around Tom. "There it is," she said. The little white church was now raw pine, its paint stripped clean by windblown sand, its off-center tilt precarious. She opened the door and jumped out of the still-moving truck.

"Abbey, wait! That building's not safe." Tom jumped out behind her. The sheriff parked a safe distance in front of the building.

"There's a pretty good chance they're in the attic," the sheriff said when he caught up. "Roof looks like it's partially gone on the rear. Let's go around back." They followed the driveway.

"Hey," a voice called from above. "Sheriff, up here!" A young black man peered over what remained of a wall.

"Otis Simmons, that you?" the sheriff asked.

"Yessir." Otis turned and yelled over his shoulder, "Sheriff Tanner's here. I knew somebody'd come for us."

The sheriff glanced at Abbey and Tom. "Let's go."

Reverend Isaiah appeared beside Otis. "Praise the Lord. You're a gift from God, Sheriff. We're kind of stuck up here. The pull-down ladder tore off when the water rose."

Abbey hesitated. *"Simmons" was the name of the dead woman, the one with all the children. Dear God.* Somewhat unnerved, she shouted, "Reverend, is Blix with you?" Reverend Isaiah barely shook his head. Abbey's stomach knotted.

The sheriff and Tom pulled an extension ladder from the back of the truck and leaned it against the church. Each pressed a foot on the bottom of the ladder, then held on to stabilize it and assist people toward the bottom. Otis and the pastor helped folks down from the top while Abbey stood back and coaxed them. "Take it slowly, ma'am. That's it." The oldest came down first. "Be sure to hold on with both hands, then step down one rung at a time and move your hands as you go. Good. That's it. Go at your own pace. We aren't in any hurry."

One by one, the elderly made it down. Abbey offered a hand for them to hold as she led them to a high mound of ground. She had just delivered an elderly woman when a child's giggles drew her eyes to the top of the ladder. A young black man encouraged a string of small children who laughed and teased as they descended. He started down next, with a fist-flailing little boy grasped firmly to his chest. She'd recognized the young man and his pink T-shirt when he'd been talking to the sheriff. He was the same fellow she had been curious about days earlier at the fish market, and here he was with a child in his arms. When he stepped from the ladder, his eyes moved around the rescue party as he mouthed "Thank you" to each of them. The little boy in his arms reached both hands toward Abbey and kicked and grunted and continued to reach for her. With eyebrows raised as though to ask permission, the teenager held the little boy out to Abbey.

"Are you Miss Blix's friend?" the young man asked. "I saw you at the fish market the other day."

Abbey said, "Yes. I believe I heard Ben call you Otis."

The child's curious fingers explored Abbey's hair and face. "My name's Otis Simmons. Joseph really took to Miss Blix, too. I don't reckon he sees too many white ladies up close."

"Otis, where is Blix?"

Otis was taken aback by her question. "Oh, well, she was helping everybody—sort of running a taxi service." Abbey nodded and took a deep breath, then hugged little Joseph, who continued to touch her face and hair.

Still at the foot of the ladder, Tom lent a hand to the young woman who descended next. She thanked him, then walked over to Otis, who said to her, "Latisha, this Miss Blix's friend."

The woman grinned. "You're Miss Abbey, then."

"That's right."

"She told me 'bout you. And Mr. Tom. My baby likes you just like Miss Blix." Abbey bit her lip when the baby's mother made no move to take him from her, but rather folded her arms about her waist and turned toward the sheriff. "Thank you, Sheriff Tanner. We was afraid ain't nobody coming for us."

"No problem, Latisha." The sheriff looked up at the top of the ladder. Male voices still came from the attic. "Who else is up there?"

Otis said, "Sam and Franklin are into a card game. I guess the reverend's trying to get them to stop."

Abbey had had enough. "Latisha, where is Blix?"

"Oh. She went to get Esther yesterday afternoon, and something must have happened. They never made it back to church." Abbey handed Joseph back to his mother and went to Tom. "We have to go," she said.

Reverend Isaiah bellowed from the attic, "Hold on. We're on our way."

"I suppose you have blankets and pillows up there, Isaiah," the sheriff said. "Throw them down, please." To Otis, he said, "I'll take everyone to a shelter. I imagine they'll have some means to dry things, and you'll need the blankets and pillows there." Women and children scurried around to grab the raining bedding material; the men and women shook out and folded the blankets and quilts.

When Reverend Isaiah was down, Abbey asked him, "Do you have any idea where Blix is? Latisha told me she went to get someone."

"She's probably stuck on that dirt road just past Bennie's Red Barn Restaurant."

"Trees is down all out that way," Otis said. "I could see from the attic, and all I saw was broke trees and water."

Sheriff Tanner glanced at his watch. "I hate to pester, but you two had better keep an eye on the time if you're planning to try to make it home."

"I'm not leaving here without Blix," Abbey said.

"The sheriff's right, Abbey. We might have to come back tomorrow to look for her. It's getting late."

Tom and the sheriff grabbed the ladder. "Y'all stay here," said the sheriff. "I'll bring the truck around, and we can throw your blankets and pillows in back for you to sit on and make yourselves comfortable for the ride. It's a pretty good way to the shelter."

TOM WALKED WITH the sheriff to get the truck.

"If you want to start walking," the sheriff said, "which it sounds like your wife wants to do, head out to Frederica Road, and I'll get back to you as soon as I can. Turn right at Bennie's Red Barn and follow that dirt road to the end."

"I think we'll stick with you," Tom said quietly. "Don't even mention us walking to Abbey, or she'll want to do it."

"Got it."

AS IMPATIENT AS she was to go find Blix, Abbey realized she should help get this group to safety. She was distracted by an older woman trying to gather two little boys and a little girl. Abbey was reminded of a mother hen collecting her chicks. The woman was very insistent with Otis. "Why can't we just go home?" she asked. "I need to go home. These children needs clean clothes."

"Not yet, Granny," Otis said. He raised his eyebrows at Abbey and shook his head. "Everything will be all wet and muddy, and you can't stay there until it has had a chance to dry out some." Abbey half-expected the woman to stomp her foot.

"But I can at least open windows and doors to air it out." The woman hurried over to her wards, who had found an inviting puddle.

Otis said to Abbey, "I reckon ain't much left of Granny's house. I should have been able to see it from the attic. I couldn't see it this morning."

The woman continued her tirade about going home when she returned with the children.

"It'll wait, Granny." Otis followed his firm tone with a gentle pat on his granny's back.

Reluctantly, his granny said, "Okay. I reckon you the man of the house now."

Fighting a grin that only Abbey saw, Otis said, "Yes, Granny."

Sam shuffled up to Abbey and pulled something from his pocket. "Ma'am, I believe this belongs to you." He handed over her Smith & Wesson. She took the pistol; her expression begged for an explanation.

"Miss Blix picked up me and Franklin, and when we got back to church, they was a situation, but Miss Blix took your piece and managed it." He smiled. "With one bullet. Sure did."

Abbey asked, "She actually fired it?"

Sam said, "Yes, ma'am." Franklin nodded.

"Don't forget that snake, too," Otis said.

"Uh-huh," Sam said. "Then they was this snake on the island in the kitchen, and I done used another bullet on him." There were murmurs and nods throughout the group.

"Well, I'm glad it came in handy, Sam, and I'm glad Blix knew how to use it."

Sam's upper lip curled. "That's right. Sure did. Didn't even hesitate."

Franklin laughed out loud. "Well, Miss Blix knowed how to pull the trigger anyhow."

"You got that right," Sam said.

"I believe there's a story there," Abbey said.

TOM AND SHERIFF TANNER got into the truck. The news was on the radio. The hurricane had strengthened over the Atlantic and was circling back to Brunswick. "Seek shelter!" the reporter said. The two men glanced at each other.

Tom said, "Damn." The sheriff whipped the truck around to the rear of the church and threw it into park. They jumped out.

"It's coming back on us," the sheriff said. "Otis, we need someplace to go. Now. Something low, a ravine or creek bed or something."

Otis squinted. "I know a place."

Abbey was already arranging blankets and pillows in the back of the truck; Latisha, who had the elderly lined up and ready to climb in, said, "You children stop shoving. Get away from the truck and come line up behind me. Let these older folks get settled up there first, and then we'll go. Quietly."

Otis spoke to his siblings, and they took off running. "Follow them, Sheriff."

CHAPTER 34

Late that afternoon, ferocious winds again screamed toward Brunswick. The sheriff had packed as many of the elderly as he could in the cab of the truck while Abbey and Tom rode in the back with the others. Abbey held one of Tom's hands with both of hers. Sheriff Tanner followed the coltish child-scouts far back into a section of woods inhabited by ancient live oaks, their limbs sleeved in resurrection ferns and draped with Spanish moss and arm-thick vines. There were no signs of development, though long-cold campfires, beer cans, and scat—animal feces visible to the knowing eye—made it clear the woods sheltered both man and beast. When the dense forest prohibited driving farther, the truck stopped, and everyone got out.

While Tom and Sheriff Tanner lagged behind the group and strategized, Abbey and Latisha helped the ill-equipped elderly negotiate the woods behind Otis, Reverend Isaiah, Sam, and Franklin, who attempted to clear the way. Abbey strained to hear the children's voices over the growing wind, their small bobbing heads the only assurance they still forged ahead.

Suddenly, she lost sight of the heads. When she and the rest of the party arrived at the edge of a deep cut in the forest floor, they found the children splashing in a small pool of water in what had obviously been a dry creek bed at one time. A rusted vehicle picked clean of tires and any other usable parts housed a sapling that poked through a broken window.

Dented hubcaps and shot-up beer cans had laid claim to the crevice long before.

Otis, Tom, and the pastor helped folks navigate the descent down the crumbling sides of the depression, some on uncertain legs, others who giggled timidly as they derriere-bumped their way down. At the bottom, Latisha and Abbey settled everyone, as well as could be expected, on the gentle slope above the soggy bottom. As human nature would have it, men took the protective perimeter, their backs against a steep wall that was held in place by the roots of a massive live oak; women and the less able-bodied occupied the bottom row with the children nestled among them. Latisha and Abbey adjusted pillows and distributed blankets. Over the years, several trees had fallen across the gulley and gave the space the feel of a room with a patchy overhead view. Abbey told everyone to use the blankets to cover their heads and protect their ears and eyes, should things begin to swirl around.

Abbey watched the sheriff pick his way down the bank then go down on one knee beside Otis. He talked quietly, his voice private, meant only for Otis to hear. The teen's head turned slowly toward the sheriff; he said something. The sheriff shook his head, then clapped a hand on the boy's shoulder and continued to talk. Otis dropped his head and clasped his hands over his knees. When the sheriff stopped talking, Otis nodded. *Poor kid.*

Abbey looked around for Tom and found him with several rambunctious boys that he had ushered a safe distance away from the others. They crawled on hands and knees and flicked bits from the creek bed's wall with their index fingers. Abbey knew what Tom was up to. She had seen him do the same thing with their boys along the cliffs near the Chattahoochee River at home. Tom spoke to those young boys as though giving his opening argument to a jury of archaeologists with fossilized bones marked "Exhibit A" on a table nearby. *God, I love that man.*

"What are y'all looking for?" Abbey asked.

One of the boys looked up. "Mr. Tom says there might be sharks' teeth in the wall. Real old ones. He said all this was under the ocean a long, long time ago, when dinosaurs was running around everywhere."

"Ah," Abbey said, "is that right?" *Tom, the teacher.* She nodded. Tom was great at entertaining their boys. When she'd had a long day showing houses and their two little ragamuffins demanded her attention, Tom would rummage in the toy chest and then Pied-Piper them out the back door with their tiny footballs in his hands as enticement.

One of the junior archaeologists whooped then crawled to Tom with one flat palm outstretched. Tom nodded, looked Abbey's way, and grinned, and then he roughed the boy's head and spoke to him. The boy nodded, tucked the prize into a pocket of his shorts, and double-fist-pumped the air before he went back to his search.

A sound overhead caught Abbey's attention. She looked up, puzzled at first by leaves that swirled through what looked like a horizontal screen of textured air. She listened and heard the indistinct peppering of small things on a hard surface—the same sound she'd heard at the cottage when she and Tom had awaited the storm. *Sand.*

"Tom, I think it's coming. Look up."

Tom glanced overhead, then tapped the boys on their shoulders and thumbed toward the group. When they protested, he said something and pointed. The boys looked up. Their mouths and eyes opened wide; like a pack of pups, they scrambled to their mommas. Tom pushed slowly to his feet and grimaced—an old sports injury occasionally tightened up on him. The sound of the wind changed. Abbey watched Tom brush dirt and leaves from his hands and take a deep breath. His face relaxed, and he started toward her.

Reverend Isaiah led the group in the recitation of the twenty-fourth Psalm. The children followed along, their sing-song voices rising and falling as they mimicked the familiar words.

There was a rolling, rumbling noise. Envisioning a tidal wave, Abbey looked up into the branches of the ancient oak whose leaves shook as though the magnificent old-timer had taken a chill. She looked back for Tom. He hurried over the tangled forest floor, caught his toe, and fell.

"*Tom!*" Abbey's scream arced and blew back in her face. Tom scrambled to his feet. When her terrified eyes locked onto his, he instinctively flattened on the ground. A millisecond later, an ear-piercing wind rocketed through the ravine.

CHAPTER 35

In what remained of Esther's boys' treehouse, Blix and Esther huddled on lichen-covered floorboards and leaned against age-worn walls. Wind passed through gaps where boards were missing, more like through a sieve than a house. The gaps were an acquired feature that allowed the treehouse to give, rather than succumb, to the wind. "So, I don't know how much of my jaw I'll lose. I'll definitely have to take food through a syringe again."

Esther shook her head and patted Blix's arm.

"And the doctors can't tell me how disfiguring the surgery will be. They won't know much until they get in there and look." Blix looked straight into Esther's eyes. "Now you know a whole lot more about my life than you bargained for."

"When do you have to make this decision, sweetie?"

Blix shrugged. "As soon as I get home. The cancer is aggressive, so if I agree to surgery, the sooner the better."

"Sweetie, you'll know what to do when the time comes. Until then, enjoy those boys of yours. Every day God gives us is a blessing. Remember that."

They stopped talking. The leaves no longer tapped; the wind no longer howled. Blix looked out the opening in the front of the treehouse. The creek had receded and was within its banks. "I think it's time to go down. I'll go first and lead."

Blix sat on the edge of the floor and wondered how to position herself to step out of the treehouse. Then she realized what the handle on the edge of the floor was for. *Esther's boys thought of everything.* Grasping the handle, she made the turn and stepped down to the nearest rung. Then it was a simple matter of going down the ladder. That treehouse had been a haven and had kept her and Esther well above the raging waters of the swollen creek. Esther listened attentively as Blix told her what to do, then she made small humming noises and rippled her way down the tree like a gray-muzzled grandmother raccoon.

"You're doing great, Esther," Blix said from just below her. Blix stopped and panted for several seconds and reminded herself to renew her gym membership. *Is that a worthwhile investment, all things considered?* She was very tired. *Damn, I'm out of shape.* She looked up and watched Esther make her way down and marveled at the older woman's stamina. The ankle didn't seem to bother her, or if it did, Esther didn't let on. *Renew the damned gym membership.* It seemed the perfect opportunity for Blix to chide herself for all the years of cigarettes and alcohol. *If I had it all to do over again... don't I wish.* "A night in that oak tree seems to have done your ankle some good, Esther."

"Lawd, I don't know as I'd say that, but I do all right." Esther chuckled. Wind whispered through branches. Clumps of Spanish moss drifted by on the way to new attachments. "Why we leaving up here?" Esther said. "Ain't nobody come for us yet, and I was just getting comfortable. I can keep a lookout for them from up here just like an eagle."

"I'm changing your name to Jane, Queen of the Jungle. You can go on back up there if you want. I'll yell for you when somebody shows up to rescue us."

"You teasing me? I'm ready to get down for a while, I reckon. Stretch my legs. Get something to eat. My stomach feels like it's got a hole in it."

"We'll take care of that first thing. I'm about to starve, too. The water has gone down and the tide should be going out now, but if the wind picks up again, I don't want us stuck in the top of the tree. I'm afraid you'll get blown away, and then what would I tell Reverend Isaiah? 'Yessir, I had her, but we were up in a tree and she just blew away.'"

Esther laughed and continued her descent.

Blix said, "This limb has protected us so far, and I trust it. We'll be safer inside your house, where we won't get conked on the head by anything flying around."

"Oh. That's good. At least we can use the bathroom. I'm about to bust!"

Blix laughed. "I hear you. But remember, there's no back wall. Not that anybody is around to see us, but it is a little open-air."

Esther said, "I used an outhouse most of my life, so that's not a problem."

"Good. Let's take care of that first, then I'll look for something to eat."

"There's peanut butter in the cupboard near the refrigerator and saltines in the round tin on the kitchen counter."

When Esther's foot finally reached the bottom rung, Blix gave her a hand the rest of the way. "You were impressive up there, Esther. You're an inspiration, that's for sure."

"Lord, honey. You're the inspiration, coming over here to rescue me when you don't know me from nothing, and all you got going on. I imagine they would have found me a shriveled-up little lump of black leather, if you hadn't come along. Don't you be telling me I'm something special. You risked your life to come after me. I'm the one's indebted."

At that moment, the air went still; it became strangely quiet. Blix held fast to Esther's waist and helped her inside. The wind came back to life again, as though to finish the job it had only just begun earlier.

CHAPTER 36

After what seemed an eternity at the bottom of the ravine with the wind howling overhead, Abbey heard something different. Silence. She removed the blanket she had pulled over her and Tom after he had army-crawled to her. Her lungs filled with the smells of newly turned earth and salt air. The wind had mustered out, tail between its legs like a chastised hound. When Abbey sat up, Tom gave her thigh a squeeze.

"I think the coast is clear," Abbey said.

Otis tossed off his blanket and looked around. "Dang."

Sheriff Tanner emerged and said, "It looks like we made it, but that was a damn close call. That wind could have picked any one of us up and carried us away."

"I thought Tom was a goner when that old oak started shaking like a twig," Abbey said.

Reverend Isaiah removed his blanket. "That old tree shaking like that was the good Lord warning us to take cover because that wind was coming. He was looking out for us, that's for sure."

"Being down in this ditch didn't hurt," Tom said. "Thanks, Otis."

Otis flipped Tom a no-big-deal wave. "Dang, that felt like another hurricane came right through this ravine."

"It could have been, the way the air blasted through here," Sheriff Tanner said.

Otis scrambled up the bank by jamming his toes into its crumbly sides, grasping overhanging branches, and pulling himself up. "Coast looks clear," Otis said from the top.

"For the time being, anyway," Tom said to Abbey. "I wonder how often these winds just keep coming and going until they eventually die out." Abbey frowned. "Just kidding, honey." She punched him playfully in the arm.

The sheriff said, "I suggest we all go to the shelter, settle in, and get in front of a radio or television."

"Okay by me," Tom said.

With a look that dared them to deny her, Abbey glanced at Tom and then the sheriff and said, "It's not okay with me. We have to go find my friend. Now."

"It's too late to go looking for anybody today, and even if you did go and you found her, it'd be suicide to try to make it back to Kings Bluff today," the sheriff said. "There's no way in hell you two are getting back in that boat anytime soon, and I'll arrest you both if you try. Let's go get food and rest, and I'll take you two to look for your friend first thing in the morning." Sheriff Tanner stood there like Birmingham's famous Vulcan the Iron Man statue. The expression on his face said, "Don't even think about testing me."

Abbey looked up at the fading afternoon light and said, "I guess you're right."

Tom gave the sheriff a nod.

When the three of them had helped everyone make it up the embankment, Abbey sidled up to Sheriff Tanner and said, "Crack of dawn tomorrow. O-dark-thirty. I'll be your alarm clock."

"You got it," the sheriff said.

IT WAS NEARLY dusk by the time they pulled into the high school parking lot in Sterling, two-and-a-half miles from Brunswick and the closest Red Cross shelter. Abbey and Latisha checked everyone in and then helped them find cots. After volunteers served them a hot meal in the cafeteria, they gathered around several television sets and watched film footage of the hurricane ransacking Brunswick. "Damn," Otis said. "We made national TV. Cool."

When they'd had enough news, Abbey, Otis, and Latisha took the children to the school parking lot, where other youngsters ran around and organized games. "These little folks are probably exhausted already, but let's make sure," Abbey said. "They need a good night's sleep in a bed."

Sometime later, Tom found Abbey in the parking lot, watching the children playing tag. "There's a payphone in there. Why don't you call Boonks?"

"Great idea. Thank you, darlin'. I've been so worried about Blix... I just forgot about calling. The school won't mind?"

"No. Everybody's putting calls on their credit cards. Did you bring yours?"

"You're kidding, right? I'm surprised I remembered underwear."

He handed her his Mastercard. "Tell her we're very happy the boys are with her and not here." Children stampeded past them, laughing. Latisha smiled and waved when she ran by with her group. He added, "Though they might like all of this."

Abbey waited patiently in the phone line. Luckily, Lila's number was easy to remember. After several rings, Boonks picked up the receiver and said, "Hello." The quaver in her normally perky response nearly brought Abbey to her knees.

"Momma, it's me."

There was a gasp on the other end of the line.

"Tom and I are fine." Abbey heard her boys' laughter in the background. Bracing her free hand against the wall, she fought back tears.

"Abbey! Oh, sweetie, we've all been so worried." Boonks's voice cracked. "We didn't have television to see what was happening there, but we have called around, so we sort of know what's been going on. It sounds awful. Of course, I knew you'd be without power if there was any sort of bad weather." She paused. "Abbey, you didn't mention Blix. Is she okay? I'm sure this is more than any of you bargained for."

"Momma, we got separated. She was helping at this church in Brunswick, and when Tom and I went to get her, she was off picking someone up. We're at a Red Cross shelter in Sterling with a sheriff who offered to take us to look for Blix first thing in the morning." The line had grown behind Abbey. "Listen, Momma: we're in a school gymnasium and there's a line waiting to use the phone. I'd like to talk to the boys for a minute." Boonks handed over the phone.

Abbey smiled as James and Walt handed the phone back and forth and breathlessly accounted for their fun-filled days in the mountains. "We rode the *burros*," "We threw sticks to Lila's dogs," "We showed Lila how to make pully candy." She was relieved they didn't seem the least bit concerned about their parents.

When her mother was back on the line, Abbey said, "Momma, thank you for not alarming the boys needlessly. We will tell them all they need to know when we get home. Please thank Lila for me. I am so grateful that the boys were up there with you and not here during this ordeal. Tom sends his love."

CHAPTER 37

The next morning, Abbey leaned over Tom's cot and patted his shoulder. "Let's get moving, Tom." She whispered so as not to disturb others in the tightly packed rows of cots. She was ready to go. Upon their arrival, the Red Cross had handed each of them a goodie bag with travel-sized toothpaste and toothbrush, shampoo, deodorant, and comb.

"Come on, darlin'. Rise and shine." Abbey gazed around at what looked like a huge spend-the-night party in the gymnasium, then back at Tom. He blinked.

"Does Little Mary Sunshine always wake up like that?" Sheriff Tanner mumbled from the cot next to Tom's.

"Always," Tom said. "And she has probably already been for a ten-mile run or something." Abbey punched him in the thigh. "Ouch. Would you please bring me a coffee, love of my life?"

"Right, and I'll pick up a dozen hot glazed from Dunkin' Donuts while I'm out, Snoogums."

Tom's head popped up. "Would you?"

With a hand on her cocked hip, Abbey said, "Come on. Get up, you two. We have a lot to do today. I've been smelling coffee for about an hour, so I bet there's a fresh pot on."

She grabbed the bag that held Tom's shoes and said, "I'll meet you in the kitchen. I've got your shoes, so come on." The school welcomed the refugees with the stipulation that street shoes not be worn on the newly refinished gymnasium floor. Volunteers had bagged shoes at the doors to the gym with instructions to store them under the cots along with whatever meager belongings people had with them. Local hospitals had donated boxes of hospital socks for their use.

On the other side of the gymnasium door, volunteers buzzed around like it was an airport terminal. Abbey yanked off her hospital socks, pulled on her running shoes, and followed her nose to the coffee pot. She chatted with a volunteer who had been at the shelter since noon the day before and still smiled and acted gracious. Abbey thanked her for volunteering, then moved from the growing line back to the rear for a second cup.

Moments later, she watched Tom grimace when he walked in. Odors of fried fish and spoiled milk permeated the air—smells of a school cafeteria. Abbey waved Tom over. One corner of his lip curled up when he saw her. *There's that grin I love.*

He pecked her on the cheek. "Good morning."

"Here." She handed him the bag that contained his shoes. "You can take off your slippers now."

He looked at his feet. "Oh. Thanks." He slipped on his shoes. "No good-morning smooches yet, honey. My mouth feels like a polecat bedded down in it."

"Yuck. I brushed mine first thing. Where's the little goodie bag they gave you when we got here yesterday?"

He frowned. The volunteer with whom Abbey had been speaking earlier stood nearby. She disappeared and came back with a handful of little bags. "This might help, sir. Compliments of the Red Cross."

"You're a life-saver," Tom said.

"Happy to help."

"Abbey, the sheriff said he'd drive us over to where Blix was headed."

Abbey was distracted by Latisha and Otis, who were involved in whispered conversation as they came toward her.

Latisha's face was always expressive, but this morning, she'd added her hands.

"Miss Abbey, he's going to show y'all the way over to Esther's," Latisha said with one head bob and a bottom-lip pout aimed at Otis.

Otis said, "I'm ready when y'all are."

"Okay then," Abbey said. "Let's go." She stopped at the lunch table and filled her pockets with packets of peanut-butter crackers and Oreos. Then she grabbed two Diet Cokes and two regulars.

Tom said, "I'll grab coffee for Sheriff Tanner."

"Good," Abbey said. "Why don't you take something to eat, Otis? You're sure you don't mind going with us?"

"No. I don't mind. Your friend's a nice lady. I hope she's okay."

"Thank you," Abbey said.

"Latisha thinks I might be able to help if there's a problem, trees down or something."

Abbey had noticed the looks between the two young people and figured the rescue would be worth brownie points for him.

"Let's go, then," she said.

THE SHERIFF'S TRUCK puffed diesel fumes into the dark, humid morning air. Abbey and Otis hopped into the back seat. While they drove, Abbey explained to the sheriff how Blix had become separated from her and Tom. The closer they got to Brunswick, the more precarious driving became. The road was littered with limbs, signs, boat parts, and children's yard toys. It was obvious how high the water had gone by the distinct water lines on buildings. Marsh grass and trash had piled up and clung to anything left standing.

"We're bound to see a lot of unusual things when we start digging out from this thing," the sheriff said. "A patrolman called me and said he'd found a red convertible hung up on some lady's mailbox, just stuck right there on top of it like a lollipop on a stick."

Otis sat up.

"No joke," Tom said. "A little sports car or something?"

"No, man—vintage fire-engine-red '64 Chevy Impala, four on the floor. Dang. It was a beauty. Totaled now."

Otis lowered his window, rested his arm on the door, and closed his eyes.

"Any sign of the driver?" Abbey asked.

Before he answered, the sheriff glanced into his rearview mirror. "Nope, but whoever it was left a few things behind." He continued to look in the mirror as he talked. "Of course, we'll run the plates to see who owns it. Interesting thing is, there were two pillowcases in the trunk, one filled with nothing but little plastic stands and small boxes lined with this slick white fabric."

Otis seemed to have found something interesting outside his window.

"Sounds like satin," Abbey said. "I have small jewelry boxes that are lined in white satin."

"That would make sense because of what was in the other pillowcase," the sheriff said.

"What was that?" Tom asked.

"Oh, about a hundred thousand dollars' worth of jewelry."

"What?" Tom asked.

Abbey shook her head. "A few always take advantage of a situation."

Otis remained silent.

"Honest to God," the sheriff said.

They went across the causeway to St. Simons and were the only vehicle on the normally busy connection between Brunswick and the islands. When they reached the other side, Sheriff Tanner asked, "Okay, who knows where we're going?"

Abbey took a deep breath. "Well damn. I don't know the address, but I think the reverend said the turnoff was near Bennie's Red Barn Restaurant." She placed a hand on Tom's shoulder.

"Well, I sure don't know, honey."

Otis said, "She went for Miss Esther."

"Yes, Otis," Abbey said. "That's what the reverend said. Do you know where Esther lives?"

"She lives on a creek just past that restaurant you said. Her house is on the left side of the dirt road—has a big old live oak near the front porch. My granny and me went fishing over there with Miss Esther once."

Otis directed as the sheriff maneuvered around obstacles in the road. After what seemed hours to Abbey, Otis said, "Right up yonder's the restaurant." Bennie's Red Barn came into view. "Take a right there."

Abbey scooted up to the edge of the seat. The sheriff turned onto the dirt road, where deep mucky ruts were filled with water. The diesel churned on without a slip. "What kind of car do you drive, Abbey?"

"A Jeep."

"I see it dead ahead," Tanner said.

"I see it," Abbey said over Tom's shoulder.

Tom said, "There's another car there in what used to be the road, I think."

"That might explain things," the sheriff said. He pulled up beside the Jeep, and they hopped out. The pond had begun to drain. "It looks like the road washed out and that car got hung up on the high part in the middle."

Aided by the early-morning light, Otis led the way, with Abbey close on his heels.

Otis said, "There are trees down up yonder. Might be on her house."

Abbey broke around Otis and jogged until she came to a cedar that lay across the road. There was a small house. *Left side of the road. Beside a big oak tree. That has to be it.* She stood there and stared at the devastation. *There's no way...*

CHAPTER 38

Getting to the front door of Esther's house was like running a foot race through a furrowed field of corn after a week of heavy rain. The men in their mud-clumped shoes caught up with Abbey only because she stopped to consider her options.

Sheriff Tanner said, "I know what you're thinking, Abbey, but these little houses are sturdier than they look. Most of them were built out of heart-pine boards from trees cut right here on the island. They're tough. They've withstood a lot of pretty bad storms."

She glanced at him, wanted to believe him, but couldn't imagine anyone inside being alive. Mud had turned her running shoes into clunky black blocks. She stepped onto the porch and called out, "Blix. It's Abbey. Yell so I know where to look for you." Ahead of her, the front door hung by one hinge from its frame.

She squeezed herself through the opening and stepped into a room occupied almost entirely by a limb with what looked like a sheet draped over it. That was enough of a sign of life to encourage her. She scrabbled ahead, barely aware of the men's voices behind her. Otis did most of the talking, which seemed odd. She launched herself up on top of the limb. The sheet felt like silk. *This is a parachute. Way to go, Blix.* She dropped down on the other side, where the parachute draped to the floor. She lifted the edge of the chute and peered into a makeshift rabbit hole fully lined with wool Army blankets and sofa cushions on top of a tarp. She reached inside. The cushions and wool blankets felt damp. When her eyes adjusted to the dim light, she saw a not-so-white Adidas walking shoe. She reached out and shook it by the toe. It jerked back. There was a startled gasp.

"Blix, it's me."

"Bunns?" There were scrambling noises. Blix emerged and grabbed Abbey in a hug, then pushed away. "We've got to get Esther to the hospital. She has congestive heart failure. And a sprained ankle. This has been way too much for her. She needs medical attention yesterday." Blix looked in need of a shower and that hairdryer she loved so much.

"Okay." Abbey squeezed her friend's shoulder. "You can relax now. I am so glad to see you. The sheriff is with me and he will call in for help."

"Honey, we heard all of that," Tom said nearby. "The sheriff is already on it. Otis and I will see what we can find... or we'll make something to carry her out of here. Y'all sit tight. Hi, Blix. Fancy meeting you here."

"Hi, Tom. Glad you decided to stop by," Blix said. "There's a little garden shed out back. There are too many trees down all around the house to get there easily outside, so go through the living room to the hall and turn right. The wall is missing in the bathroom, so you can jump down into the garden, and you'll see the shed. You might find a cart or a wheelbarrow or something there."

"There's a sturdy wheelbarrow in the shed," Esther said.

"I'll go look, Mr. Tom."

While Otis searched, Abbey and Tom removed and discarded the parachute. Blix introduced Esther, then gave her water and explained what was happening.

"I guess you get to chalk this up as another one of your rescues, Bunns. You're pretty good at this."

"Yeah, but my rescues never involved a friend before."

"I'm glad you got here when you did," Blix said. "I was running out of ideas."

AN HOUR LATER, Sheriff Tanner reappeared, medical kit in-hand, and handed it to Blix, who went to work on Esther. "Is she okay?" the sheriff asked.

"Holding her own," Tom said. "What's the plan?"

"Well, I made a call. Help ought to be here any minute." Tanner looked to the sky. "The hospital isn't really opened back up yet, but the doc on call is going to meet us there. I, uh, I didn't know the lady's exact address, so the guys sort of followed the flashing light on my truck. Ah, there it is."

The unmistakable *whop-whop-whop* of a helicopter grew louder by the second. Tom looked at the sheriff. "I like your style, Sheriff." They high-fived.

Otis watched open-mouthed as a black-and-white chop-per with "Georgia State Patrol" emblazoned on its side slid to a hover overhead. A door opened. A stretcher emerged and lowered inch by inch to the ground. "Now I done seen everything," Otis said.

Abbey and Blix stood beside the wheelbarrow that en-throned Esther, who watched the helicopter proceedings wide-eyed. When the sheriff gave the word, Blix and Abbey walked alongside the Otis-powered wheelbarrow to steady it. Blix said, "They'll strap you in good and tight, Esther, so you won't fall out. Then they will lift you up. It's a short ride to the hospital."

"Oh Lawd," Esther said. "You'll come with me, baby, won't you?"

"I'd better not, Esther. An emergency airlift is one thing, but taxpayers might frown upon me riding along for company."

"But I am a taxpayer."

Blix laughed at Esther's protest. She'd become accustomed to Esther's spunk.

Within minutes, Blix and Esther were strapped in for the ride of their lives, with Blix secured to the head end of the stretcher like a deity figurehead on a Viking ship. She grinned and did the royal wave to her rescuers below.

"Damn ham," Tom said with a grin. "She looks like a homecoming queen or something."

"If you only knew." Abbey said.

"Knew what?"

"I saw her do that for real once," Abbey said. "She's the same dear boob I knew in high school." She watched the stretcher rise. "You go, girl!" Abbey clapped and waved until the stretcher was safely inside and the helicopter swooped away.

CHAPTER 39

Late that afternoon, the Carolina Skiff skimmed around the bend of the river. Like a mother at the back door with arms opened wide, the familiar docks and cottages were a welcome sight on that hot, sultry afternoon. After they'd made sure Esther was settled in at the hospital, Sheriff Tanner had taken the three of them back to the skiff and wished them safe passage. Tom cruised slow and easy the whole way back to Kings Bluff from Brunswick. Abbey and Blix stood at his sides, all three on the lookout for floating and near-submerged objects. They'd seen bottom-side-up boats, doors with knobs and knockers still attached, logs, and sections of docks, all of which would travel on the tides until they wound up in someone's backyard miles from where their journeys had begun or in the Atlantic, where a whole new journey began. The sun was low in the sky, and the river was calm. It was the time perfect for reflection.

Abbey thought of the final pages in her book, where Scout stood on Boo Radley's front porch and imagined the world as Boo saw it from inside his shuttered home. Boo observed the lives of others; his interactions were few and far between. Abbey listened most of the way back that afternoon. It wasn't that she didn't have anything to add, but she respected how Tom and Blix verbalized what they had experienced, what they'd felt and feared and learned, their interpretations seen through their own shutters.

She enjoyed Tom's telling of the brief period of time when she'd been knocked out. That filled in the small gap she had lost. She turned her head and watched his face when he said he had to admit that of all the harrowing events of the past several days, his biggest takeaway had been when he'd watched a boy become a man. Otis, of course.

While Abbey had climbed over the limb and into Esther's living room, Otis had confessed the jewelry-store break-in to Sheriff Tanner. He'd known the police would fingerprint the red Chevy convertible, but he'd said he could save them a whole lot of time and expense. The sheriff had nodded and asked why Otis supposed one of the pillowcases had contained nothing but plastic display stands. Otis had admitted that he couldn't touch the first piece of that jewelry because he didn't want to end up in jail like his daddy... and he didn't want to disappoint his granny. The sheriff had told Otis they'd found the blond-haired driver trapped inside the upside-down vehicle. It was obvious the car had been underwater at some point in time. The sheriff had spared them the details.

By her own account, Blix had been dropped into the middle of a big-screen hurricane film. She'd seen action: she'd rescued two little old men, fired a gun to stop a bad guy, and helped save the life of a dear little old lady. And by her own admission, she'd never felt more alive and purposeful in her entire life and wouldn't trade the experience for anything.

Abbey looked at the smiles on both their faces, then bumped Tom's hip with her own and blew him an air kiss. *I am so lucky*. He gave her a shoulder-squeeze and a grin. Snag must have heard his familiar motor when it had rounded the bend. Abbey watched his black truck whip out of his driveway and churn dust as it headed to the dock to meet them. And he wasn't going any twenty-five miles-per-hour, either. Abbey figured no one was paying much attention to rules today. Snag would want every detail. She would let the other two hit the high spots, since their voices were already primed. There'd be plenty of time for her to talk later, but there was much she wanted to savor and let mellow, for the time being.

CHAPTER 40

Two Months Later
Kings Bluff, Georgia

An uneasiness Abbey couldn't name came over her—not a pain-in-the-gut warning, more a knowing. She ran harder, as though that might put distance between her and the gnawing feeling. Her marks in the road's soft sand mingled with those of deer and raccoons and the wavy squiggles of snakes. Select pines, as though they'd been singled out from the others, rested at forty-five-degree angles in otherwise soldierly rows. Massive cedar and oak limbs lay dead on the forest floor, ignored and left to disintegrate among lesser detritus or consumed in the next controlled burn. Maybe seeing the desecration again after such a short period of time was what unbalanced her. Or it was something else entirely.

In the early-morning light, she emerged from the woods into broad open daylight and jogged past docks that stood on tall mantis-leg pilings. She breathed complex, heady air that said much in layer upon layer of details: of smoke, decaying plant debris, and her own sweat. She loved the smell. Marsh hens chattered unseen among tall marsh grasses. A loud thump nearby sent prickly tingles down Abbey's arms. She jumped sideways. A red-tailed hawk squared off with her in the grass and blinked; in his talons, a gray squirrel whipped his bushy tail frantically. The hawk lifted off, dangling the squirrel's limp tail, and landed in the top of a hickory tree. *Damn.* Abbey's heart raced. *Life—death. Here—gone.*

She jogged on. In front of her mother's cottage, she slowed then stepped onto the walkway to the dock. Some people liked beaches. Rivers were her thing—forever on the move, constantly changing. Like life. The water looked bottle-green; there had been no rain lately to disturb the pluff mud and send it along with the tide, but the dark gray sky foretold precipitation. Thunder had rumbled since before sunrise, and though it was well into autumn, November might recall the heat of late summer and create a mild Indian summer. Or birth another hurricane.

Abbey glanced at her watch. Almost seven-thirty. Her mother had scheduled workmen that week to repair the damage to the cottage that had happened over Labor Day. They'd promised to be finished by today, and it looked like they'd meet their deadline. Abbey had driven down from Atlanta on Monday to oversee the work and to pay the foreman with a check from her mother. Before she'd left for her jog earlier that morning, she'd taped a note to the kitchen door that had told the men to come in, the door was unlocked, and to grab a cup of coffee and to please eat all the donuts or take them with them. She didn't want the temptation on her drive back to Atlanta.

Footsteps on the dock's walkway announced company. She turned and watched a young man approach with a hammer in his hand, not a fishing rod. She recognized Frankie, the foreman's son. The look on his face concerned her. *Problem with the house?*

"Ma'am," he said, "you just got a call. I only heard the last part because the saw was running." His eyes pleaded with hers. "It got recorded. I think you need to come listen."

Abbey's heartbeat quickened as they headed to the cottage. "Who was it, Frankie?" She thought about her boys, whom she'd left with her mother, and Tom, who was due back from a business trip this morning on a Delta flight into Hartsfield. "Was it Momma, Frankie?"

He clutched his hammer with both hands. "You'd best listen yourself, ma'am."

The feeling she'd had all day burned through her like uncut vinegar. Her head went light. She reached for Frankie's arm.

CHAPTER 41

Frankie thanked Abbey for the check and the donuts and said he'd lock up when they finished the work that afternoon. He understood her need to get on the road.

Five hours later, Abbey drove up to the Stouvers' home in Atlanta. She recognized Blix's Monte Carlo in the driveway—the only car in Buckhead whose horn blasted "Dixie" when pushed. The back door to this house was never locked. Family and friends had always come and gone with such frequency that a burglar dared not waste time or effort here. She knocked twice, then pushed the playroom door open and walked into cool air and semi-darkness and the faint odors of stale beer and cigarettes. This room had been a gathering place for Blix's friends throughout high school and college.

Blix sat on the sofa watching an old movie. Paul Newman wore his sexy grin and stared at his wife, Joanne Woodward, with mischievous yet adoring eyes. "Why go out for hamburger when I have steak at home," Abbey said as she walked in.

It took a minute for Blix to look up. "Oh, hi, Bunns. I thought you were Momma. She just ran to the store." Blix remained seated. Over her lap lay a red-and-black UGA throw with a big jowly bulldog at its center. "What did you say when you walked in? Something about hamburger?"

"It was an old quote I heard by Paul Newman. He was asked how he'd not gotten involved with other women. He said because he had steak at home. Joanne Woodward."

"I remember that one." Blix chuckled. "Why aren't you at Kings Bluff? I left you a message there."

"I'm not there because... well, I *was* there for a couple of days. Anyway, when I got your message, I called you back several times, but I kept getting a busy signal. Abbey moved a corner of the blanket and sat by her friend. *Your message and the way you sounded scared me.* "So, what's going on?"

"I'm sorry you left Kings Bluff. I didn't mean to drag you home."

"Don't be silly. The only reason I went was Momma scheduled contractors to repair storm damage, and she wanted her check hand-delivered so the fellows would have money for turkeys, so I volunteered. Not much was going on at work, anyway. I took some me-time."

Blix picked up the remote and turned off the television. "I know. You told me the other day you were going. Remember when you said if there was ever anything I wanted or needed, all I had to do was ask?"

Abbey studied her friend's face, tried to anticipate what might come next. "Yes, Blix. I said as long as it was legal." *Where is this headed?*

Blix nodded. "You didn't have to come home on my account. I figured you'd just call me back."

"I was finished down there anyway." She thought about what to say. "Your message concerned me, dear one. What's going on?"

Blix gathered the throw, folded it into a neat square, and tossed it onto the end of the sofa. "I'm sorry. It's just..."

Abbey studied Blix's expression. Something had changed. "You're sorry for what?"

Blix shook her head.

"Talk to me, you goof."

Blix said, "I was upset, you know, about everything. I shouldn't have called you. I know better, but I just got to reminiscing about the hurricane and picked up the phone. I guess I wanted to relive it with you."

Abbey patted Blix's leg. "Well, we can do that, but explain something to me. I listened to your message several times, but you were pretty upset, so I missed a lot of it. Of course, your boys will be okay, no matter what. You have nothing to worry about there." She went to the kitchenette across from them and came back with two glasses of water. "Here. Drink up."

"Yes, Mother." Blix smiled as she took the glass and dutifully drained half.

Abbey said, "Tom was due in from a trip this morning. I should call to let him know I made it to Atlanta okay, but do you want to go for a walk or something first? It's beautiful out, and my legs could use a stretch after the drive."

"Sure. Maybe later, but I have something I want you to do with me first." Blix placed both of her hands on the coffee table and pushed up. She wobbled. Abbey was surprised. This was a new move. She followed Blix to her bedroom, which Abbey remembered as neat and orderly, everything in its place. Now, it looked as though Blix planned to move. Scissors, clear packing tape, and empty folded boxes were arrayed on the dressing table like a UPS store. Other boxes were taped and labeled and stacked in the bedroom's corners. Blix said nothing, and Abbey didn't ask, though the feeling she'd had early that morning on her jog at Kings Bluff came back—a knowing she didn't want to know.

Photographs were neatly stacked in separate piles on the bed, beside a brand-new red photo album. "Will you help me put these pictures in my new album?"

Abbey knew how much Blix loved her photographs. She would save them in lieu of a lot of valuable stuff, if she ever had to make the choice. Abbey picked up one of the piles and thumbed through the images, careful not to touch the glossy fronts. There were black faces, live oaks, a little white church, and her cottage and the dock. This was not Atlanta. Abbey stopped at a picture of herself, pistol in-hand, a determined look on her face, and one of her old real-estate signs in the background. "These are all from the hurricane weekend."

"Well, duh, Bunns. They're my new favorite memories. Why do you suppose I was thinking about that weekend?" Blix tore the plastic wrap off the album and tossed it into the trash can. "Will you help me put them in the album? Give me some names to write beside them?"

A lump rose in Abbey's throat. *At the cottage, Blix said she wanted her boys to remember her happy and whole, not disfigured by surgery that might buy her a little more time.* "I'd be delighted. Let me check in with Tom first."

"Phone's right there by the bed."

Abbey saw the receiver lying on the floor between the bed and the bedside table. It had been there long enough for the dial tone to have died. She replaced the receiver in the cradle for several seconds, then dialed Tom's office. When he picked up, she said, "Hi. I'm glad you got home safely."

"Hi yourself. Where are you?" Tom asked.

"At Blix's. I left Kings Bluff early and got here a little while ago." She smiled at Blix, who looked on from the foot of the bed.

"How is she?"

"She's great. We've been having a chat, and now we're going to sort through photographs and put them in an album. I'll tell you all about it when you take me to Houston's on West

Paces Ferry for dinner tonight—that is, if Momma doesn't mind keeping the boys for a few more hours until I get there."

"Sounds good to me," Tom said.

She nodded to Blix and gave a thumbs up. "Great, darlin'. I will see you at Houston's at six. I'll be the good-looking one at the bar in jeans, Topsiders, and my fishing hat. You'll know me."

CHAPTER 42

Seven days later, Abbey sat in the first row with her old friends from high school. It was odd how humor escaped like birds from a cage at times that might seem inappropriate and irreverent to some, but to those in the inner circle, the levity fit this occasion. Blix would prefer it that way. A photograph made its way down the pew. Each recipient studied the picture, and then her shoulders shook for a moment and she passed it on. Chuckles were more-or-less stifled. Abbey received the photo last. She was on the aisle—the first to speak. She glanced at the snapshot, remembered the night.

The Kodak photo had been taken during college in the living room at Kings Bluff. Blix smiled back from the print. Dressed in a short summer dress, her long, skinny legs were bent in a plié; she was sockless in white tennis shoes. Her braided pigtails had been wired with a bent coat hanger and pointed straight up. Her grin was huge. It was obvious she was laughing. Blix and laughter went together. Abbey looked down the row and met the teary-eyed smiling faces of friends she had known most of her life. Abbey had thought a lot lately about the feeling she often got and decided it was from an angel who kept watch over her, looked over her shoulder and gave her insights, nudged her in the right direction when she was at a standstill and needed answers. *The piano music stopped. That's my cue.* An elbow punched her right side. "I'm going," she whispered back.

Her low heels felt like spiky stilettos as she walked to the pulpit. The college-ruled paper she had written on stuck to her fingertips as she laid her notes on the podium with the wordy paragraph version on the bottom of the stack, a one-page bullet-point sheet on top. She'd never considered herself a good toast-maker and certainly not a great eulogizer, but she wasn't afraid to stand in front of a group and talk about a topic with which she was comfortable and familiar. She had this one covered.

"Most of you know me. For those of you who don't, I'm Abbey Taylor Bunn, the lunatic who encouraged Blix to join me and Tom, my husband, on Labor Day weekend at my mother's cottage on the coast of Georgia. You all might remember that weekend, though you probably didn't pay as much attention to it here in Atlanta as we did down there. The Storm of the Century hit Brunswick, just north of where we were staying. As luck would have it, the eye of the storm blew right over the cottage where Tom and I quaked in an old clawfoot bathtub. It hit Brunswick, where Blix and her new friend Esther waited for it to pass in a dilapidated treehouse in the top of a live oak tree." She glanced at the second row behind Blix's family, where Tom and Boonks sat with Esther, Otis, Latisha, Joseph, Sam, Franklin, Sheriff Tanner, and several others. Sheriff Tanner had rented a minibus so they could all drive up together.

"From what I have gathered, Esther's life isn't the only one Blix saved that weekend." There were amens from the second row. "I got a call from Blix last week, and to be honest, the message she left frightened me. She sounded like she was in a hurry to finish things, as though she was running out of time. If you knew her well, you knew what she had gone through over the years. She'd faced death before and knew it was coming the final time. But she decided not to have the surgery that could have extended, but drastically changed, her life. She wanted to fully enjoy every day she had left. After I got her message, I went over to her house, and she asked me to help her put together an album of photographs she'd taken during the storm. Her album is here today. I hope you'll look through her pictures at the reception following this service. You'll see her happy, and goofy, and full of life, the way we all knew her and how she wanted to be remembered. She told Tom and me she had never felt more alive and purposeful than in those days of the storm. Blix was an amazing woman who touched a lot of lives. I'll finish with this quote from Henry David Thoreau that I think sums up Blix's life. 'Time is like a river. You cannot touch the same water twice because the flow that has passed will never pass again. Enjoy every moment in life.'"

Abbey swallowed and took a deep, tear-staunching breath. Someone clapped, then another. Abbey looked up. Blix's two sons were on their feet, their hands slowly, rhythmically clapping. More joined them. Abbey smiled, gathered her notes, and stepped down.

Others spoke, and the lightheartedness continued. Esther's soulful a cappella rendition of "Amazing Grace" sung in her rich alto closed the service. The church emptied slowly, everyone in quiet conversation or sharing a chuckle as they made their way to the Fellowship Hall. Blix's family stood together and received hugs and condolences. Folks nibbled cheese straws, finger sandwiches, and an array of sweets—typical southern fare.

Abbey hugged family members, then made her way around the room and spoke to friends she hadn't seen in a long time. They traded Blix stories and cried a little. An hour or so later, when the crowd began to thin, Abbey told the Brunswick crowd goodbye, and then she found Boonks and Tom standing together, ready to go, and asked them to give her a minute. She wandered over to the table near the entry doors, where Blix's family had displayed photographs of her childhood and of her with her two sons. The album she and Abbey had recently compiled lay open. Abbey started at the beginning and lingered over each page, savored every picture. The room grew quieter as more and more people left. The sensation, the odd one she had experienced recently at Kings Bluff before she'd heard Blix's message, was back. The knowing. But this time, the feeling wasn't urgent. A calmness settled over her.

At the last page in the album, she smiled. Blix had added one photograph that hadn't been in the stack she had gone through with Abbey. The six-by-eight glossy was the photograph Abbey had taken of Blix before they had gone to the firing range, bowed chicken legs and all. Hand-printed below the photograph in gold letters was *"Tidewater Tempest,"* and below that in black block letters was "ALL OR NOTHING" and Blix's signature. Abbey shook her head and sighed. *Blix, the Tidewater Tempest.*

Click. Her eyes narrowed. She looked around the room. Boonks and Tom were talking to Blix's family. They were the only other ones there. Above her, a ceiling fan moved drowsily; other ceiling fans in the room were perfectly still. She looked overhead again. The fan slowed, then stopped. *Click.* She placed her fingertips on the gold lettering. "See you later, dear friend."

ACKNOWLEDGMENTS

Thank you to those who read early drafts of the manuscript and made insightful comments: Lila Bird Allen, Emily Clement Davenport, Linda Fraser, Rebecca Parham Kiefer, and John Worley.

Thank you, Jeremy Turner, for police rescue advice and Billy Badger for introducing me to Erik Larson's wonderful book *Isaac's Storm*.

Novels are made better by good editors. A big thank you goes to Emily Carmain, my friend and editor, who made my novel presentable for the next round of critical eyes. To Pinckney Benedict, Hayley Swinson, and Mandi Jourdan, I say thank you for being critical but fair and for teaching me a lot about what makes a novel better.

And a special thank you to Steve McCondichie. Good luck in your endeavors.

M. Z. Thwaite shares her life-long love affair with Georgia's Golden Isles as the author of the Tidewater literary suspense series. A licensed realtor for nearly forty years, she continues to enjoy the simple pleasures of the hunting and fishing club cofounded by her maternal grandfather. She grew up in Atlanta and lives in Beaufort, South Carolina, with her husband, Steve Weeks, of Riverton, New Jersey.

SHARE YOUR THOUGHTS

Want to help make *Tidewater Tempest* a bestselling novel? Consider leaving an honest review of this book on Goodreads, on your personal author website or blog, and anywhere else readers go for recommendations. It's our priority at Hearthstone Press to publish books for readers to enjoy, and our authors appreciate and value your feedback.

OUR SOUTHERN FRIED GUARANTEE

If you wouldn't enthusiastically recommend one of our books with a 4- or 5-star rating to a friend, then the next story is on us. We believe that much in the stories we're telling. Simply email us at pr@sfkmultimedia.com.

Do You Know About Our Monthly Zine?

Would you like your unpublished prose, poetry, or visual art featured in *The New Southern Fugitives*? A monthly zine that's free to readers and subscribers and pays contributors:

$40 Per Book Review
$40 Per Poem
$40 Per Photograph or Piece of Visual Art
$15 Per Page for Prose (Min $45 and Max $105)

Visit **NewSouthernFugitives.com/Submit** for more information.

THE NEW
Southern Fugitives

SFK
PRESS

ALSO AVAILABLE FROM
HEARTHSTONE PRESS

Sanctuary: A Legacy of Memories by T.M. Brown
Testament: An Unexpected Return by T.M. Brown
Purgatory: A Progeny's Quest by T.M. Brown
Tallapoosa: A Southern Novel by Mike Corwin
Ariel's Island by Pat McKee
Paper & Ink, Flesh & Blood by Rita Mace Walston

Forthcoming from Hearthstone Press in 2021:
If the Light Escapes by Brenda Marie Smith

CPSIA information can be obtained
at www.ICGtesting.com
Printed in the USA
JSHW020026230621
16058JS00002B/12